King of Diamonds

Anthony Davis

Copyright © 2014 Anthony Davis

All rights reserved.

ISBN:1505523400
ISBN-13: 978-1505523409

DEDICATION

To Barney Barnato who died too young and to my wife Judie who encouraged me to write this book.

ANTHONY DAVIS

BARNEY BARNATO – KING OF DIAMONDS

Access to the diamond diggings – Kimberley Mine circa 1880.

De Beers Mine after rain has flooded the lower levels. C1880

ACKNOWLEDGMENTS

My thanks go to all descendants of the Barnato family who have helped with information on Barney Barnato. A special thank you to my grandfather Alexander Jonas Morton and grandmother Josephine (Pick) Morton for passing down the wedding photograph of Barney Barnato and Fanny Bees which hangs on my wall today.

Solly's eyes glared at me. I'd seen that look before in other men's eyes; he wanted my blood. If he thought he could take me, I had no doubt that he would try. Instead he turned on his heel and appeared to back down. I relaxed and turned to look over the rail of the ship. "Murder!" Barney Barnato's final word.

PROLOGUE

Hope Town, Cape Colony, 1866

The high tablelands of Eastern Cape Colony in Africa are lush with crops that grow easily in the temperate climate of the region. Sheep graze on grassy verges, aloes and stapelias are seen in abundance. Large trees; willow, acacia, pendoorn, zwartbosch, ebony, capparis and wild juniper, provide shade and timber for the farmhouses in the region. The area is irrigated by the Great Orange River flowing majestically east to west across the tableland and beyond.

On the De Kalk farm, leased from the local Griqua natives, Daniel Jacobs struggles to unblock a water irrigation pipe. Mud, stones and silt have clogged the pipe and he calls to his son, Erasmus, to get a long stick and help unblock the pipe. The pipe brings water from the river and is essential for the sheep and crops, mainly cereals, growing on the farm. After helping to clear the obstruction, Erasmus is attracted to a brilliant pebble lying on the ground, reflecting in the bright sunlight of Southern Africa. Fascinated by the light playing through the stone, Erasmus picks it up and shows it to his father. His father admires the stone, but he is busy and hot.

"It's beautiful Erasmus, but we have much work to do before the sun sets."

He gives it back to Erasmus, who puts it in his pocket and returns to working on their planting.

A few evenings later, Schalk van Niekerk, a neighbor is visiting the Jacobs family, and Erasmus shows him the stone he has found.

"That is an interesting stone, Erasmus. Can I buy it from you?

"No, Mr van Niekerk, you can have it. I'll find another."

Van Niekerk insists that he give him something for it. He takes a few coins out of his pocket and gives them to Erasmus, who is delighted with the transaction. He has never had his own money before. Van Niekerk is not sure what the stone is, but he knows someone he can ask. It may be worthless, but it cost so little. He thinks it might make a nice present for his wife.

Later that week, van Niekerk meets John O'Reilly, and shows him the transparent stone. O'Reilly examines it, but he has never seen anything quite like it.

"I don't know, van Niekerk. Could be anything. If you like I can show it to the Commissioner in Colesberg. I'm seeing him next week. I would think he'll know what it is."

"By all means take it and show him. It's a curiosity and I'd just like to know more about it. Who knows, it might be valuable."

"I don't think so, but its hard to say really."

O'Reilly shows the stone to the Acting Commissioner, Lourenzo Boyes, who examines it carefully. O'Reilly watches him go to the window and run it over the glass. It leaves a distinct scar on the glass.

"Well, we can see that it is hard enough to scratch glass, but I've never seen a stone like this. It has something about it that makes me believe that it could be a diamond, but I'm guessing. It might be wishful thinking on my part. It would, however, be exciting to think that there were diamonds waiting to be found in our territory. Let me send it to Dr. Atherstone, the mineralogist in Grahamstown, and see what he says. He has the training and the equipment to test it properly. I'll tell you this, if it is a diamond, then it is indeed very valuable. Where did you find it?"

"Ah, that would be telling. Let's wait and see what it is first."

"As you wish, but you know as Assistant Commissioner, I will have to make a report on it."

"Why don't you hold off till we know if it worth you making a report. You don't want to create a lot of paperwork for something that turns out to be worthless." Boyes nodded in agreement.

Dr. Atherstone received the stone by post a few days later and after careful examination, writes to the Assistant Commissioner and confirms that the stone he received, was in fact a diamond, weighing more than twenty-one carats, considered a substantial size for a rough diamond.

Several weeks after having acquired the diamond for just a few pennies, van Niekerk sells it to the Governor of the Cape Colony for five hundred pounds. The Governor gives it the name *Eureka* and takes it to England where it was cut into a cushion-shape weighing 10.73 carats.

Having made a substantial profit, van Niekerk decides to keep a look out for other diamonds in the area. He puts the word out to families and traders to keep a look out for bright transparent stones of any size, offering a substantial reward for any that are found.

Society of Arts, meeting, London December 2nd, 1868

A report to the members of the Society by Mr. Emmanuel:

"As to the existence of diamonds in the Cape Colony, Mr. Gregory, President of the Institution of Civil Engineers has searched very carefully the whole of the places where they were reported to have been found and he failed not only to discover a single diamond, but even such soil as diamonds are usually found in."

Colesberg, Cape Colony, 1869

A native Griqua tending his sheep finds a big transparent stone. He sends word to van Niekerk, who loses no time to go and see it. On this occasion, he does not get the stone for next to nothing. The native demands a substantial payment, not in gold, but in animals. After lengthy negotiations, van Niekerk gives him 500 sheep, 10 oxen and a horse, in exchange for the stone.

He took some risk as his knowledge of diamonds was minimal, but he was convinced that this was a diamond. Luckily for him, his instincts served him well. Dr. Atherstone identified it as a diamond, weighing 83.50

carats, and suggested that the stone be given the name Star of Africa. He confirmed to van Niekerk, that it was a magnificent and rare gemstone.

The diamond had been found on the slopes of the Colesberg Kopje, a small, conical hill in relatively flat country. This was on a farm owned by the De Beers brothers. Word of the find spread quickly and the stampede to find diamonds was on. Men rushed to see if they could make their fortune by literally picking it off the ground. The area around the Colesberg Kopje became known as New Rush. Within a month, more than eight hundred claims were filed and several thousand men toiled away searching for diamonds. The kopje disappeared, quickly replaced by a large hole in the ground.

The Star of South Africa, was sold for £11,200 to a London dealer, who in turn sold it to the Earl of Dudley for £25,000.

Hoxton, London. 1871

Mayday celebrations in England and all of Europe go back thousands of years to pagan times. Traditionally in England, the first day of summer is celebrated by crowning a beautiful, young maiden the Queen of the May. The festival is marked as a holiday, where food and drink is consumed in large quantities. For many, it is one of the few times in the year; they can afford to celebrate in such a lavish way. Fairgrounds are setup with rides, games of chance, and sideshow booths. 1871 was particularly important for its Mayday celebrations. That was the year Queen Victoria proclaimed Mayday as a national holiday.

Various booths are set up, many containing wild animals, some real and some not so. It was not uncommon to entice the crowd to see mythical unicorns; ponies with narwhal tusks tied on to their head. And mermaids; scantily clad young girls wearing fish skins. And everyone's favorites the freak shows, showing off the monstrosities of nature; people with horrible deformities, whose only way of making a little money, was to be shown off to the public. Bearded ladies, people seriously obese or extremely malnourished, tall giants and tiny midgets, were all part of the attractions.

For a few pennies, the public could stare in wonder at things that they could never imagine.

The most important element to all of these sideshows was the showman; the man whose silver tongue could persuade the gullible to pay,

"Just a few pennies to see this incredible, no, not incredible, but unbelievable sight. Not for the kiddies, ladies and gentlemen, this is for adults only. Far too grotesque for the faint at heart."

Sporting and gambling booths were among a number of attractions at the fairs. In particular, bare knuckle boxing with Marquis of Queensbury rules abandoned, was most popular.

It was a beautiful, warm and sunny Monday at a fairground in Hoxton, London. Standing outside the boxing tent of Mr. Hill "The World Famous Boxing Promoter," is a diminutive young man, five feet, two inches tall, with a pleasant face and light mousy-colored hair. Mr. Hill rings a hand bell and shouts to the crowd.

"Roll up, roll up. Beat champion Barney Isaacs in a five-minute fight and win a gold sovereign. Roll up, roll up."

The "champion" does not look very much like a boxer, far from it. This is Barney's story.

Chapter 1

"Be not afraid of greatness: Some are born great, some achieve greatness, and some have greatness thrust upon them." William Shakespeare (1564 – 1616).

I really love the roar of the crowd when I am in the ring or performing on stage. There is something about the excitement that I know I can create. Looking at the faces of the men deciding if they can beat me is hilarious. My physique is hardly threatening, I am short and stocky, but I can handle myself. Winning the fight is all I care about, and the bigger they come, the harder they fall. The man I fear the most is someone who has my build, is fast on his feet and who knows a trick or two. But they rarely take the chance. It is always the biggest bruisers that feel they can beat me to a pulp. Hold up, here comes one now!

"Oi'll beat your man, sir, is it a gold sovereign you be paying?"

Wouldn't you know it; a group of Irish laborers has lumbered up to Hill, pushing the biggest of their gang to the front and up the steps onto the platform. My guess is my opponent is over six feet tall and weighs well over twice my weight. I think this Irishman must have breathed in Hill's face, as he has stepped back a pace to avoid the foul smell of the man's breath.

"Beat him, will yer? You beat him in five minutes and the money is yours."

"Looks like a little runt, should be the easiest money I ever made," the challenger boasts.

They can all stare at me and poke fun, but I'll have the last laugh. I watch as Hill holds up the contender's arm so the crowd, and particularly the bookies, can see the man.

"We have a challenger, sixpence to watch the fight. You will be able to place your bets with the bookies inside the boxing tent."

I look around for my favorite bookie inside the tent. I spot him and can see money changing hands quickly as he and the other bookies take the bets. The Irishman is odds on favorite at five to four. He nods and shouts out the odds to me.

"Three to one on you, Barney."

"Too soon, I'll wait till when it is five to one"

The tent is full of excited, shouting men crowding in. They can't wait to see the damage that this huge opponent is going to do to me. Nothing like a bit of blood and guts to get the crowds screaming for more. In less than ten minutes the tent is completely full. My bookie saunters over to me with a big smile on his ugly face.

"I can give you five to one."

"Great, here's a pound on me to win."

"Are you sure, this Mick is huge, he'll make mincemeat of you!"

"Don't you worry; I've fought bigger'n him."

I move to the center of the ring as Hill leads the Irishman to join me. The crowd goes quiet. As quick as a flash, I clobber the Irishman with a left to the kidneys. He lets out a scream of pain and lunges at me.

"Come here you little shit. I'm going to break your scrawny neck."

I'm a southpaw with a distinctive stance, leading with quick right jabs to the Irishman's head, but it is having no effect. I'm fast on my feet. I dance around my lumbering opponent and strike him with a hard left cross, followed by a stunning right hook to his jaw. There is a crunch of breaking bone and the Irishman's mouth spurts blood and spittle. He looks as if he is about to charge me. Instead, he staggers forward and falls face down onto the dirt floor of the ring.

The crowd goes wild, hooting and shouting for the Irishman to get up. After all, this Mick is twice the size of me and should have easily managed to knock me flat.

Hill moves into the ring, throws a bucket of water over the Irishman who is still out cold.

"I declare Barney Isaacs the winner of this match."

"Barney, you could have given the crowd a bit more of a run for their money."

"Are you kidding, did you see the size of those mitts?"

The largely disappointed crowd leaves the boxing tent. The bookies look pleased; I'm a favorite with them. Once again I've made them money and shown them I'm no ordinary boxer.

My father made sure that my brother Harry and I learned to fight when we were really small. He used to set up a boxing ring in our small back yard. Three nights a week after he finished work, he would teach us the rudiments of boxing, well actually fighting. I think I was five when I started, Harry was seven. My father always said never allow anyone to put their hands on us. Always hit first and make sure that whoever it was, big or small, they did not want to come back for more.

At that time, we were too young to understand why. Jews had been persecuted for hundreds of years by anti-Semites, who would pick on us just because we were different. As I grew older, I encountered anti-Semitism and my father's years of training paid off. Yes, I had gotten hurt a few times, but never seriously, and I always gave better than I got. One of the reasons I can box all comers, is that I am not scared of anyone. I make good money boxing and now I have another more important reason to do this. I need the money for my passage to South Africa.

Four years ago, someone found a big diamond near the Vaal River in South Africa. It took some time before the news reached the big cities in England, thousands of miles away. Personally, I don't think it made much of an impression in my neighborhood in the East End of London. There are very few people who can afford to buy diamonds, and they wouldn't know a real one if they saw it. My father reads day-old newspapers that he gets for free. He told Harry and me about this huge diamond.

"This diamond they found is as big as a hen's egg."

"What's a diamond?"

"It's a bit of coal that had made good under heat and pressure over thousands of years. This causes the coal to form a transparent crystal. An expert diamond polisher turns it into a sparkling jewel. Diamonds are valuable. People that find diamonds can get very rich."

I thought about this for a couple of seconds, trying to imagine what very rich meant. Everyone wants to be rich, people say that all the time, but I really had no idea what that meant.

My mind flashed back to the pictures, Father showed us, of the High Priest breastplate in the Temple in Jerusalem long ago.

I never gave diamonds another thought till a few weeks later when Harry announced after dinner on *Shabbos,* Friday night, that he was going to travel to South Africa to try his hand at diamond mining.

You can imagine that my father was a bit surprised by this and my three sisters were aghast at the thought of Harry, their big brother, travelling to the wilds of Africa.

"Why do you want to do this, Harry?" my father asked.

"I've been reading about the thousands of men that are travelling there. Some have already been lucky enough to make substantial diamond finds, there are so many of them. People are just picking up stones off the ground. I think I can make a good living, performing in the local theatres at night and searching for diamonds during the day. Who knows, I might become incredibly wealthy."

The whole family was silent for a few seconds as we all took this in. It is never that quiet at our dinner table.

"Harry, you're of age, so I can't stop you doing what you want to do. However, I advise you against such a rash decision."

"I don't feel that this is a rash decision," Harry replied.

"Please be so good as to hear me out before you make any more comments."

"Sorry, Father."

"You're a hard worker, but I am sure that you have no idea how hard a venture this is. You will need money for your passage, for food and equipment, but most of all you will have to fight for what you want."

"Father, you've taught me to take care of myself. You've taught me how to make a living buying and selling. Please believe me when I say I've given this a lot of thought, and I'm confident that I can do it."

"I'm glad to hear that, but I urge you to give greater consideration to this idea of yours."

"I've saved enough money to pay for my passage, and I will earn more before I leave. If I fail, and you agree to it, I will come home and resume my life here. I really want your blessing on this."

My father glanced at my sister Sarah, who was close to tears. Saying nothing, he looked around the table at my oldest sister Kate, at her husband Joel, at me and back to Sarah, whose husband Isaac was trying to pacify her. Lizzie, my youngest sister, sadly was rather sick and crying miserably. Kate shook her head in disagreement as the rest of us just sat there, not uttering a word.

"I'm going to consider this all very carefully. Your wish to better yourself is admirable. My fear is that you will be unable to continue to practice your religion. I'm concerned that you will abandon your faith out of necessity and hardship, that you will no longer keep *kashrut* and eat kosher food, as it may not be available. Our family has lived in England for many generations since we travelled here from Eastern Europe where we were persecuted for our faith. We have been fortunate to be able to do so without that fear here in England. I'm not sure that this adventure to South Africa is in your best interest."

With that he got up from the table and left our small dining room.

"Harry, can I come with you?"

"I'm sorry Barney; I have to do this alone. I promise that as soon as I have established myself, I will send for you and we will work together. Father will not allow both of us to go at the same time. He will want me to pave the way for you as you will be my responsibility."

"You promise to send for me as soon as you can, though?"

"Don't worry; if I say I will, you know I will."

Chapter 2

My home is in Whitechapel, a very poor area in the East End of London. We are close to the docks at Irongate Wharf, where so many immigrants literally got off the ship and settled. Buildings in our area are shabby and squalid. The front doors of the small two-up, two-down terraced houses open directly onto the street. The small houses back onto other houses. There are few windows, making the interiors really dark. Poor ventilation traps the smell of cooking, smoke, body odors and sewage. We're used to it, but in the cold of winter it is worse.

My family has lived in this neighborhood for close to a hundred years. We are considered well-off by most peoples standards. My father Isaac Isaacs makes a good living buying and selling used clothing and off cut fabrics. In fact he trades in anything legal that can turn a profit. He owns a shop on Cobbs Court close to Petticoat Lane, and our home is over the shop. Mother died some years ago. I live here with my older brother Harry, my youngest sister Lizzie, and Father of course. Two of my sisters, Kate and Sarah, are married and live nearby. Mother died giving birth to Lizzie when I was very small. I really don't remember her much. Kate helped to raise us.

Harry and I help father in the business since we left school at the age of fourteen. All three of us buy and sell in the neighborhood street markets. We are successful at what we do. I hate to brag, but I have a good eye for stuff that can be sold at a profit. Both Harry and I have had a pretty good education in the three R"s at the Jews Free School in Bell Lane, and I am quick at making calculations. This helps a lot when I am dealing with the public.

Many of my father's generation moved east out of the area, to Hackney and Dalston. My father stayed here because my grandfather was the rabbi at one of the many local *shuls*. When my grandfather died, my father decided that he would rather not move away from his regular customers and familiar streets.

According to the newspaper, ninety percent of all Jews in England live in this area of Whitechapel, Spitafields, and St. Georges in the East End of London. I don't know how true that is, but it would not surprise me. We have dozens of synagogues in our neighborhood and many *chevrot* societies based on towns of immigrant origins. These people help the new arrivals find somewhere to live. The narrow streets and alleyways are as familiar to me as the back of my hand. I can't imagine what another country, thousands of miles from here, might be like, but if Harry thinks he can make a go of it, I'm with him.

Harry and I perform at Wilton's Music Hall on Wednesday evenings. Wilton's is one of dozens of local theatres in the East End. It is a beautiful little theatre and we both love the audience. It is an easy walk from our home. We discuss our act every step of the way, sometimes changing part if that needs to be improved. The walk is the time we have together to make those changes. We never have enough time to rehearse like real actors. Fortunately, it all comes quite instinctively to us. We know what each other thinks.

We have a double act; Harry is the magician and the main attraction with his conjuring, sleight of hand, and all kinds of tricks. My contribution is helping Harry, juggling and reciting Shakespearean soliloquies. For the past three or four years we have been performing at Wilton's where the audience is great. We're not paid very much, but the crowd, if they like you, throws you pennies, cigarettes or sometimes an apple or whatever else they have at hand. Of course, if they don't like you, it can be a rotten egg.

The stage is not very large. There is a long balcony that runs the length of the theatre. This is where the more up-market clientele, sit and watch, Then there is the pit in front of and below the stage, where people mill around, drink, eat and generally have a good time. They don't sit down, so the pit is a constantly moving mass of people. These are the best of the audience. They love you or hate you and they do it with enthusiasm. I particularly enjoy playing to this crowd."

Second-hand or third-hand evening clothes sometimes come through our shop. Harry and I have pulled a few of the better ones to dress up our stage performances. We look like the "cat's whiskers", all dolled up in top hat and tails. Sometimes we use old curtains and get Kate to sew them for us into exotic Eastern style costumes. She can do anything with a needle and thread.

For the longest time, Harry has been introduced by the master of ceremonies, as the Great Henry Isaacs. I'm always added as "and Barnett too". I told Harry I'm fed up with this, how about we use a play on words and call ourselves Bar-na-to, the Barnato Brothers, instead of Isaacs. It makes us sound much more important and mysterious, the name conjures up (pardon the pun), exotic places and far lands. Harry didn't have a problem with it, so we are the Barnato brothers. Now we could perform under our new name.

I was not sure how things would be once Harry leaves for South

Africa. My act is all right, but it might need improvement to make it more appealing to the audience. I will have to think hard about that. My dearest desire is to be a Shakespearean actor. I recently heard about a performer who walks on his hands on stage, whilst reciting Shakespeare. How difficult can that be? I know the words. All I have to do is practice walking on my hands!

New Years Eve 1872

A letter arrived from Harry today creating much excitement for me. The letter took almost two months to get here. It was sent from a town called Dutoitspan in South Africa, so many thousands of miles away. It is not surprising that it took so long. The sea voyage alone takes four or five weeks, sometimes longer, depending on how many ports of call there are along the way. Looking at the map of the world that I keep beside my bed, I can see roughly where it is. There is no town on the map called Dutoitspan. Harry described the location, close to the Vaal River, in the northern part of the Cape Colony, next to the Orange Free State.

Harry says he's doing well, whatever that means. What he doesn't say is what it is that he is doing. Most importantly, he says that I should join him at the earliest opportunity, and that there's hoards of money to be made in the diamond fields.

Father must have read the letter a dozen times. I know that he's concerned I will follow Harry, and that he will have to run the business on his own again. He's not scared of hard work, not at all. He has done it all his life, but he is getting on in years and suffers from rheumatism. It is not so easy for him now. When Harry left, Father was unhappy, but stoic. With both of his sons half way round the world, it will be ten times harder on him.

At dinner that evening, I said very little about joining Harry. In fact I did not bring up the subject at all. We all knew what was on everyone's mind. I decided to talk privately to Father the next day to find out if he would agree to let me go to the Cape Colony. Money is not too much of a problem; I have worked at building my funds, performing three or sometimes four nights a week in the Music Halls. Added to that, I've made money boxing at a lot of fairs. When I checked a couple of days earlier, I'd reached my target, and I have a little more than one hundred pounds. I feel like a wealthy man. There are not too many twenty-year-olds around here who have even one tenth of that saved up.

Checking into the cost of the ship's passage, I can travel steerage for fifty pounds, which includes all my food. That will leave me fifty pounds to travel to the diamond fields and set myself up in business. My mind is made up. I'm going to join Harry. My real concern is that Father is not going to agree to it, even though I am of age and able to support myself. My sisters miss Harry, so it is going to be much worse for them once I leave. There is no avoiding it: tomorrow will be decisive

Chapter 3

After dinner the next day, Father and I sat in our small front room, the best room, as he called it. I laid out my plan to meet up with Harry in the town they call Dutoitspan, in the Cape Colony. I brought my map to show him where it was located.

My Father, is always the pragmatist. He wanted to know how much money I had to pay for my voyage. How much I anticipated I would need to set up in business. Showing him the hundred pounds I've saved, impressed him. I really have amassed a small fortune.

My cousin, Barney Harris, has agreed to join me on this journey so I won't be travelling alone. Barney is a couple of years older than me and he's going to join his brother David, who is doing well trading in diamonds. I think that helped make my father more comfortable, although he gave me a long lecture, probably the same he gave to Harry.

"There are so many men rushing to make their fortune in the diamond fields, Barney. What makes you think you can compete?"

"I've as much chance as any man. Besides, Harry is there and doing well. If I'm unable to make money in diamonds, I'm sure there is plenty of opportunity to buy and sell the everyday commodities that miners need." Father sighed before speaking.

"During the gold rush in Australia, twenty years ago, men I knew got on the first boat they could, in anticipation of making a fortune. When they got to the goldfields, they found that it was a dreadfully hard life. One, possibly two had any success. The rest returned to England, as soon as they were able to earn enough to do so."

"Is that why you don't want me to go? You let Harry do it."

"I wouldn't stop Harry and I won't stop you, if that is what you are determined to do."

"Then it's settled?"

"No, not quite. Mining is extremely dangerous. Men get killed, not just mining, but at the hands of rogues and thieves who go after those who are successful - even marginally successful."

"I can look after myself, you know that."

"Yes, with your fists, but you will be in great danger from the villains using guns, knives and ambush tactics." I stuck to my guns.

"There are villains here in London that use the same tactics. I can just as easily be killed by one here as I can there."

"You always have an answer, Barney. I am also concerned that your sisters will be heartbroken when you leave. With both Harry and you, thousands of miles away, and in jeopardy every day, they will worry themselves to death."

"I know that, Father. I can't let that stop me, though.

"You have to be careful about sleeping with women who may have syphilis and gonorrhea. They are impossible to treat and your life could be ruined forever."

"I know all about that. You have warned me for years. Don't worry, I won't ruin my life." But he kept on.

"It will be hard to practice our religion, to keep the Sabbath and find kosher food in a country that is obviously quite primitive. You have to try, though."

"I will, Father, I promise you that."

"Then I wish you well. You have my blessing."

"Thank you, thank you. You won't regret it." He smiled.

"I think if I were thirty years younger, had no family, I would not hesitate to get on the next ship leaving for South Africa and seek my fortune, too."

With that, he hugged me, wiped a tear from his eye, and left the room. He was allowing me some time to reflect on his words of wisdom. My father is a wonderful, understanding man not prone to emotion. The tears in his eyes were quite a surprise to me. Somehow, I did not expect it; neither did I expect that he would stand in my way. After all, we're Jews, who have roamed the world for hundreds of years. Why should I be any different? I made up my mind that I would try my best to be everything my father expected of me.

Later that week, I went out with some of my friends I had grown up with. We were out to celebrate my decision, and my father's agreement to let me go. We decided to go to the Music Hall on Cambridge Heath Road. I have played there with Harry and on my own, so the proprietor let us in for free. He couldn't believe that I was leaving in a few days, time.

The entertainment was varied as always, singers, jugglers, acrobats and comedians. We had a lot to drink and thought everything was either good, or very funny. I couldn't believe my friends when Joe, the loudest one of the bunch, handed me a small box, wrapped in fancy paper.

"A going away present, something to remember your old pals everyday of the year."

I removed the paper very carefully and opened the box to find a beautiful, silver pocket watch. I put it to my ear to see if it was working. The steady tick confirmed that it was. For once in my life, I was speechless for several seconds.

"Thank you for such a generous gift."

I shook hands with them all. Laughing, Joe gave me a bear hug.

"Don't worry, we didn't pinch it. We bought it from Mr. Cohen in the Lane."

"The thought never crossed my mind."

I lied to them because the first thought that came to me was they had stolen it. Some of the lads were not too particular about that sort of thing; however most of them earned an honest living in one way or another."

Actually, I felt guilty about thinking they may have stolen it. I vowed to keep the watch for the rest of my life.

It seemed like everyone in the neighborhood wanted to see me before I left on my voyage. I had no idea that I was so popular. It's important to my family that they get to see me and wish me well. Kate is married to Joel and together they run the King of Prussia, one of the local pubs on Middlesex Street. From time to time, I had worked there to earn extra money, especially when they were very busy.

I find this quite funny really, because there can't be many Jewish publicans in the entire world. Many Jews think it a strange choice of profession, but my kin had the opportunity to take over the pub and jumped at the chance. I'm sure the beer company that owns the pub, had no idea. Most of the brewers would take exception to Jews running a pub, in case they decided to close for the Sabbath or a Jewish holiday. Kate and Joel have a non-Jewish couple that helps out for the important days.

Joel used to be a cigar merchant, nothing fancy, no Havana, cigars that are a good inexpensive smoke. He thinks there will be a great demand for luxuries like cigars when I get to the diamond fields. So he gave me forty boxes of cigars to help me get a start. I have no idea how old they are as he hasn't been selling cigars for quite a while. I am sure I will be able to sell them. Joel can get more if there is a demand. Who knows what will sell?

My passport arrived by Royal Mail and I couldn't wait to open it to show everyone in the family. When Harry got his, he didn't make much of a fuss about it. To me this was the most beautiful document I had ever seen and I was proud to show it off.

Lizzie was the first to see it.

"Can I get one too?"

"When you are old enough, and ready to come and visit me and Harry in Africa."

A British passport is a small leather bound book, that has a flap to keep it closed. Inside is a large fold-out page complete with Queen Victoria's Coat of Arms, and it is very impressive. It states: "Request and require in the Name of Her Majesty, all those whom it may concern to allow Barnett Isaacs travelling to the Cape Colony to pass freely without let or hindrance and to afford him every assistance and protection of which he may stand in need." It was signed by the Foreign Office, London, and bears its Coat of Arms. Mine is numbered 171436 and is something I am very proud to own.

Time flies and I am packed and ready to go. I've said my goodbyes to everyone and now I can't wait to leave. My father, bless him, has given me a set of heavy flannel underwear because he said it could be very cold in South Africa in the wintertime. I tried to tell him that it's hot there, but he insisted. I packed them in my trunk around the cigar boxes. My little sister, Lizzie, cried non-stop. She is still not well and has this really bad cough for months now, and looks really thin. I told her I will come home and visit as soon as I can. I will write to her regularly, even though I hate writing letters. It means a lot to her, so I promised myself to make the effort.

Chapter 4

Cousin Barney and I took the Great Western Railway from Waterloo Station to the port of Southampton, a distance of sixty-two miles. This was our first time on a long-distance train. I think my cousin was more excited about it than me.

"I love the speed. Do you know that this train can reach a speed of forty miles an hour?"

"Fantastic isn't it? Beat's driving a cart."

"How would you know, you've never driven one," he scoffed.

"Actually, I have."

"Yeah, pull the other leg; it's got bells on it."

"I'm not lying, I got to drive Bert Cohen's cart once."

The journey gave me a taste of train travel, firmly planting the idea that I would like to do more sometime in the future, even though I had no idea when that would be. I don't think they have any trains in the Cape Colony.

Once we arrived at the station in Southampton, we had to lug our heavy steamer trunks to the port. An official directed us to the Union Line pier where our ship, the R.M.S. Anglian, was moored.

I talked to a lot of the merchant sailors in my sister's pub, about sea voyages and they all told me the same thing: steerage was cramped, decks and bunks were dirty and often rotten, especially on some of the older ships. They gave me tips on what to do, and what not to do; sleep in an upper bunk, be as close to the hatch to get fresh air, and away from the toilet facilities.

We were surprised to find that we are sailing on a brand new ship, in fact it was the maiden voyage of the R.M.S. Anglian.

Ships in the London docks all look pretty big to me. This one looked quite small, but I am no judge of ships.

I asked a sailor who was working some ropes,

"How big is this ship?"

"She's a 2200 tonner, mate."

"That doesn't mean much to me. All the ships I've seen ships in the London Docks all looked much bigger."

"Well this beauty is a new mail packet taking the Royal Mails to the Queen's Colonies. She's only three hundred or so feet long, but she's fast. That's the thing, being fast, she'll easily make the voyage to Cape Town, three or even four days faster than the older ships."

I was impressed and thanked him for telling me.

In the offices of the Union Steamship Line, cousin Barney and I paid our fare of ten pounds each, and were given a ticket, which was not much different from our railway tickets.

We had to show our passports. The officer hardly glanced at them, obviously he wasn't impressed. Seen too many of them to appreciate their beauty.

With the formalities taken care of, we had to wait around on the dock to board the ship. It was to sail on the tide at midnight. Surprisingly, there were not a lot of people travelling third class in steerage. I counted that there were only twenty-five of us including Barney and me. Not the overcrowded numbers that sailors had told me about. Most of my fellow travelers were men; three were married, with wives and kids in tow. The rest were on their own.

Nobody talked to each other. Barney and I kept our voices low, so as not to disturb others who, like us, were probably thinking about their families and loved ones they were leaving behind.

We watched as the well-dressed, first class passengers drove up in their carriages. They were helped out and escorted onto the ship by the officers. I wondered what it would be like to have a carriage and be treated deferentially, travelling in luxurious surroundings, enjoying fine food knowing that there would be more of the same awaiting you, when you arrived at your destination.

Late in the afternoon, just before dark, all of the steerage passengers were ordered up the gangway to board the ship. Once on board, an officer directed, no, ordered us down a flight of steep steps to the center of the ship.

Our accommodations consisted of wooden bunks, each with straw to sleep on and a rough horsehair blanket as a cover for warmth. The single men were in the forward section. The married couples with kids were in an area partitioned off behind our section. In the center of the ship, there were two long fixed tables and benches, which was our communal eating area. Everything was new and the rich dark wood was evenly stained and had the smell of linseed oil. The decking was clean! Not at all as it had been described by the old tars. I'm sure over time this will change.

There was not much privacy, and the shared toilet facilities in one corner of our section did not look adequate. I'm used to shared facilities and I hoped the other men were, too. There is nothing worse than having to wait when you're busting to go. The families had their own separate facilities and we were told in no uncertain terms that this was not for our use. I grabbed a top bunk and Barney took the one underneath.

We sailed at midnight. I checked my new watch, on the dot we got slowly underway, out into the Solent and the English Channel beyond. Standing on the small area of deck, where we steerage passengers were allowed, we watched the land slip away. I could not help the tears that welled up and the lump in my throat. I know that I will miss my family terribly. I fear for little Lizzie whose health seems to be deteriorating and for my father, who is getting on in years. I said a prayer for all their safety and hoped that I would see them again.

Our £40 fare included all our food, but we did not expect much. Breakfast was oatmeal, bread and butter, with tea or coffee. Dinner always started with soup, followed by either meat or fish, with potatoes, and on most days, some kind of pudding. For tea, we had to be content with plenty of bread and butter and lots of strong tea or coffee. Mind you, the coffee was bad, and the tea not much better. For the most part, the meals were plain, but wholesome.

For the first couple of days, some of my fellow passengers, including my cousin, were seasick. The rolling movement took some getting used to, and the smell of vomit made everyone feel queasy. I spent most of my time on the small deck, staring out into the distance, looking for land or another ship that might be nearby. I had no problem with balance and found my sea legs quickly.

Other steerage passengers frequented the deck to get some fresh air, and I quickly got to know their names. It seemed to me that all of these people were going to the Cape for the same reason: diamonds!

The weather was fairly good, although the Bay of Biscay was rough with swells of eight to ten feet high, causing more people to suffer from sea-sickness. Our ship seemed to cut through the waves like butter. Cousin

Barney was back on his bunk again in between spewing out his guts. I realized that we had spoken little during the first few days of our voyage. Barney is not much of a talker anyway.

Fortunately, there was always another passenger to talk to. This was a mixed bunch of people with high hopes of striking it rich. Nobody wanted to admit that failure was a possibility. They all had stories to tell and I spun a yarn or two. I even entertained in our dining quarters in the evenings, showing off some of my juggling, not so easy with the swaying of the ship, and when it was too rough, I quoted Shakespeare. One man remembered seeing me and Harry at the Cambridge Music Hall.

Barney was finally finding his sea-legs. We were chatting away about how we were going to spend our fortune. Surprising to me, was that he wanted to marry and have kids. This was the furthest thing from my mind. I guessed it was because he was a bit older than me.

Seven days out, the sea was calmer and we saw land. There was the Rock of Gibraltar off in the distance, rising majestically out of the water. It is a magnificent sight when you approach from the sea. This was our first port of call, although we were not allowed off the ship. A tender was lowered and several sacks were loaded onto it. I concluded that this must be the mail for Gibraltar. After three hours or so the tender returned. It was winched on board and we slowly continued on our voyage.

A couple of days later, we passed the island of Madeira off to the east and although clouds covered most of the peaks of the island, we could see much of it. As another day passed, the weather was getting much warmer. We passed another island which I could be seen in the distance. It was one of the Canary Islands. I was pleased I'd packed my atlas. Somehow, I had expected to see much more land.

After passing the Canaries, there was nothing to be seen other than the vast expanses of ocean and sky. The temperature inside our ship was continuously hot. We got some relief by going on deck. Many of us were spending our nights out there as well. In fact, Barney and I only went below to have meals, and then we were back on deck.

Our skin was getting dark from all the sun, which I don't think is a bad thing. I expect we will be spending many hours in the sun once we get to the diamond fields.

One day, with the temperature rising to over one hundred degrees, the cook announced to us at dinner, that we were crossing the Equator.

Almost without any warning, the weather turned. Strong Trade Winds kicked hard and started to blow. The ocean got extremely rough and even I felt sick, but it did not come to anything. Barney surprised me by being alright with the rough seas, and had no further attacks of sickness.

Twenty-seven days after leaving Southampton, I was standing on deck and thought I could see land. I wasn't sure, but within a few minutes, way off in the distance, I could see a flat top mountain mostly covered in cloud. I knew from my atlas that this was Cape Town and I had spotted Table Mountain. I shouted to Barney to come quickly. He was looking over the opposite side of the ship. We stood there in awe, watching as Table Mountain grew nearer minute by minute.

Chapter 5

My cousin told me that he was going to spend a few days in Cape Town before going on to the diggings. He wanted to stay in a hotel, take a bath and sleep in a real bed. For my part I just wanted to go north as soon as I could.

We docked early morning. Barney said he would keep an eye on my trunk while I went to look for transport to the diamond fields. It did not take me long to find out that I would have to travel more than six hundred miles to get there. The price for a seat on *coach and four* was twenty pounds, a ridiculous amount considering I'd travelled more than six thousand miles from England for twice that amount. I really couldn't afford to spend so much. I walked through a market selling all kinds of supplies and food. One of the stall holders told me the cheapest way to get to the diamond fields is to go with an ox wagon. They take up to forty tons of supplies at a time and will take the occasional passenger.

"Where can I find a wagon going to the fields?"

"Go to the Diamond Fields Transport Company, ask for De Kalk."

It did not take me long to find him. He was a big man, a head taller than me, with a beer gut, red face and a skin that looked like worn leather. I guessed he was in his late forties or so. He was a Boer and spoke with a strange accent. Of course he could say that I do too. We haggled a bit on the price, and finally struck a deal for him to take me for five pounds, paid in advance. What I did not realize at the time, was that we would walk the whole way. De Kalk told me he would provide me food in return for my help. Also, he allowed me to sleep under the wagon at night in bad weather.

"How long before we leave?"

"In about two hours, as soon as my wagon is loaded."

I rushed back to the docks to get my trunk. Barney was sitting on it watching the hustle and bustle of a busy port. We said our goodbyes and told each other we would meet up soon. Then I lugged my trunk over to the Transport Company where De Kalk threw it on the wagon as if it weighed nothing.

The ox wagon was an impressive sight, there is nothing like it in England. De Kalk's wagon had eight pairs of oxen.

"Very strong animals, as they are all castrated bulls. Much stronger than horses and not as prone to injury."

"Do you give them names?"

He laughed at me.

"They are beasts of burden, not pets. I don't have to love them, only make sure that they are fed and watered. They will do the rest. If you look you can see that the harness is made in such a way that the load is spread evenly across the team. The older experienced oxen are at the front of the team leading. These animals know the way as good as I do."

The wooden wagon was well made with metal axles and wheel rims, a necessity for the dirt roads we were on. Small wheels at the front allowed for steering and large fixed wheels at the back for strength and stability. A canvas tent like cover went over the top of the wagon. We walked alongside the wagon from sun up to sundown, eating only twice each day before we started and after we stopped. De Kalk introduced me to mealie porridge, a thick maize porridge and biltong, dried spiced meat which I became very fond of. It is hard to tell what animal the meat is from, and I am sure De Kalk's supply is from different animals, judging by the varied taste. My father was right, it is impossible to keep kosher out here.

For all that my companion said about his beasts, he looked after them well and cared about them. He liked to sing softly to himself for most of the day, and the oxen responded to his voice. During our supper, we chatted about our lives and how different they were. I told him my life story so far and he told me his. He particularly like my recitation of Shakespeare, telling me that he liked Hamlet best.

We travelled across the Karoo, an area that has little vegetation other than stunted shrubs. Dried river beds were covered with mimosa; otherwise the landscape looked drab in the bright, African sun. One night, after a particularly heavy rainfall, the bush burst into color, with yellow and purple flowers everywhere. Suddenly the Karoo was transformed. We saw buck feeding on the flowers, and wild birds seem to come from nowhere to sing their songs. De Kalk told me that the Karoo was part of a much larger region to the north called the Groot Karoo, a huge plateau, three thousand feet above sea level, that extends hundreds and hundreds of miles to the north. The rain slowed our progress as the wheels got stuck in the mud. The temperature was comfortable during the day, but the nights were cold and I was pleased to be able to sleep under the wagon when the rain came.

There were some days when I questioned why I was doing this. I was heading for an uncertain future. What if I'm too late and there are no diamonds left to find? What if I fail, where will I get the money to get back home? So many questions raced through my mind on this long, tiring march across an inhospitable, foreign land. For all my doubts, I felt that no matter what happened, I was able to make a go of it. I was young, healthy and could wheel and deal in anything. So these uncertainties never lasted longer than a few minutes. But they were there, creeping around in the back of my mind.

Nearly two months after leaving Cape Town our wagon rolled into Dutoitspan.

"It is hard to believe when you see it now, but only a year and a half ago there was nothing here but a single farmhouse where Du Toit, the owner, eked out a bare living farming about one hundred acres. Close by is another farm that used to owned by the De Beers brothers and then there is an area called New Rush for obvious reasons. This year the town got a new name of Kimberley, and Dutoitspan will be getting a new name as well. You will still hear the Afrikaaners calling it Vooruitzigt though."

"Thank you for this, De Kalk."

"This area of the Cape Colony is known as West Griqualand after the Griquas that inhabited the area. They are mostly half-castes and you will hear people call them bastards, for that is what many of them are. Other than the Griquas, there are more than thirty thousand men living here, searching for diamonds."

"Now there are thirty thousand and one."

"Just so you know what I have been told Barney, the best diggings are not here, but about three miles west at the Colesberg Kopje and on the old De Beers farm in Kimberley."

"Mr. De Kalk, I consider my journey with you the highlight of my adventure, so far. You take care of yourself and those hard working oxen."

I removed my trunk from the wagon, and dumped it on the ground in front of a corrugated iron shed whose sign read Cohen and Company, Diamond Buyers.

Chapter 6

"There's place and means for every man alive." William Shakespeare (1564 – 1616).

My first impression of Dutoitspan was that it looked like nothing I had ever seen. It would be hard to call it a town; it was an ugly assortment of corrugated iron shacks and hundreds of tents in varying condition. The streets, if you could call them that, were dusty, rutted dirt tracks, which I was sure that when it rains, were a river of mud.

It was the middle of the day and the streets were empty. People were working their claims and wouldn't be out in the town until after dark. Across from where I stood was a shack with a painted sign *The Pig and Whistle*, a pub. If there is one thing that any publican will know, it's their customers, and I was sure that I could get information on where to find my brother Harry. I crossed the road and entered the shack, a one-room affair about fifty feet long and twenty-five deep. After the bright sunlight outside it took me a couple of minutes for my eyes to focus in the gloom. My eyesight isn't the best and I know that I would have to find some kind of glasses that will work best in dim interiors.

I walked up to the bar, a well built affair with a slab top and even a brass foot rail. The publican immediately asked what I wanted to drink. There was only one other man in the pub, standing at the far end of the bar, nursing a beer.

"I'll have a beer."

The publican slid a bottle to me.

"Two shillings."

"How much?"

"Two shillings!"

"A beer costs three pence in London."

"This ain't London."

"Perhaps you can help me, I am looking for someone."

"Owe you money or something?"

"No, it's my brother, Harry Isaacs."

"Don't know 'im."

"He might be calling himself, Harry Barnato."

The man at the end of the bar perked up. I couldn't see his face as it was so dim.

"I know him, your brother you say?

"Yes, I'm his younger brother Barney. Do you know where I can find him?

"Possibly."

"Could you take me to him?"

"I ain't done drinking yet."

I thought for a minute, this could be a long process. It was the middle of the day and this man was not working. He could be at it for hours and I was anxious to find Harry while it was still light outside.

"How about I buy you a beer and then we go and you find him for me?"

The man limped toward me. He was about my age and really dirty, not that I looked much different I'm sure. At least I had the opportunity to bathe three days ago in a muddy stream. When he stood next to me, he was at least a foot taller than me and his breath was foul. I stepped back just enough to be out of direct range.

"How about two beers?"

"No can do, don't you worry, I'll find somebody else to help me."

I finished my drink and started to walk out of the pub. It's an old trick but you have to know when to use it, generally it works.

"Don't be so hasty, I'll settle for a beer."

The publican served up a bottle to the man and I paid him.

"Another?"

"No, not now, thanks."

I waited patiently while this man sipped his beer. At last he finished it, wiped his hand across his mouth then down his jacket, picked up his hat, and we went out into the bright afternoon sun.

It was then that I thought about my trunk that was still sitting where I had left it. I walked back inside the pub.

"Can I leave my trunk here, somewhere?"

"Put it in the corner away from the bar. Don't worry, no one will steal it, they're all pretty honest around here. The only things people steal here, are diamonds."

"It's full to the top with them."

"I believe you, thousands wouldn't."

He laughed as I dragged it to the corner. Apparently, it looked like it would come in handy, as there were few chairs for the patrons to sit on. I wasn't too sure about leaving it, but I had little choice.

My guide turned out to be an Australian.

"What's your name?"

"Morant, and yours must be Barnato."

"Barney Barnato. You know you have a funny accent."

"Huh? I've a funny accent! What about yours? You must be a cockney, judging by the way you talk. Hardly much different to my ear. My grandparents were "*pommies*". You know what that is?"

"Prisoners of her majesty. They were convicts deported from England to Australia for the petty crime stealing a loaf of bread."

Funny thing, he was quite proud of his convict heritage, not something I would want to boast about.

"How do you know my brother?"

"Most of the time he works in the Music Hall, does conjuring tricks and the like. He's been dabbling as a *kopje walloper*."

"What the hell is that?"

"Men who go around the diggings, buying up some of the inferior stones to resell at a profit. Of course, that's if they know what they're doing."

"Does he know what he's doing?"

"Hard for me to say, but if he was, he'd have given up the vaudeville stuff, wouldn't he?"

We walked along a wide, dirt road lined with a mix of corrugated iron shacks and large tents. These served as shops, selling all kinds of supplies, with a number of pubs mixed in between. Most had hand-painted wooden signs nailed to a post, or propped somehow on the roofs.

To my delight, I spotted a sign over a tent reading Athenaeum Music Hall. We walked inside. It was dark and smelled of mildew. The place was empty. There was a stage at one end, with a fancy velvet curtains open in the center.

"I was hoping my brother might be here."

"He must be out working."

"Doing what do you think?"

"Buying diamonds would be my guess."

I thought about that as we went outside again into the bright sunlight. Farther down the street, we walked past row upon of row of tattered and bleached tents of varying sizes, mostly deserted with the exception of stray dogs, sleeping in whatever shade they could find. Dust covered everything. It was in the air and I could taste it in my mouth. I needed another beer.

Morant chatted incessantly about his experiences on the goldfields of Bendigo in the State of Victoria, Australia.

"I got to the goldfields much too late. Large conglomerates already controlled all the mining. There was plenty of work to be had in the mines, but I wanted to have my own claim. So I came to the Cape Colony. The same thing will happen here within a few years."

"Really?"

"Yeah. All these thousands of claims will end up being owned by a handful of wealthy companies. The small men will be squeezed out. You mark my words. Diamonds, gold, it makes no difference. A man can get rich with hard work and a lot of luck, but you gotta do it fast."

"Why aren't you working today? Surely everyone works in the daytime?"

He shrugged his shoulders, pulled his hat down further to keep the sun out of his eyes.

"I was nearly killed when the reef caved in two days ago. At the moment I'm a bit scared to go back to it. Next time I may not be so lucky and end up dead! I need a few days to get my nerve back."

"What do you mean the reef caved in?"

"Cor, you're obviously a novice in these parts."

"I've only just arrived and have no idea what you are talking about."

"Why don't we go take a look at where all the action is; that way you'll have a better idea?"

"After I've found my brother. Then you can show me if you want."

But it was pretty obvious that we weren't going to find Harry before the evening. So I agreed to give up the search for the time being and let him show me the diggings. I was not prepared for the sight that spread out before me as we approached the area.

As far as the eye could see, there were square pits of different levels, each one immediately adjacent to the next one. Some of the pits were twenty feet deep, but the one that abutted it could be sixty feet deep. Around the edges of what looked like a giant crater, were piles of rock that had been dug out, making the pits look even deeper. At the bottom of these pits men hacked away at the rock with pick axes, shovels and hammers, breaking the rock into fist size pieces.

A yellowish dust covered everyone. It would be hard to tell if the men were white or black if they were dressed the same. However, the *kaffirs*, Morant's word for the natives, wore almost nothing, just a loin cloth. The white men dressed in shirts and work pants, had their hats pulled down well over their faces. The noise was overwhelming with all of the hammering going on.

An elaborate system of ropes was set up on the outer rim of the area. Attached on top of each pair of ropes were crude box cars that could be hauled up and down carrying rock or people from the bottom of each pit to the rim. It looked like some giant spiders had incredibly woven this.

"Each of these squares is thirty by thirty Cape feet in size, which is equivalent to thirty-one by thirty-one English feet," Morant explained.

"See how there is a thin strip of land between some of the pits. That is called the reef. Do you know what a coral reef is?"

"Sure I do, you have them in Australia."

"Right on. Well here in the diamond fields that pathway is referred to as the reef. There is meant to be a seven foot six inches wide pathway to allow a Scotch cart to be wheeled along it, letting the diggers take the rock to the outer edges for weathering. Because it is so narrow, and the rock is being continually removed from below, it has a tendency to collapse. Mules and carts constantly fall into the diggings and when that happens men get buried in it. Often it is fatal, by the time anyone can dig 'em out, they've suffocated."

"Sounds horrendous. I can't imagine being buried alive."

"That's what I was telling you about. Happened to me only last week. Now you know."

"What do you mean by weathering?" Morant shot me a look of contempt.

"Oh shit, you don't know nothing. The rock is taken to depositing floors; these are areas that diggers have to rent. There it is tipped out, broken up, and put through mesh sieves. The yellow rock is quite soft. It is left out in the sun and rain to weather. Then it is shoveled onto tables and sorted through and the diamonds are picked out."

"Sounds like a lot of work with a lot of risk."

"Yeah better believe it, mate, but that is only one of the risks of mining. It doesn't matter what you do here, there are huge risks. It gets worse when the rains come. The dirt becomes mud which washes down to the lowest level, taking men and equipment with it. Take a look at the graveyard here and you'll see several hundreds of graves of men who died trying to make the big find. At the moment they say there are twenty thousand men working the diamond fields, ten per cent are whites, the rest are *kaffirs*."

"I'm beginning to see that this was not going to be as easy as I may have thought. In my mind I thought you could literally pick diamonds off the ground."

"At the beginning men were doing that, picking diamonds off the ground, particularly by the Vaal River. These here are what we call dry diggings. The diamonds are in the soft yellow ground. At some point a few of the miners have hit a hard blue color rock that's the devil to break. The theory is that its the bottom of the deposit. If you have a claim that has hit the blue ground, it's all over. You can pack up and go somewhere else."

"Are there any claims that can be bought?"

"Yes and no. Diggers in Dutoitspan and Bultfontein mines are abandoning their claims because they cannot find enough stones to pay the overhead of ten shillings a month. So those can be bought, but you don't want to waste your time and money on those. Good claims in Kimberley or De Beers cost a lot of money. I don't suppose you have that. Of course you could buy one that has been worked out. You might get lucky and find a few stones."

"Are there any diamonds in the blue ground?"

"Some say there are tiny stones, but they are too small to make a profit and they are too damn difficult to get out."

"You are giving me quite an education. Where's your claim?

"Further east, you can't even see it from where we are standing now."

I looked at my watch to find that we had been here for much longer than I realized. In this part of the world, it gets dark quite rapidly, not like in England where we have a long twilight. That is, when we can see the sun.

"We'd better be getting back into town. Get there before the rush," Morant advised.

Men were stowing their gear and making their way out of the pits after a long, hard day's work. I could see how they winched the box cars up to the rim, not an easy task when fully loaded. I could imagine that some had found a lot and were excited at what their prospects would be. While others may have found nothing today, but hoped for better things tomorrow. It was time to get some food and rest and start again at daybreak. The natives walked along in groups, some of them singing, some laughing. They appeared much happier than the whites, who were heading in the opposite direction.

"Where are the natives going?"

"They have their own camps on the west side of the rim. We don't mix with them. The *kaffirs* are only interested in earning enough money to be able to buy a gun and some good gear. That's how they consider they are wealthy. After that, they return to their tribes and find a wife. Every day they are nearer to their goal. Diamonds mean nothing to them; it's what they get paid that matters."

There was quite a crowd walking along into Dutoitspan, I looked at their weary, leathery, unshaven faces. Covered in yellowish dust, they were filthy. Insects buzzed around them all, but hardly anyone batted them away. As the sun went down a few of the men lit flaming torches to light the way. To my surprise there were a few women among the crowd, dressed like men. It was hard to tell until they took off their hats now that sun had gone down. For the life of me I could not understand how any woman could do this backbreaking work. I was curious about it.

"Are there are many women miners here?"

"Not that many?"

"Surely it's too hard for a woman to do this kind of work!"

"They want to get rich like everyone else. It may not be something that you'd want for your mother or sister, but its honest work. They have as much chance at striking it rich as anyone else.

There were women working in the goldfields of Bendigo. Of course, there were a lot of women working in the bars and whorehouses too. That's a different kind of work, but it can be just as dangerous considering the peccadilloes of some of these men when they act like animals."

"I've no doubt, we've had our share of murdered and battered prostitutes in London, especially in the area around Limehouse."

"Well if we are going to find your brother, I think we should go back to the Pig and Whistle. He often stops in there on his way to the Music Hall. If I am not mistaken, he will be playing there tonight.

Chapter 7

The Pig and Whistle was packed from wall to wall by the time we got back. My trunk was, as predicted, being used for a seat for a pretty young woman of indeterminate age. She could have been anything from sixteen to twenty-five. Her long golden hair hung down over her bare shoulders and she had the most beautiful blue eyes. She flashed me a smile when I went to check that the trunk was still there.

"Don't worry luv, I won't break it. Thanks for giving a lady somewhere to sit."

"Thanks for looking after it."

"Anytime."

I surveyed the bar looking for Harry. More and more people were squeezing through the door. This place was busier than any pub I'd ever been in. Men were eating from tin plates that contained some unidentifiable meat and vegetables. It was then that I realized, I was very hungry.

"Morant, you want to get something to eat? I've had nothing since the early hours of this morning."

"Good thinking mate."

We pushed our way up to the end of the bar where two men were ladling out food onto battered tin plates. It took a while to get to the front of the line and get our food. As I turned to move away from the bar, a shout went up and a familiar voice called out my name.

"Barney! Barney, I don't believe it, you're here."

Harry grabbed me in a bear hug, picked me up and spun me around, my food spilling on the floor.

"Watch it, you're making me drop my supper."

"Sorry Barney, I'm so excited to see you. Why didn't you let me know you were coming? I wasn't sure if my letter had got to you. In fact I was going to write another letter tonight. How's dad? And how are Kathy, Sarah and Lizzie?"

"When I left England, what, two and half months ago, everyone was in good health except Lizzie. She has been really sick with a cough that does not seem to go away. Dad took her to the doctor who gave her some medicine, but she has not got any better. If anything she is worse. I'm terribly worried for her."

"That doesn't sound good. I'm glad to hear everyone else is fine. I share your concerns and we should send a letter quickly, let the family know you have arrived in one piece."

I looked at my brother who appeared to have lost a lot of weight since I had seen him last. He had a full beard, his hair was long and matted. His skin was darkened by the sun.

"How are you, Harry? You look much changed since last time I saw you."

"I've had a touch of camp fever, but I am better now. It is one of the problems of our life here. No sanitation to speak of. Lack of clean water, but you don't want to hear about that now. "

We moved out of the way of the men trying to get to the bar. There wasn't much room anywhere, so we stood outside in the street. Harry kept looking at me.

"Look at you, skinny as ever, but you look fit. Are you ready for a few prize fights? "

"Not with this mob. They break rocks all day and some of them look like they do it with their bare hands."

"Not to worry, we can play on the stage at the Music Hall together. The Barnato Brothers from the London halls. Sounds good. You want to play tonight?"

"Harry, I'd love to, but I'm knackered. I've walked all the way from Cape Town. A long bloody way, and I only arrived this morning. What I would really love is a hot bath and a comfortable bed."

He started laughing, so much so I had to laugh with him. I was not sure what was so funny.

"First off, there is a big shortage of water here, it all has to be brought in from the river several miles away. So you have no chance of a bath until the rain comes again. Next off, there are no comfortable beds here. The lucky ones have camp beds or hammocks, we sleep on a dirt floor."

"Okay then, no bath and no bed. I'm going to finish my grub. Then you can help me pick up my trunk and go to wherever it is that you sleep. Is that okay with you?"

"No problem, where's your trunk?"

I pointed to where the pretty young woman was holding court around my trunk. She looked my way again and winked.

"I see Roseanne has commandeered it."

"You know her?"

"Every man in this town knows her."

"Oh, I should have guessed."

Morant had been standing off to one side, eating, watching and listening to our conversation. I thought it would be polite to introduce him to my brother.

"By the way Harry, this is Morant, he has been kind enough to show me around and help me find you."

The two men shook hands, but Harry's attitude was quite cool toward Morant. Later, I would have to ask him why.

With that we pushed our way over to my trunk to rescue it. Roseanne was reluctant to give it up. Sitting, perched on top, she was showing off her best features.

"I'm not sure I'm going to let you take your trunk laddie."

"How about I give you a big kiss to get you to surrender it?"

"Well now, that would depend on what else you want."

"For now all I want is to get some sleep. After two months walking here from Cape Town, I have little energy for anything else."

"That's not bad for an excuse, so I will give it up. The kiss will have to wait for another day, when you are properly rested."

She laughed and flashed me her beautiful blue eyes, allowing me to stoop down and pick up my trunk. Her breasts brushed across my hand and she winked at me again.

I took one side of my trunk; Harry took the other and guided me through a maze of tents to where he lived. Fortunately, there was a full moon and it provided plenty of light for us to find our way. Small campfires glowed outside many of tents and the smell of cooking made me think of home for the first time in many days.

Harry's tent was like the hundreds of others surrounding it. I wasn't sure how he could tell which one was his until I saw he had Barnato painted on the side. Inside, there was barely enough room to stand upright and I'm shorter than Harry. It was pretty basic; fortunately he did have a couple of blankets, one of which served as a pillow. I lay down on the ground and pulled a blanket over my head.

"Goodnight, Harry. Let's talk in the morning. I'm dog tired and can't keep my eyes open a minute longer."

"Goodnight, Barney, I'm sure glad you've made it here. We'll talk all you like tomorrow. I'll be leaving before it is light, so I won't wake you."

Chapter 8

I awoke with a start. The sun was beating down on the canvas of the tent and the temperature inside was unbearable. The smell of unwashed clothes and my own sweat-covered body was revolting. I knew I'd get used to it after a while. First things first; I needed something to drink. My mouth felt like the bottom of a parrot cage. I pulled out my watch and looked at the time. It was a quarter to four! Judging by the sunlight it was afternoon. How could I have slept so long? It was time to go back to the Pig and Whistle and get somet food. Eating and drinking there every day was going to use up my money quickly, especially as the price of beer there is ten times that of London.

On one side of the tent there was a small table with a bowl of murky water, a bar of soap and a hand mirror. I washed my hands and face, opened my trunk, took out a change of clothes and two boxes of my cigars. Time to make some money, at least pay for my food for the next week. I changed and brushed my hair. I looked fresher and felt much better after my long sleep. Now I was ready for anything.

On my return to the Pig and Whistle, I found it was almost empty. Of course it was still early in the afternoon and there was at least a couple of hours of daylight left. I looked around for Morant, but he was not there. I ordered a beer and asked the publican his name.

"Albert, some call me the prince after his royal highness, but I don't care much."

"Well if you're okay with Albert, so be it. I'm Barney I. Barnato."

"Yeah, you told me when you arrived. Find your brother okay?"

"I did, although it was more like bumping into each other in your food line, than finding him."

"Not too many choices for food in Dutoitspan."

"Talking of food, is it too early for a meal?"

"Yeah, I can offer you mealie and biltong, but that's about it for another hour or so."

"Okay, I'll take that, I'm starving. Seen Morant?"

"No, he's not been around today."

I sipped my beer and Albert went and got my food. He returned with a large bowl of mealie with the biltong layered on top. Not the most appetizing dish, but I didn't care. He was eying the boxes of cigars I had placed on the top of the bar. Curiosity got the better of him.

"Planning on smoking those on your own?"

"Not really, I brought my supply with me. Can't beat a really good smoke. I wasn't sure if I would be able to get Havana cigars here."

"Havanas! They'd fetch a pretty penny if I was selling them, probably get two shillings each."

"Hah, you're kidding me, I paid more than that in London."

"Well I bet I could get double that without much quibbling by some of my regulars."

"Now you're talking. I tell you what I'll do, you don't have to pay me for them now, you sell them and we"ll split the proceeds eighty, twenty, the twenty per cent is for you."

"No, that's not enough, I want fifty per cent of the proceeds."

"Sorry, Albert, I'll have to go down the street to the Spotted Dog. They'll not be so greedy."

"Greedy, greedy, I'm not greedy, I have overhead. This building cost me a fortune. Sixty, forty that's my last offer."

"I tell you what I'll do and I will understand if you say no. Seventy, thirty or I'll go elsewhere. Remember, it's not going to cost you anything up front and I'll be in here as a regular, spending my proceeds back with you. All I'll need is a bit of spending money for supplies. What do you say?"

"Deal."

We shook on it. I handed over the two boxes of cigars to Albert who put them under the counter out of sight. Just then, Harry walked into the pub.

"Great timing I was just getting something to eat. You want some?

He looked at my mealie and biltong with distaste.

"Is that all he's got?"

"Yeah, it's a bit too early for a proper meal. You want some or not?"

"Sure, I'm pretty hungry, haven't eaten anything all day."

"Albert, same again for my brother and a beer for him too. Put it on my account."

Harry's eyebrows went up.

"You've been here a day and you have an account with Albert?"

"I did a little bit of business with him, sold him some fine Havana cigars, well sort of. Let's take our food and sit at a table."

"You have to tell me everything that you've been doing since you got here. I can't wait to start in diamond dealing, or whatever it is you're doing. I've seen the diggings and as crazy as it looks, I want part of it."

"Steady on now. There is so much that you have to learn, even though you have an advantage. You have me to show you the ropes. I've found it difficult to trade in diamonds, as it is easy to pay too much for a stone because of over enthusiasm. I've had a few successes, but I have had a number of losses too."

"But I thought that you were doing well."

"Barney, let me talk first and then you can ask your questions. There are thousands of men here digging out diamonds. Some have found really big stones and made fortunes. Many have found nothing and have been forced for one reason or another to give up."

"Well it sounds like there are still diamonds to be found."

"Of course there are. I've been able to perform here in the Music Hall and make money which at least allows me to eat. But I don't have much capital to buy and sell. So on a day that I am able to buy a few stones, I have to quickly find a buyer that will pay me a profit to let me to buy more. It's a constant cycle of buying and selling, made more difficult by living hand to mouth. Things are expensive here as you can see a bottle of beer is at least ten times that of London. Water is more expensive than alcohol and all the food that is consumed has to brought in by ox wagon at a high cost."

"Yes, I know about ox wagons, that is how I travelled here from Cape Town. My waggoneer was carrying twenty tons of produce."

"Well that's only part of it. There are dangers here that you cannot imagine. Natural disasters, like when the reef falls in and buries men underneath. Floods when the rains come in such torrents that you can't work in it without being half drowned. Or even worse when the mud buries men in their claims. Then there are the thefts, murders, and the IDB."

"What's IDB?"

"Illegal diamond buying. This is something that you have to know about when you deal in diamonds. The natives come here to earn enough money to go home to their tribal lands equipped with a gun and some supplies. Their wages amount to about three pounds a year!"

"That doesn't sound like much for a year's work."

"To reach their goal quicker, they steal up to half the diamonds they find."

"Can't they be searched?"

"In 1870, the diggers formed a group called the Diamond Diggers Protection Society to stamp out the illicit trade. They got the idea from the Australian gold miners, who had the same problem there. What they did was to impose regulations approved by British Commissioners. They do not allow any man of color to hold claims or own diamonds. If they have diamonds in their possession they have to have permission from their employer and that is rare. So what happens is that the natives steal a diamond by swallowing it, or inserting into a cut in the thick skin of their feet. Or sometimes in their arse, depending on the size of the stone. When they leave the diggings at the end of the day, nothing is easily seen on them.

"Pretty inventive if you ask me."

"Later, they sell the diamond to a tout for a fraction of the real value. He sells it for a profit to someone with a small claim who, if challenged, can say it was found in his claim. This way the claim owner legitimizes the possession of the stone."

"Cunning bastards."

"The penalties for being caught are quite extreme. Fines, three months hard labor or twenty-five lashes."

"Does it stop the thefts?" Harry laughed,

"No, not at all! More and more men and natives come here to work the claims every day, so it continues. You really have to know with whom you are dealing when you go out to buy. The best thing is to buy from the small claim holders and diggers on the outer edge of the fields. They find less and need money to continue. They'll make you a deal. If they don't make enough money, they have to sell up or worse, just abandon their claim. The people you don't want to work with are the Morants of this world, they have no visible means of support and are the most suspect."

"So that is why you were so cool to him the other day. Now I understand your reaction. You know with all this talk, I have never seen a diamond in the rough. Do you have one to show me?"

"Here take a look."

Harry slid a little pouch over the table to me. I moved the now empty plates out of the way and looked around me to see if anyone was watching. Satisfied that there was nobody, I slowly tipped out the contents into my hand which trembled slightly. It was so exciting. I know that I was holding my future and I was awe struck. Picking up the first stone, about the size of a large pea, was this clear crystal that looked like two four sided pyramids stuck together. The surface was hard and cold and etched with a pattern in the shape of the crystal. I rolled it around with my finger and then held it up to the light coming in from the open door to see how clear it was.

"That double pyramid shape is an octahedron. This is typical of what a diamond looks like. It can sometimes be quite flat, like one of the others in that group. The color will vary. Some have a yellowish tinge to them, some have a bluish tinge, and some, regardless of color, will glow in the sunlight. You have to have an eyeglass to see inside the stone to judge the impurities that will affect the value and the way the stone is cut when it is polished."

I took an eyeglass that Harry held out and tried to focus on the stone.

"No, you have to bring the stone much closer to your eye to see anything. About three or four inches between the glass and the stone."

I got the hang of it and stared at the interior of the stone. It appeared to have a few spots, of what I had no idea. This was so unimaginable; I was sitting here looking at diamonds. Up till now it had been all talk, but here was the real thing. I had no doubt in my mind that with Harry's guidance it would take me no time at all to learn about diamonds.

"What about the value? How much is a diamond worth?"

"That depends on many factors, size, color, weight, clarity. In fact, everything affects the price. Some stones are worth as little as six or seven shillings a carat; others are worth forty to one hundred pounds a carat."

"How do you know what to pay then?"

"You have to look at a lot of stones and ask prices. The more you see, the better it is. After a few weeks of looking, you can start to buy a few stones. Start by offering half of the asking price. That won't make you popular with sellers, but it will get you to a better price, probably still be more than you want to pay. Then you start really negotiating. Believe me, the diggers will try and sting you hard with high prices if they think that you know nothing. You have to look like you know what you are doing, even when you don't. That's the way I do it."

"You told me you were finding it difficult to make money. What can I do to improve our success?" Harry smiled,

"With the two of us buying there is a bit of strategy that we can employ. Every time I say I like something and want to buy it, you say no, it's not worth the price and get up to leave. I then say to the digger that my brother doesn't like the deal so give me the best price, or we walk. That is when the bottom price is reached. It still may be too high, but at least it will be as good a deal as we can negotiate. See, it's much better working as a team."

"I get it."

"I have a suggestion. For the next few weeks you should spend some time with our cousin David Harris. He's been quite successful and has been on the fields for nearly three years."

"Yes, I was going to ask you about David. Where do we find him?"

"He has a small office on Reitz Street. I will take you there tomorrow."

Chapter 9

The next morning Harry and I went to visit David at his small office right in the center of town. It was no more than a wooden frame covered by canvas, twelve feet by eight with a sign over the top proclaiming David Harris, Diamond Dealer. He greeted me warmly; we were more like brothers than cousins. We attended the same school, the Jews Free School in London, where we had received a pretty good education.

"Welcome to Kimberley, Barney, hello Harry, I was expecting my brother as well. Did he get lost along the way?"

"He decided he wanted to spend a few days in Cape Town. I presume that he did so and is on his way here now. It took me nearly two months to get here walking alongside an ox wagon. I only arrived two days ago. He probably found out how expensive it was to travel by coach and is travelling the same way. It is really good to see you again. I had a tour of the diggings and can't wait to be part of it."

"Well, it takes time to learn about diamonds. You may not want to do the actual digging. It's back-breaking work and often fruitless. Dealing in the diamonds is the best way to get started. Let me tell you, I tried my hand at digging and lost my shirt. I could not find enough diamonds to pay my overhead and workers."

"Men are finding diamonds aren't they?

"Yes, of course they are, and that is why I am sitting in an office, buying and selling every day."

Harry looked around, obviously not impressed by David's office.

"Do you think you could teach Barney how to buy and sell diamonds?"

"Why don't you teach him?"

"I'm not really doing much dealing. I am earning my money from performing."

David sat in thought for a minute.

"When I lost my claim, I went to work for Marcus Hayman. He has the general store in town and he is also a diamond dealer. I was very fortunate because I handled a lot of stones in the store. Within a few months, he allowed me to become a kopje walloper. That's a low-level, itinerant diamond dealer Barney. He fronted me one hundred pounds to buy diamonds. I had to give him first choice of the stones I purchased and half of my profit. The arrangement was initially for one month and lasted three months. In the meantime, I made enough money to set myself up in business. If you are interested, that is what I propose for you Barney."

"Well, I don't know what to say, but thank you. When should I start?"

"No time like the present. Start now."

Harry said his goodbyes and I began my career in the diamond business.

Over the next few weeks, I quickly learned the ropes from David. I acquired a good magnifying glass as my eyesight is not good. This I attached to my watch chain so that I always had it handy to take a close look at any diamonds that were being offered to me. I spent the daylight hours trudging from one diamond dealer to the next. In the evenings, I met with the diggers at the Pig and Whistle or the Spotted Dog and bought the results of their day's hard labor. Harry earned some money with his conjuring act in the local Music Hall. Funny enough, some of the diggers didn't like Harry handling their diamonds as they had seen his slight-of-hand at work in his act.

It wasn't easy walking around all day in the heat. My shoes were wearing thin and the few clothes I had were beginning to look like rags. After three months, I left David and worked with Harry. Over the next three months, we managed to make a bit of a profit together. Harry was confident that I could buy and sell without his help. Any extra money he earned at performing went back into more diamonds.

"I gotta hand it to you, Barney, you have learned fast and with your gift of the gab, you'll do fine. You may not become a millionaire but I think you'll do alright."

"That sounds like a speech to tell me you are giving up."

"No, it isn't that. I got an opportunity to work for Van Praagh, who is an important diamond dealer. Cousin David recommended me and this is great opportunity to learn. For the time being you are going to have to work on your own."

"Wait up a minute. Aren't we still partners?"

"Barney, listen to me, I need to gain more knowledge about diamonds so that I can teach you too. This is a good break for both of us. In a year or two, I will have gained far more knowledge than I can do in ten years. Then we will continue to be partners again."

"Harry, you and David have done a good job teaching me the basics and it helps that these dealers here are some of the worst business men I've ever met. They try on more tricks than any petty crook in London would do because they think I'm still wet behind the ears. But don't do this now. I think we can still make enough money to be able to buy our own claim. Then we will make some real money, not this pittance we're making at present"

"Listen kid, I know you have your heart set on diamond mining, but after the time I have spent here, I've come to the conclusion that I lack the knowledge to make it big. I'm tired of living hand to mouth, never knowing if we can make a profit or lose everything on the next purchase."

"We never needed an education. Father taught us just about everything we know."

"That's right, but think about this; he taught us what he knew. Now I can learn from someone who is rich and successful in the diamond business, and so will you." I felt sick inside,

"I can't say I blame you, but you should know I'm not happy about this. I think you should put a time limit on this education, like six months, not longer."

"I'm going to say one year, not less not more and I don't want you arguing on this. My mind is made up."

That night as I walked over to the Pig and Whistle. There was a horse drawn wagon with a string quartet playing Mozart's Requiem. At one end of the wagon was a pile of digger's tools topped with two rifles. A black flag fluttered in the wind, bearing the inscription "The Earth is the Lords and the fullness thereof." A few men walked alongside of the wagon handing out handbills to everyone in the street. I read one. "Important meeting in Market Square at six p.m. Thursday. The government must change its policy on Griqualand West. We the Diggers Protection Association demand that the government repeal, alter or mutilate recently passed ordinances. Make your voice heard!"

Harry went to tell Van Praagh that he would start working for him. I was not too happy, but I felt confident that I could still achieve my goal without Harry if need be. I know that he was right about learning as much as he could. After all is said and done, between us we hardly know anything. It's all right when we are only paying a pound or two a carat, but we knew nothing about how to value a diamond of any size. Spending fifty or even one hundred pounds a carat is out of the question. We could lose everything in one go.

I'd almost reached the Pig and Whistle when the rains came. I'd never seen anything like it in my entire life. Torrential rain so thick, I could not see a hand in front of my face. My shoes filled with water through the holes in the bottom and my clothes clung to me. Thunder accompanied the downpour, and the night lit up with flashes of lightening that gave an eerie appearance to the street. The din of the rain on the metal roofs of the buildings created a continuous cacophony and the water gushed down on anyone walking below. The rain was warm. It felt good on my unwashed body. The roadway quickly became a torrent of thick mud. It was hard to lift my feet without losing a shoe from the only pair I had.

I returned to our tent, stripped off my clothes, stood out in the rain and washed myself and my clothes. Oh, what a great relief to feel clean again. My shaving kit was lying unused on a small table, so I made use of it, removing the weeks of hairy growth from my face. I felt sure nobody will recognize me, so I kept a small moustache. Once I had finished my ablutions, I decided that something had to do be done about the mud that was flowing freely into our tent. I set to work trying to save our flimsy bedding.

Harry returned about an hour later, so wet and bedraggled that he could hardly stand up. He too took the opportunity to wash and shave in the downpour, but decided to keep his beard for the time being.

Morning came and the rain was still going strong. I wondered if anyone would be out digging in this, but realized that nothing stops these men. The sky was dark and foreboding. I'd got used to the bright early sunlight, but this morning was as dark as a London fog. And I was wet, really wet. Amazingly, I had slept well enough considering the noise of the storm.

Suddenly, a bell started clanging, seemingly coming from somewhere in the diggings. We ran out to see what was happening. Men were running and shouting something about the reef collapsing. I ran with them. As I got to the diggings, I could see that the rain had washed away part of the thin pathways that lined some of the claims.

Water was accumulating at the bottom of many of the lower level claims. At one of them, men were digging frantically. Apparently five men, two whites and three natives, had just started working when the reef caved in, burying them all. This had been seen by the diggers arriving on a higher level claim and they had put out the alarm. One by one, the bodies of the five men were pulled out of the mud. All had suffocated before they could be rescued.

Close by where I stood, another reef collapsed, washing thick mud into the hole below and swamping four men almost immediately. I slid down the muddy wall which was almost a vertical drop and tried to grab one of the men as he went into the mud. His eyes rolling in panic and his mouth filled with mud as he let out a scream. I managed to get a hold of his wrist and pulled with all my strength. Suddenly more mud flooded down, the light disappeared as it swept over my head. I still held the man's wrist, but I was in dire straits, unable to tell what was up or down. The force of the mud totally disoriented me. My lungs hurt and I was gasping for air. A pair of hands grabbed me under my armpits, hauled me out till I could see daylight. I still had hold on the man's wrist and yanked hard, pulling him from the morass.

"You were lucky, kid, I saw you go down. Another minute and you would have choked to death on mud."

I looked at the worried face of my brother. I was never more thankful to my maker that he had been there for me. Bodies were winched up to the rim where the local undertaker had already pulled up a wagon in anticipation of the outcome. Life is brutal here; many will die in their quest to strike it rich.

Chapter 10

I was none the worse for the close call with death that day, but I was a bit shaken and needed a drink. I thought about changing out of my muddy clothes, somehow it was pointless in this torrential rain. The only thing to do was to head over to the Pig and Whistle and grab a fresh bottle of Cape Smoke, the local made brandy.

I entered the Pig to find that it was really crowded. It was obvious that many men had decided not to work today. I ordered soup and a bottle of Smoke. Albert didn't recognize me. My beard was gone, my hair was slicked down and I was dripping wet from the rain. By now, most of the mud had washed off me. Then I saw the flicker of recognition in his eyes.

"Barney I. Barnato as if I live and breathe, is that you?"

"The very same."

"What happened, are you getting married or sumtin'?"

"Nah, just got tired of the all the hair. The rain gave me the opportunity to clean up my act, so I took advantage of it."

"Heard you was nearly buried alive this mornin'."

"Yeah, I had a close call, but my maker obviously has other plans for me."

"That's good. What would we all do without your smilin' face and natural wit around here. Here's your soup."

I took the soup and looked around for somewhere to sit. Albert had recently added more tables and chairs, but it looked like they were all taken. Across the room was a bench with inadequate space on it, but I figured I could squeeze in. Of course, I would have to shift the two men either side a bit. I walked over, slung my leg over the bench, sat down and wriggled my bum to fit in. The two men gave me a sideways glance and tried to push back, but I wasn't having any of it.

I slurped my soup loudly, the two men ignored me. I coughed into a spoonful, sending splatters in all directions, mostly on them. It had the effect I wanted. They both slid away from me, giving me plenty of room.

"Sorry mates, a fly got into my soup and I sucked it up. It's gone now."

They both gave me looks that could kill, but I wasn't afraid of them one bit. Across the table a young man started clapping loudly. He was laughing so much it started me off. He reached over the table and shook my hand.

"Louis Cohen."

"Barney I. Barnato. You have any diamonds you want to sell?"

"Maybe."

I looked at the man. He was about the same age as me, taller and pale in complexion. His handshake was strong, his voice was deep and sonorous with a slight accent that I placed as Irish.

"Where are you from in Ireland?"

"I'm not from Ireland, I'm from Liverpool in England."

"But I can hear an Irish brogue in your voice."

"That's because my mother is Irish, but not my father. He is from Whitechapel in London."

"Really, which street?"

"Philpot Street."

"Are you Jewish?"

"My dad is, but I am not considered to be so, as my mother isn't."

"Yes, I know how that is."

"I was brought up in both religions of my parents. We celebrated all the Saint's Days, Christmas, Easter and all the Jewish Holidays, so I guess I've had the best of both worlds."

Louis was eying the bottle of Cape Smoke in front of me. I pointed to the bottle.

"Have a drink with me, I hate to drink alone. You can tell me all about your life so far."

"Thanks I will."

We sat drinking for most of the day. The rain came in torrents outside and there was absolutely no reason to venture out in it. I was sure that my belongings would be flooded, not that I had much there to worry about. The first bottle of Smoke disappeared and we were already on the second when we both talked about becoming partners as diamond dealers.

Louis had been in Dutoitspan slightly longer than me. He had come to the Cape Colony at the age of 17. His father was quite successful in business and had paid for Louis' second class passage from England. He had given him a twenty-five gold sovereigns to help him get started and for his protection, he gave him a revolver. Louis, like me, was a kopje walloper dealing in small diamonds and had been working with his cousin Lewis Woolf. I 'd heard of Woolf, but had no dealings with him. I had the impression that Louis was not happy in this partnership and was looking to go it alone. That was difficult, as I already knew it takes capital and when you are doing the rounds buying, you need a partner who can be selling what you have already bought.

"Do you have any money?" Louis demanded quietly. I looked at his body language to see why he was asking me.

"Have some, could always do with more. How much do you have?"

"Sixty pounds. Can you match that?"

"I can, sort of."

"What's that suppose to mean?"

"So I told him about the valuable boxes of cigars. I had twenty-one boxes left and the valued them at thirty pounds. And I had thirty pounds."

"Well, what do think about the two of us teaming up. I think we could be a great team!" Louis exclaimed. I thought about this for a few seconds. I was impressed with Louis and felt that we were going to get on like a house on fire. So we shook hands and became partners.

We had no written agreement. We decided that if either of us wanted to break the partnership, we would divide up the results of our work, fifty-fifty and there would be no hard feelings; Barnato and Cohen, diamond dealers.

Chapter 11

"It is not in the stars to hold our destiny but in ourselves." William Shakespeare (1564 – 1616).

Louis and I got off to a great start. In our first month we purchased several lots of small and medium size diamonds at very good prices. There was a fear amongst the diggers that because of the large quantities of diamonds that were being found at New Rush, Colesberg Kopje and Kimberley, the world prices would take a dive. There were also rumors that the American market was going through a slump and America was the number one buyer of diamonds. The reason made sense. The diggers were anxious to sell before the market dropped. Nevertheless, every day we sold the purchases from the previous day's buys and made a decent profit.

All of the diamond dealers were getting wary of overpaying. In consequence, the diggers were much more open to negotiation and we made sure that we offered fair, but sensible offers. I always made sure that I carried a flask of Cape Smoke brandy with me to seal a deal. Somehow this became my trademark.

It was still raining heavily at the end of the first month, although that did nothing to discourage either of us. In fact, it probably was an advantage, as production was low with many diggers nervous to work when the reef was in constant turmoil. Everyday men were dying, being buried alive. Horse-drawn carts fell into the diggings and the pits filled with water and mud.

We had heard that there was a man named Cecil Rhodes who had purchased a large steam pump and was charging the diggers to pump out their claims. Personally, I couldn't see that it made sense to do this until the rain let up, but I realized that when that happened, everyone would want his services and the delay in waiting could be lengthy.

I was beginning to see how diamond mining was not an easy proposition, but it did nothing to deter me from my goal of buying a claim, as soon as I had enough money to do so. I told Louis that this was my ultimate goal. Somehow it wasn't his. He always seemed to dodge the subject when I brought it up. Still, at this point it was a long way from being a reality.

It was truly amazing to see the ingenuity of the diggers. Kimberley

Mine was criss-crossed with ropes like a huge spider's web. These ropes were set up to allow men to get to their claims and haul up the rock out of the huge crater. Wooden stagings with several platforms were constructed on the outer rim of the mine. Extending from the stagings to the claims below were ropes, actually wire hawsers, with wooden tubs hanging from them. These were hauled up and down by hand wound windlasses. As one tub is wound up, a second empty one descended, allowing a continuous flow of diamondiferous rock to be brought outside of the claim for crushing and weathering.

Someone told me there were more than a thousand in operation in Kimberley Mine and I could well believe that. A windlass is one of the oldest ways of lifting heavy objects, so it was a natural choice. It was used to get water from wells for hundreds of years.

Horse whims were gradually replacing the hand labor. This was a more elaborate and efficient set-up. Whims are a large wooden wheel fifteen or so feet in diameter, fixed horizontally above the ground with clearance for men and carts to be able to pass underneath them. A hawser went around the wheel and back into the diggings. A horse walked around in a large circle and the tubs moved continuously up and down. A whim is similar to a windlass and has been used in tin mining in Cornwall for hundreds of years. Obviously, someone had brought the idea from England. The big advantage of the whim is that it can operate at a distance from the diggings. It was truly amazing to see the ingenuity of men to get in and out of their claims and to be able to haul out the thousands of tons of rocks.

It was all very fascinating to me and essential knowledge for a successful diamond miner.

One Sunday, Louis and I decided to celebrate our good fortune and go to Maloneys for lemon syrups. These were a great treat for both of us when we were growing up in England. Maloney had his own special recipe, which included a shot of Irish whisky. Maloney had his corrugated iron shack right next to the edge of what was now being called the Big Hole at Kimberley.

The rain had let up for a bit and we sat on a couple of empty beer kegs outside and surveyed the complex riggings of the diggers. There were rail tracks around the rim of the hole with small rolling stock that a miner could push to a field close by, tipped out and spread for weathering. There were quite a lot of men working this area, searching the tailings for overlooked diamonds. The sieves that the diggers were using allowed smaller, mainly insignificant stones to drop through as these stones were considered unimportant. Everyone was after the larger, higher priced diamonds.

A patient man could make money working the tailings. There was no risk of getting buried alive or the high cost of buying a claim. I'd thought about this on occasion, but decided that this was too slow, as there was no chance to find anything but tiny stones worth a few shillings a carat.

"You know Lou; there is enough room here to put up a building alongside Maloneys. It would make a huge difference to us if we had our own office. A lot of the diggers come here for a drink at the end of the day. Why don't we ask Maloney if he would be interested in renting us the land and put up an iron hut like his, smaller of course?"

"I'm not sure, Barney. It might be too expensive. You know we can't afford much."

"Well, I'm going to ask him. What's the worst that can happen? He could say no or he could rent it to someone else."

Maloney wasn't a bad chap; he had a good head for numbers and was not averse to the idea. He scribbled some numbers down on a piece of paper and worked out what it would cost to build the hut, a twelve foot by ten foot structure split into two rooms, one for the office and a smaller room for living quarters.

"One guinea a day."

A guinea is one pound, one shilling, so I offered him a pound a day. His eyes narrowed,

"No, I worked it out, that is my price. You can think about it for a couple a days. Thanks for giving me the idea. I might as well get started constructing the building. If you don't want it I am sure one of the other diamond dealers will. Shouldn't take long to construct, no more than three weeks tops."

"Thanks, Maloney, I'll discuss it with my partner and get back to you within a couple of days."

I went outside to tell Louis the price. Deep down I knew he was not going to be happy at the cost. I also knew that if we were to expand and make it big, we had to show that we are successful. Having a proper office told everyone that we were going up the ladder, no longer kopje wallopers picking up the dregs, but proper diamond dealers. Sure enough he balked at the price.

"A guinea a day! Much too expensive, we can't pay that kind of money, it will bankrupt us."

"I don't agree. We'll be able to buy much more. You can work the office and I'll make my rounds as before, both buying and selling. I think we'll make double the rent every day. You have to see this is a good move. Besides, we'll have an office and living quarters with a little stove so we can eat all our meals there, that'll save us money."

Reluctantly, Louis agreed to do it and I went to tell Maloney we have a deal.

Good to his word, Maloney had the building constructed in less than three weeks, complete with a stove. We even had gutters with downspouts that drained rainwater into barrels, allowing us to have water for both drinking and minimal bathing. This was a much appreciated addition, knowing that I could bathe and shave from early December to mid April, when we had most of the rain for the year.

Chapter 12

There was a lot of entertainment at night in Dutoitspan and Kimberley. Of course most of it was in the pubs where liquor and beer was cheaper than water and brothels, which were plentiful. With all the thousands of men working the diamond fields, they were doing a roaring trade. I had seen the effects of syphilis and gonorrhea around Whitechapel in London, which also had its fair share of brothels, and I was not interested in partaking of any of the local prostitutes. Because of the shortage of water and the seriously unsanitary conditions, disease was rampant and many men died from the ravages of sexually transmitted diseases. A lot of men got rolled by the prostitutes, losing their money and diamonds. There were stabbings and killings almost every week. Unfortunately, there was not much of a police force to stop it, or for that matter, investigate it. This was a pretty lawless place to live.

I enjoyed the opportunity to play in the two Music Halls in town, particularly the Theatre Royal. Harry and I performed in a show at least one evening every week. Our audience appreciated our performances, which we varied as much as we could. We didn't want to discourage them from coming back the following week. Harry did his conjuring and I did my juggling and performed acrobatics. Best of all, we both did Shakespearian soliloquies. The pay wasn't much, but we enjoyed performing. The crowd would often buy us a drink or two and that saved us money.

A small group of ladies in Kimberley, started an amateur Dramatic Society and asked both Harry and I to take part in my favorite Shakespearean play, King Lear. How could we refuse? These ladies were the wives of influential men, diamond dealers, bankers and property owners. Most of them lived in a new suburb of brick built houses, situated well away from the diamond fields and even farther from the boisterous nightlife of Dutoitspan.

When we arrived at the church hall that was loaned to the Dramatic Society, we could see there was quite a large crowd. I was wondering which of these ladies would be playing the role of Cordelia, when my eyes set upon a young woman, who was the most beautiful woman in the hall. She had a perfect figure and was taller than me by at least three inches. Her hair was light and her eyes a piercing blue. With a wonderful smile that brightened up the entire room. I wanted to go and say hello to her, but knew that here, that would be considered rude. We had to be introduced formally.

The organizer of the group, a stout matronly woman called Mrs. Smythe asked everyone to be seated. She talked about her dream of a Dramatic Society to bring a little culture to the town. Apparently she had the support of the Kimberley Council officers, who promised to cover all the costs needed to get the Society started. She introduced her committee, consisting of eight ladies and three gentlemen from the Council.

I was hoping to get the name of the beauty I had noticed earlier, but Mrs. Smythe did not mention her. When asked if any members of the audience were familiar with the first planned production, Harry and I raised our hands. One of the Council members leaned over and whispered into Mrs. Smythe's ear. She beamed.

"It appears that we have some professional actors amongst us. Perhaps you could tell us who you are?"

Harry and I stood up.

"We are the Barnato Brothers. We are not professionals at all, although we do have experience on the Music Hall stages both in London and here."

The group applauded and we sat down again while Mrs. Smythe talked about the play King Lear. I wanted to recite some of the lines I had memorized to show off a bit, but thought better of it.

Later, as everyone was leaving, I went over to Mrs. Smythe to thank her for inviting me. Then I casually asked her who the beautiful young woman was and she told me her name is Fanny Bees. Harry and I left and as I walked down the road, I could not get her out of my head.

A travelling circus arrived in Kimberley in mid April. The rains were dissipating and the daytime temperatures were comfortably warm, although it was still very cold at night. It had been a while since I had boxed, although on occasion, I had got into a couple of drunken brawls.

The star fighter of the circus was billed as the Champion of Angola. I vaguely knew that Angola was somewhere in Africa. He was huge, well over six feet tall, had arms like tree trunks and fists like sledgehammers but I was tempted to take him on. I felt sure I could make some money with the bookies, providing I could knock him down. I watched this gorilla dispatch three big diggers in quick succession. None stood up to him longer than a minute. He was awesome, so I had to have a go.

When the bookies got a look at me, and I asked what the odds were on my winning, they laughed. One offered ten to one and another said he would give me twenty to one, but told me to save my money to pay the doctor I was going to need when the champ was finished with me. I placed a bet of five pounds for me to win. The bookie walked off, making gestures to his mates that I was obviously crazy.

I entered the ring stripped to the waist and wearing my bowler hat. The crowd was enormous and broke into laughter and applause. I could hear them saying that's Barney Barnato who plays at the Music Hall and he's obviously madder than a hatter. I bowed to the referee and to the Champion of Angola. As I did so, my spectacles fell off my nose, and I groped around to find them. The champ did the same, bending down to pick them up. This was what I was waiting for. I hit him as hard as I could with a left and a right into his solar plexus.

The Champion of Angola buckled, first on his knees and then flat on the ground. The referee gave me a knowing look. I guess he had seen that trick before. I picked up my spectacles and carefully placed them on my nose. The crowd went wild shouting and jeering. All the bookies had cleaned up with the exception of mine. I quickly sorted him out, just in case he chose to make a run for it and not pay me my fifty pounds. He saw me coming and knew I meant business. He peeled off fifty one pound notes from a thick wad and made his departure. Not a bad day's work, and I had extra funds to buy more diamonds tomorrow.

Chapter 13

Everyone had heard about Cecil Rhodes' steam pump, and I was curious to actually see how it worked. Rhodes was nothing like I could have imagined. He was a tall, gangly young man with a high-pitched voice and an accent of an English gentleman. His pallor was yellowish and he sweated profusely. Not surprising considering he was wearing a heavy Harris Tweed jacket when the temperature was in the mid seventies and climbing. He greeted me as a colleague.

"Good morning to you, sir. Cecil Rhodes is my name. How do you do?"

"Good morning to you too. My name is Barney I. Barnato of Barnato and Cohen, diamond dealers."

"Excellent. What business brings you here today?"

"Two things really. First, I wanted to inquire if you have any diamonds for sale."

"I'm afraid not. My time recently has been taken up with my steam pump. There has been much flooding in the mining area from the torrential rain. Currently, I have the only pump in this part of the country."

"Yes, I had heard about your pump. In fact, that was the second thing. Can I see it?"

"Surely, you can. It really is a magnificent piece of machinery. If you care to follow me, I will show it to you."

Rhodes claim in the middle of the De Beers farm was much higher than the pits of the surrounding claims. It was obvious to me that he was not working his claim very much, if at all. He pulled a cover off the machine to show me the pump. He then led me acroos the uneven ground to the far side of his claim.

"It is quite portable, as you can see. It has wheels on both sides. The greatest difficulty is getting it along the narrow walkways when the reef has already collapsed. Needless to say, it is very heavy. Fortunately, I have a couple of hard-working native Griquas, who help me move it around. They are strong enough to be able to lift it when it gets stuck in the mud. Do you have a claim that needs to be pumped?"

"Alas no, I have not saved enough to be able to afford one yet, but I am going to buy one soon. Is yours available for sale?"

"No, dear boy, I am interested in buying more claims as they become available."

"You have obviously done well then."

"You may not believe this, but I have not made much money from mining. So far my profits have come from this pump and supplying other miners with their everyday needs, including, I might add, ice cream."

"Really, that's very interesting. So why did you buy this claim?"

"My dearest aunt insisted on giving me two thousand pounds to get me started in my new life here. I really did want to mine diamonds and I know that this claim will produce a good return on my investment. Sadly, my health is a problem and the work is too arduous for me at present. Perhaps with warmer, dryer weather I will feel strong enough to continue. In the meantime, my steam pump is bringing in a satisfactory income."

I actually felt quite sorry for Rhodes. As I had noticed when I first saw him, his pallor was not good. It made me wonder why he had come here, to a place that he surely would have known, was not the healthiest place to live.

"What do you think of it?"

"I think it's fantastic, I'm sure there will be more of these working here in the future. Thank you for showing it to me. I won't take up any more of your time." I started to leave.

"Come and visit anytime, I enjoy a game of chess. Do you play?"

"No, but I am sure I could learn."

"Well, goodbye, Mr. Barnato, I am sure we will meet again."

"Goodbye, Mr. Rhodes." We shook hands.

I liked Rhodes; he was so different from anyone I'd ever known. He was obviously well educated, yet he treated me like an equal. He didn't look down on me as many of his peers would do and do all the time. It is easy to tell where I grew up. My cockney accent is the giveaway. I have tried to speak better, especially on stage and particularly speaking Shakespeare. Thinking of Shakespeare brought my mind back to Fanny Bees again. This is ridiculous, why can't I get her out of my mind?

I was up before dawn most days. It made sense to get an early start considering the area I was trying to cover. It was a Thursday and I decided to see what I could buy in Kimberley. That seemed to be the place where larger diamonds were being found, and I wanted to spend my winnings on one big stone.

Close to Rhodes claim in Kimberley was a pit that was near to sixty feet deep and was owned by John Alvernon, an American who was a forty-niner and apparently had been quite successful in the California gold rush of '49. He'd been serving on a ship that was docked in San Francisco at the time. Apparently, the entire crew had abandoned the ship and headed for the goldfields.

I spotted him near his diggings.

"Morning, Alvernon, got anything for me today?"

"Hiya, Barnato. I have something, but it is out of your league!"

"Says who?"

"I say it is out of your league."

"Try me."

He took out a small leather pouch from his belt, which also held his Colt revolver. Alvernon tipped out three diamonds into his rough, blistered hand. The sunlight caught the largest, reflecting a spectrum of colors. He turned so the sun was at his back and lifted his hand to show them to me. I picked up the smallest first, turned it in my fingers, feeling the hard cold surface.

I reached into my jacket and pulled out my magnifying glass, I'd recently gone to a ten times magnification as my eyesight was getting worse. I brought the magnifier to my eye and peered into the stone. It took me several minutes to realize that the stone had absolutely no imperfections that I could see. The diamond was colorless, absolutely no hint of yellow, a true gem, a real beauty. I guessed the weight around seven carat. I put the diamond back in his hand and took the next one.

This had some imperfections that were hard to see without a magnifier, but showed once I looked with it. The stone had a hint of yellow, and was at least double the size of the first stone. I gave that one back and picked up the biggest diamond, a large double octahedron. It was at least thirty carats, way beyond my means as Alvernon had said. It had some imperfections and was yellowish, but a beautiful stone nevertheless. Something I would be happy to find, if this was my mine.

"Okay, now you've had your fun, what did I tell you? Out of your league, kid."

"Hold on a minute. How much for the small one, the one with all the imperfections?"

My guess was that Alvernon did not have a strong magnifying glass and that his eyes were not great. Digging away in the sun all day leaves you a bit blind until nightfall. If he had found the stones in the last day or two, probably nobody else had seen them.

"Seventy pounds. It weighs seven and a half carats."

"That's a bit high considering all the black specks in it, I'll give you thirty-five pounds."

"You must think I just got off the boat, kid. It's worth sixty pounds in anybody's money."

I took the fifty, one pound notes that I had made fighting the Chanp of Angola, out of my pocket and waved it before Alvernon.

"Look, here's fifty pounds, take it or leave it. That's my absolute final offer."

He took the cash and shoved it into his pocket.

"You got a deal."

We weighed the diamond; I checked it and he handed it to me. I walked off with a smile on my face and at least a fifty pound profit in my pocket. I was right. He'd not looked closely at the smaller diamond, probably so excited at finding a large one that he had virtually figured the seven carat as insignificant. I had no doubt the big stone would fetch two hundred pounds or even more. But I'd got the one I wanted.

The Diamond Market in town was a two-story building with large windows along its north side, allowing the best light into a long trading room on the second floor. When I arrived a dozen or so diamond dealers were hanging around outside, waiting to do business. I knew most of them, but one man was not familiar to me, so I approached him first.

"Good afternoon, my name is Barney Barnato."

"Good afternoon, Mr. Barnato, I'm Abraham Konijn from Amsterdam."

Abraham squinted in the bright sunlight.

"Here to buy diamonds, Mr. Konijn?"

"Yes, of course. Do you have some you want to show me?"

"I certainly do."

We shook hands and went inside the building to the trading floor and sat at a long narrow table where the light was best to see the stones. Mr. Konijn had an accent like the Boers. He was a dapper middle-aged man and his clothes were immaculate, even in our harsh conditions. He must have just arrived.

We sat opposite each other at the table. Earlier in the day, I had purchased a small group of diamonds for fifteen pounds. I'd put the one larger diamond from Alvernon together with them. Carefully, I laid them on a sheet of white paper on the table. Konijn took a hand lens from his pocket and examined each of the stones.

He didn't say much. I like to allow a buyer to look without banter or talk. That way it does not interfere with the accompanying mental calculations. Some of the dealers are nonstop chatterers and it is very annoying. Konijn took out a portable hand scale and weighed the larger stone first. Now I knew that this was where his interest was. Next, he weighed two more of the stones and finally the remainder. These would not be what he was after.

"Mr. Barnato, how much do you want for the large diamond?" He eyed me steadily.

"I really want to sell them as a lot."

"Okay. How much for the lot?"

"I'll take one hundred and twenty-five pounds."

He was silent for a minute and re-examined the large stone.

"Your price is not unreasonable, but I would like to make an offer close to your asking price, if that is alright with you?"

I put on my best poker face.

"I can't be insulted with an offer and I can always refuse it if I don't like it."

"Very well, my offer is one hundred and fifteen pounds."

Of course I was happy to take his offer, but I sat for a few seconds as if I was considering refusing it.

"We've not done business before so I made you an exceptionally good price in the hope that we will do more in the future. I will take one hundred and twenty pounds."

Konijn put out his hand and shook mine.

"*Mazel* and *brocha*."

With the traditional Yiddish blessing of Luck and a prayer, the deal was concluded. He counted out the money in gold sovereigns and handed them to me. Meanwhile, he folded the diamonds into the paper, tucking it carefully into his wallet and then inserted the wallet inside his jacket pocket. His face broke into a triumphant grin.

"The larger stone is exceptional and will yield a perfect diamond close to three carat when we finish polishing it. You might want to buy more of this quality when you have the chance. Please give me the opportunity to buy other stones from you."

Chapter 14

A horse, a horse! My kingdom for a horse! William Shakespeare (1564 – 1616).

My cousin, David Harris, was quite prosperous now. He had met a delightful young woman named Rose Gabriel, on a return voyage from England. Rose was born in Germany. Her father was a mining engineer and like so many men of this time, emmigrated to the Cape Colony. He believed that there were great opportunities to be had in a country that was just discovering the wealth beneath their feet. David and Rose had a whirlwind courtship and married in the new Griqualand West Hebrew Synagogue in Kimberley in March of 1873.

David had built a beautiful brick house in the best suburb of Kimberley. They had five bedrooms, two huge living rooms, a dining room, library, the very latest designed kitchen, morning room and best of all, indoor plumbing complete with a large tub bathroom and a water closet. A verandah surrounded the house, which made a comfortable place to entertain and to sit on warm summer evenings. The gardens were spacious and planted with native trees and shrubs. It was the most beautiful house I had ever seen and I vowed that one day I would have one even better.

Every Friday night he would invite, Barney, Louis, Harry and me to *Shabbat* dinner. In addition, David would invite an assortment of friends, mainly diamond dealers, to add to the mix. Rose had a pretty younger sister Martha who was being paid a lot of attention by my cousin Barney, even though she couldn't have been older than ten or eleven.

One Friday, I was sitting next to Mr. Gabriel, Rose's father, and we got into a conversation about diamond mining. Miners were abandoning their claims because they were hitting what they thought was bedrock. The first group of diggers that came to the area found diamonds in the soft yellow ground, which was easily broken away to expose any diamonds there. They used sieves to remove the clumps of worthless rock. That changed when they hit a hard bluish color rock. The blue ground as it was called, was blunting and breaking their picks and shovels. As a result, they believed that they had worked out their claims.

However, Mr. Gabriel put forward a theory that in fact they had only just begun to find diamonds! The hard blue ground was part of a vertical diamond bearing cone or pipe, formed by volcanic activity. After all, a diamond is only a piece of carbon that has crystallized under tremendous heat and pressure. Mr. Gabriel told me that this was not just his theory, but was first put forward by Dr. William Atherstone, a respected geologist and expert on diamonds. It was he that identified the first diamond found here in 1867. This was very important piece of information and I wondered how many men knew about it.

I was most interested because it meant that men were giving up mining at a time when there was much more to be had. In that case was it possible to purchase a claim that appeared to be almost worthless for very little money?

My partnership with Louis was quite turbulent at times. Lou was a penny pincher and was constantly on me about saving money. He didn't like it that I always carried a bottle of Cape Smoke to seal a deal. He criticized me for paying too much for everything I bought. I had purchased a beautifully new set of portable diamond scales, which came in a small wooden box seven inches long by four inches wide and two inches thick. The fittings and weights were all brass. I explained to him we were often being cheated by unscrupulous dealers when they used their scales. This way the price we paid was based on my accurate weights. The final straw in our partnership came when I decided that I wanted to purchase Jack Saunders old pony.

Jack Saunders had been dealing in the diamond fields of Kimberley, New Rush and Colesberg Kopje from the early days when men could literally pick diamonds off the ground. But he had a serious drinking habit and was getting on in years. He claimed his age was fifty, but he was probably closer to seventy. His eyes were failing and he wanted to retire to Cape Town. I had talked to him about selling me all his contacts, but he wanted too much money for them. I asked him what he was going to do with his old pony, as I was tired of walking miles and miles every day. I negotiated a price of twenty-seven pounds and ten shillings, but told him I would have to check with my partner first before making the deal.

"Twenty-seven pounds, ten shillings! Are you stark raving mad?"

"Listen, Lou, Saunders is drunk from early morning and that pony knows all the stops that he makes. It will literally take me from one contact to the next without me having to guide it. He wanted two hundred pounds for all his contacts. This way we are getting them for a fraction of the cost. Regardless of your decision, I'm buying the pony." Lou became livid,

"It's a complete waste of money and I'm not going to pay one penny towards it."

"We're partners and half the cost is down to you. I walk hundreds of miles every month buying and selling diamonds. You sit here in the office all day in comfort."

"Comfort, you're joking!"

"Well, what's it to be?"

"I'm sorry, Barney. You buy the pony and we are through as partners."

"Then so be it. You can divide up the funds and the diamonds and let's part on good terms."

"Don't you want to divide things up with me?"

"No Lou, if I didn't trust you, I wouldn't have gone into partnership with you in the first place. You take care of it and tomorrow we'll go our separate ways."

That was it, the end of our partnership of thirteen months. We parted on good terms. Louis didn't want the expense of the office, even though I had proved to him that it was a good deal. Over the period, we had been able to buy and sell much more than we would have done without it. I had accumulated almost enough to purchase my first claim.

The pony turned out to be a godsend; I could cover three times as much territory in a day. As I had predicted, this pony stopped at all the familiar places it had been to for years and I let the horse take me.

It was time to go back into partnership with my brother. Harry had been working for Van Praag for more than a year now and he promised me it would only be for a year. So I went to find Harry and tell him the news. A week later we painted over the sign above our office and Barnato Brothers Diamond Dealers was painted in its place. It was 1874 and we were both happy to be in partnership once again and vowed to make a fortune or die trying to do so.

In a week old newspaper there was the news that Benjamin Disraeli, the Earl of Beaconsfield, and a Jew, had become the prime minister in England. Not that it made much difference to the population of fifty thousand white people living in Kimberley. In another column there was an item that said the Cape government was going to change the name of Dutoitspan to Beaconsfield after the new prime minister.

Kimberley had grown to become the second largest town in the Cape Colony. Back in England, parliament declared West Griqualand to be part of the Cape Colony, with Kimberley as the capital. This had yet to be fully approved by the government. To me it made no difference. I went out every day buying and selling diamonds, a job that I had grown to love. I like meeting and talking with people from different parts of the world, especially from places I have never been to. My circle was widening, having a pony to get me around really made it easier to cover the distance. Now it was possible to make the journey north to the Vaal River, where the first diamonds were discovered. Men were still finding diamonds in claims alongside of the river.

A number of wealthy individuals from Europe had recently come to Kimberley. European diamond dealers with large amounts of money were setting up offices in the town. I recently met Alfred Beit, who came from a wealthy Jewish family in Hamburg, Germany. He'd been apprenticed to Jules Porges and Cie, a large and influential diamond brokerage company in Amsterdam, where he had learned to sort and grade diamonds. The company recognized that his sharp eyes and innate ability to evaluate diamonds would be put to better use in Kimberley, where high volume and quality stones were being found every day. Beit told me that I should bring him all diamonds that I considered were of quality. He assured me that he would pay the best price in town. What a great offer! I also had a request.

"Mr. Beit, I wonder if you would teach me how to evaluate diamonds better?"

"Mr. Barnato, you bring me all your stones and I will explain to you what I see and how I evaluate them. The diamonds you have shown me so far, tells me that you have a good eye for them. This is not something that is easily taught. It is a combination of how your eye assesses and how your brain utilizes the information. You have a great future ahead of you."

"Thank you, sir. I will make sure that I come to you first."

Beit purchased a piece of land in Kimberley when he first arrived. He had constructed a row of twelve corrugated iron structures. Of these, he rented out eleven of them and kept the best one for himself. This man was a shrewd operator and obviously had the funds to do what he wanted. Definitely, someone to watch and learn from.

I quickly realized that the majority of the diggers had no idea of the value of the diamonds they found, not surprising when you think about it. Most diggers had other professions before coming here to try and make their fortune. They equated size with price, rather than the other factors that influenced the price. The clarity of the stone was critical. When a cutter polishes the rough diamond; he has to consider how to get the maximum yield with as few defects. No color, or as close to colorless as possible, is a huge factor; the more yellow or brown the stone, the less desirable and less valuable. There were diamonds that were smoky and even after polishing were of little value. Diamonds are so hard that only a diamond can polish a diamond. Many of the diamonds found were non-gem grade stones that were good for polishing other diamonds, these are known as bort. All the knowledge that I could acquire from men like Alfred Beit was to my advantage.

Chapter 15

Towards the end of 1874, gold was discovered by Alec "Wheelbarrow" Patterson, in the upper reaches of the Blyde River in Boer controlled Northern Transvaal. Within a few days, word spread faster than cholera and every miner was talking about it.

It did not surprise me that many of the hardened, experienced diggers who had worked the goldfields of California and Australia, would want to try their luck. Stories about finding large fist-size nuggets abounded in the establishments in Kimberley but diamond mining was anything but easy. Many of the diggers had little to show for years of work.

At the same time, worldwide prices for diamonds were falling. Too much production with too many men working the diamond fields. More importantly, there were not enough buyers for the cut gemstones.

As far as I was concerned, it did not matter. Harry and I were content to continue dealing in diamonds until such time we could reach our goal of owning our own claim. Many of the wealthier dealers were picking up claims for next to nothing. Of course, there was no guarantee that those claims would ever produce much, as it was the unsuccessful that were selling at this time.

It turned out the gold found at Eersteling were fine particles of alluvial gold, whereas most of it or was embedded in quartz. If the men found diamond mining difficult, extracting gold from quartz required heavy equipment, which none of them had. Slowly, some of the miners drifted back to Kimberley with disappointment showing in their faces. I talked to some of the returning miners to find out as much as I could about gold mining. Who knew, when this information would come in handy?

The Diggers Protection Association was organized in the early days of diamond mining in the Cape Colony. It was a mutual protection association with established rules for the regulation and management of the diggings in the diamond fields. The diggers wanted an independent Digger's Republic. However, the Cape Governor was not going to allow any such thing and decided to curb the power of the diggers.

Alfred Aylward, an Irishman and quite a colorful character, boasted that had been implicated in the death of a Manchester policemen, though this was never proven. He arrived in the diamond fields and initially posed as a doctor, with no training as one. Aylward who wanted a republican form of government, preached revolt against British government rule.

William Cowie, a local hotel owner, was charged with supplying the Diggers Protection Association with twenty guns without a permit and was being held without bail. In response to these charges, Aylward hoisted a black flag as a signal to his followers to start a revolt, and they marched to the prison and blockaded the road. This forced the Cape governor to muster volunteers and soldiers to put down the revolt, but for ten weeks in 1875, the rebels controlled the streets of Kimberley. Finally, they surrendered to the government forces. Aylward and all the ringleaders were arrested, but later were acquitted by a jury of their peers, as was Cowie.

These distructive events had their effect on mining in Kimberley and it wasn't a good one. A number of the miners, who did not agree with the revolt, got into fights with those that were supporting it. When things finally got back to normal, we were all thankful.

Our Amateur Dramatic Society performed Shakespeare's King Lear to a full house and an appreciative audience. I was disappointed that Fanny did not act a role in the play. She took on the job of prompter, a necessary job, but I would like to have played opposite her.

In our next production "The Bells," Fanny was billed to play opposite me in my role of Mathias. I guess they thought I was suited to the part better than anyone else in the company, being that Mathias is a Jew. The play is about a man who is haunted by a murder he committed. Mathias has the star role of the Polish Jew that Henry Irving had played so well to rave audiences in London. Once I read the part, I knew that this would be my role and that I could play it well.

One night after visiting Cousin David for *Shabbos* dinner, Harry and I got to talking about marriage, as Fanny was still on my mind.

"I think I would like to get married," I told him.

"You have to meet a girl first, before you can contemplate marriage."

"I think I have!"

"What, where, when?"

"Fanny, Fanny Bees, the cute blue eyed, blonde at the Amateur Dramatic Society." His eyes widened.

"You're kidding me, right?"

"No, I'm deadly serious."

"You haven't even taken her out, have you?"

"No, but I have got to know her, working with her in the last two plays. I think I love her."

"I think you don't know what you're saying."

"No really, Harry, I'm serious. As soon as I set eyes on her, something happened. I can't get her out of my mind. I know that she is young, but she has a wonderful sense of humor, her laughter is infectious. She is a real delight and I want to marry her."

"She's not Jewish, Barney. You know if you were to marry her you would be an outcast from both her family and ours." I winced.

"Would you do that to me, Harry?"

"I wouldn't, but I think father and our sisters would."

"I'm not so sure. He is very forgiving and has modern ideas about religion."

"What about her family, what is their religion?"

"They're Huguenots and her family has been in the Cape Colony for many years."

"Seems to me that they are hardly going to allow you to marry their daughter, any more than father would allow it. What are you thinking? You know this can never work."

"I'm sorry, I don't agree. Fanny will convert to Judaism."

"You've already discussed this with her?"

"Of course I have."

"Barney, she is only what, sixteen?"

"That's old enough to marry."

"Yes, but being married and living here in Kimberley. Where do you think you two are going to live? I don't think you have thought this through."

"You're wrong, I have thought this through. Haven't you ever thought about getting married?"

"Actually, yes I have, more than you know."

"How come you have never talked to me about it then?"

"I've been waiting to tell you."

"Alright tell me. When have you met a girl that you want to marry? I've never ever seen you in conversation with any girl here."

"She is not here, she's back home in London."

"Who are you talking about?"

"Rachel Pollock."

"Rachel Pollock! You haven't seen Rachel in more than two years, she could be married with kids by now."

"No she isn't. We've been writing to each other regularly. She and I are unofficially engaged." I gasped.

"You never fail to surprise me Harry. I thought I knew you so well and you spring this news on me. If I hadn't brought up the subject, when were you going to tell me? And another thing, does our family know about this?"

"I sent them a letter about a month ago to tell them. They have not responded yet. You know how long it takes for a letter to get here."

"I'm stunned; you have to tell me more. Are you going to go back to London or stay here? Where are you going to live? When do you plan to marry?"

"I'm sorry I didn't confide in you sooner, that was a mistake. I can see that you are upset about it."

"I'm not upset, just shocked that you could keep something like this from me."

"Really, Barney, I'm sorry I didn't tell you sooner. I met Rachel a few months before I left England, and I promised her that if things went well, we would get married. She understood that I had to do this, that it was important to me to prove myself. When I got the job with Van Praagh and started earning good money, I wrote to her that I wanted to continue our courtship. When you and I went back into partnership and started to do really well, I knew that I could marry her and be able to support her. We're worth more than one thousand pounds now and that is a lot of money."

"Harry, Harry, Harry, that's not a lot of money. It's more than we have ever had in our lives and certainly it looks like a lot of money. The reality is that we need to have our own claim and be mining our own diamonds, not buying other peoples finds. It is going to cost money to get married, for either of us. I won't contemplate marriage until I have a steady income from our own mine, I can wait 'cause I know we'll make that happen."

"Well, I plan to sail to London early next year to get married and bring Rachel back to Kimberley. I'm going to buy a small house near David and Rose. You and I will still be partners and we'll build a big business together. When you're ready to marry, we'll be there for you; we will help with Fanny's conversion to Judaism. We'll be one big happy a family together."

I saw no reason to push him further.

"Whatever you say Harry, you are my big brother and I am happy for you, but I am a little taken aback with this news that has shaken me to the core. I'm going to sleep on it and I am sure we will be talking about this for a while."

"I don't want to keep apologizing Barney, I should have told you sooner, now I have and I'm really pleased. Don't worry about father, when I return home I will discuss it with him and tell him your intention regarding Fanny. In the meantime, I suggest that you meet with Fanny's father and let him know too."

I couldn't sleep that night thinking about our conversation. Things were not going exactly to plan. Yes, we are doing well and our funds are building nicely, but all the extra expenses are definitely going to delay our venture into actually mining our own diamonds. It's a setback, but the more I thought about it, I realized that it was inevitable. Both Harry and I see how happy David and Rose are, and now they have a child on the way. Naturally, we want to have the same, maybe not the lavish style that David can afford, but certainly not as bad as living in a corrugated iron shack for the rest of our lives.

I was still reeling over Harry being able to keep his courtship a secret, He was usually such an open book. My concern was that Rachel will find it hard to adjust to life here. She is a delightful young woman and comes from a good family. Living in Kimberley was a challenge because of the climate, disease, sanitary conditions and the rough population. It was easier for Fanny. Her family has lived in the Cape Colony for more than a hundred years, and since the first diamonds were discovered here. Tomorrow evening, I will go and visit Mr. Bees and ask him if I can marry his daughter.

Mr. Bees was a humorless man who took an instant dislike to me. I'm not sure what the problem was, but my guess was that there were several. The first was that I'm a Jew, the Bees family are Huguenots, whose people have had their fair share of religious persecution in Europe. Like so many others, they migrated to the Cape Colony to escape the unfair treatment they experienced. I told him that the Jews had the same problems and had been persecuted for thousands of years, but this didn't change his attitude.

He wanted to know if I would change my religion, to which I refused. I may not be a practicing Jew, but I would never renounce my heritage. Bees asked if I expected Fanny to change her religion, and although I tried hard to skate around this question, I had to admit that my family would insist on it. As if this wasn't enough, Fanny, the idol of his eye, was just turning seventeen, in his opinion, far too young to marry. He wasn't interested in how much I am currently worth, and judging by his living standard and large family was probably struggling as a tailor in this town.

Concluding my short visit, he told me to forget his daughter and find myself a nice Jewish girl back in London. With that he showed me to the door and soundly slammed it behind me. My thoughts were that it would take time. There was no way I would give up the idea of marrying Fanny.

Several weeks later, Harry made the voyage back to England with the intent of marrying Rachel. Now that he had talked about his intention, he could not wait. He had become impossible at the thought of delaying any longer. It got to the point where I had to tell him to go, I could manage the business in his absence, and we both agreed that it would not be possible for both of us to go at the same time.

Back in England, he wrote to me that the wedding would take

place in a month. I checked the postmark on his letter to find the wedding had already taken place.

Harry was gone almost five months by the time he returned to Kimberley. Rachel was a delight; she was an attractive young woman, intelligent and had a sense of humor, an essential element for the life we lead in Kimberley. She showed no fear of the unknown and had every confidence that Harry would take care of her. Best of all Rachel and Fanny got on well together and that endeared her to me. I knew it was only a matter of time before I would marry too.

Chapter 16

Around this time I met Julius Wernher, who was a colleague of Alfred Beit. Apparently they had both come from Germany to Kimberley around the same time, but our paths had never crossed. I would see Beit quite often, but Wernher stayed in the background. It appeared that he preferred it that way. He spoke English extremely well, with hardly a hint of accent. I was curious to find out more about him. How could he spend nearly two years in Kimberley without us meeting each other. Admittedly there were more than fifty thousand men here now, but we were all diamond dealers at one level or another.

It turned out that Wernher was the money man. He had borrowed a large amount of money from his half-brother, a doctor in Hamburg and a man of private means. He had worked for Jules Porges, a rich and important diamond dealer in Paris, who had realized the importance of the diamond finds in South Africa. Porges had sent Wernher and Beit to Kimberley to buy for his company. Wernher was extremely knowledgeable when it came to diamonds and had attended many jewelry auctions in Europe whilst buying for Porges & Cie. He quickly realized that if he had his own financing he could purchase quantities of high quality diamonds.

Cash is king in the diamond fields and Wernher not only obtained financing from his half-brother, he also obtained a line of credit from a London bank. Rumors had it that it ran into hundreds of thousands of pounds, but rumors were rife in Kimberley. Now he was buying on his own account.

Wernher hated Kimberley; he hated the whites who he considered a lazy bunch of drunkards. In my opinion, he hated the Jews who dominated the diamond industry. He complained to everyone he came in contact with how lax the postal system was, how registered mail was left lying around the post office just waiting for someone to steal it when the postmaster left at the end of the day.

Apparently, he had lost a valuable parcel that was being sent to Jules Porges in Paris and he was very angry about it. He hated just about everything in Kimberley, other than the promise of huge riches to be made here.

When I met him he told me that the authorities had just caught a thief in Cape Town who had more than two thousand diamonds hidden in the barrel of his rifle and powder horn. This thief had arrived from Cape Town a couple of months earlier and had managed to steal that many diamonds from the post office. His big mistake was that he got greedy. He had stolen one hundred pounds from a man he shared a room with at the Royal Hotel. He had returned to the same hotel when his ship had been delayed and was subsequently caught. Wernher told me the man should be strung up and hanged.

Our big chance to buy a diamond claim came early in 1876. Worldwide diamond prices were continuing to drop. It was estimated that diamonds in excess of one and a half million pounds sterling had been mined by the end of 1872. That this figure had nearly doubled by 1875. Two Canadian brothers named Kerr owned four adjacent claims in Kimberley. They were veterans of the Klondike gold rush where they had had some success. Most of the money they had made was now gone. Decades of rough living and poor conditions were taking their toll on their health and mental state.

Late in 1875, they had hit the hard blue ground and believed that their claims were now worked out. Needless to say, the decision was made to sell out and work the new gold fields of the Transvaal.

I had met with them many times; in fact, it was Saunders old pony that had led me to them in the first place. We haggled for several days, I knew they wanted to get out and they knew that I wanted to buy, so none of us was conceding ground. Finally, after a long bout of arguing and drinking, we came to an agreement at twelve thousand pounds. Harry and I were worth fifteen thousand now and after paying for their claims, we would be left with three thousand.

The Kerrs paid off their native African workers with a generous bonus, at least by the standard that was being paid to them. They immediately purchased rifles and left for their villages, rich men by their standards.

That left me to find my own native workers, but I had no idea that there was, in fact, a labor shortage. Brokers contracted with the influential tribal chiefs for the services of their young men and brought them to Kimberley, where they held regular auctions for the natives' services. These brokers were paid a premium of one pound for each man, hardly something that I wanted to shell out at this time.

African natives from poorer tribes were arriving in Kimberley every day. Generally, they were very young and had walked many miles, barefoot, to get there. They were emaciated and hardly fit for the twelve or fourteen hour days that diamond mining demanded of them. They came from different parts of South Africa, representing different tribes: Zulu, Xhosa,

Ndebele, Sotho and Venda. I had difficulty distinguishing one from another.

What did I know about natives? Most spoke a minimal amount of English, or sometimes none at all. Fortunately, I hired a native named Haji from the Lemba tribe, who not only spoke English reasonably well, but was able to communicate in all their other tongues. Of course, I made him my foreman.

Haji told me that he was Jewish, I'm not sure I believed him at first. How could he possibly be Jewish; he's black and I'm white. He told me more about his tribe, that they are one of the lost tribes of Israel that came to this part of the world by travelling south along the coast of Africa. Their traditions, including not eating pork, circumcision, following a lunar calendar and celebrating holidays timed with the phases of the moon, were just like my tribe, the Jews.

Always willing to learn what to do, I found myself pitching in with my native workers, hardly the sort of thing that whites considered proper. They would sit under some kind of shade and watch as the natives toiled away, shouting at them if they thought they were slacking. I fed them better than the average natives. They lived on mealie-meal and the occasional game meat. I wanted strong men, who could handle the vigors of a life for which they had no experience.

I was taking care of the production jointly with Harry and looking after some of the selling too. My natives broke the hard blue ground with sledge hammers and chisels, always careful to watch out for the diamonds that were picked out carefully. When we started working our claims, there were disappointingly a few small diamonds. Within six weeks, we were finding larger stones everyday and our yields increased exponentially.

By the time we had reached our first year anniversary our income, even considering the slump in prices, was in excess of nine thousand pounds a week! I was realizing my dream and Harry, now married to Rachel, and I could finally afford decent homes. Fanny and I were still courting, and I purchased a carriage, so that when I took her out, although never alone, she was taken in comfort and style. We met regularly at the amateur Dramatic Society where we could meet without her old man giving us grief. Mr. Bees still had not warmed to me, probably never would.

Chapter 17

Now I could afford to take my first voyage back to England. I had been away four years and I desperately wanted to see my family again. Harry and I decided that we would buy father a beautiful house in a good part of London and buy or lease a proper shop for him. We didn't think he would want to give up work completely.

My sister Kate Joel had three sons. Harry and I decided that we should bring them out to Kimberley to help us in our business. You can trust family, but strangers will always rob you blind. Diamonds were of such value that they corrupt people easily. We needed our own family and this was the opportunity of a lifetime for our nephews. After all, we'd done all the donkey-work. These young men would not have to go through the hardships that Harry and I experienced.

I arrived in England on an early autumn day. The weather was much cooler than Kimberley and it felt really good. I checked into the Ritz Hotel in Piccadilly, London. My suite was large and had a private bath and a view of Green Park.

It was hard to believe that I had returned to London as a wealthy diamond merchant and mine owner. After having a bath, haircut and shave, I had a carriage take me to Saville Row to order twelve suits. I walked down Jermyn Street and purchased things for my wardrobe: hats, shirts, shoes and gentleman's accessories from Trumpers. At Dolland and Atkinson's, I had several pairs of pince-nez spectacles made to compensate for my poor eyesight. I paid extra to have everything expedited, telling the shopkeepers that I was leaving in a few days.

It was hard for me to not rush over to see my family, but I wanted to show them that Harry and I had made a success of our lives. Five days later, I hired a carriage to take me to my family home in the East End of London where I had grown up. My emotions got the better of me and I was so choked up seeing my father again, I couldn't speak, probably the only time in my life that this had ever happened to me. He scolded me for not letting him know I was coming sooner. I'd sent a short letter two days previously telling everyone to expect me. The whole family was in the front room of his tiny house.

We had a very emotional reunion. My father shook my hand and then hugged me tightly to him, something he had never done in my entire life. Sarah kissed my cheek as tears poured down her face. She couldn't talk for several minutes. Kate kissed me and Joel and Isaac pumped my hand warmly. Lizzie, looking really well, was all smiles. Everyone was pleased to see me.

Kate laid on a feast for us all. I gave out presents that I had purchased the previous day in Regent Street and Knightsbridge. They were extravagant things that I knew they would never buy for themselves, albeit things that were not very practical.

My newfound wealth was now very obvious to my family and I told them that I had big plans for them all. I explained some of those plans, which they did not reject, but didn't exactly agree with them. It was very selfish of me to think that now I had the ability to do so, I would want to change their lives.

We ate, we drank, we laughed, we cried. I told them about Fanny and my plans to get married, that it would be some time in the future and that the wedding would take place in London, after Fanny had gone through conversion to Judaism.

Before taking my leave, I invited father to have tea with me at my hotel on the following Sunday, as I wanted to discuss my special plans for him away from the rest of the family. I hinted to Kate that I wanted to talk to her about her sons, but gave no details, that would have to wait for another day when Joel, Kate and I could get together without the rest of the family. This was not the time or place. Of course the whole family would know about it once we had some agreement. The last thing I needed was everyone giving their opinion. Jewish families never seem to agree. Put twenty family members in one room and you get twenty different opinions.

With that I left, promising to see them all quite soon. I felt drained; my emotions had been so overwhelmed. I climbed into my carriage and watched out of the window as the grey dull streets of Whitechapel faded into the elegant buildings of the City of London. Finally on to St. James and my hotel on the beautiful Piccadilly. At this moment in life, I realized that if all went well with our enterprises, one day I could afford to buy an elegant house in this area or in Mayfair.

Kate and Joel came to the hotel later in the week. They walked into my suite and I could sense that they were unable to comprehend the luxury of the Ritz. Kate could not believe that her little brother was able to afford such an extravagance.

"Barney, don't you think your money could be put to better use than wasting it on hotel costs. We can certainly find you a room at the *King of*

Prussia."

"Thanks Kate, I appreciate your offer, but after the hardships of Kimberley, I want to indulge myself for a short while. You cannot understand the deprivations of a town like Kimberley without seeing it."

Kate threw her arms in the air in exasperation. I ignored the gesture and we all sat down.

"The main reason I invited you here is to talk to you about your boys. Harry and I need to expand our enterprises. We need people we can trust and we don't want to bring strangers into the business that may ultimately steal from us. The diamonds we are mining are valuable and easily stolen, so we want to bring in family members to help us. We feel that one of your sons, or all three if you agree, are just the ticket."

"I don't think so, Barney, I want the boys here in London, not thousands of miles away in the Cape Colony," Kate demurred.

"Why Kate? This is a wonderful opportunity for your sons. They won't have the hardships that Harry and I experienced, they'll be starting on a career that will make them wealthy men. We'll pay them well and cover all their travel expenses."

Joel shook his head.

"Kate is very close to Isaac, Woolf and Solly, who are still very young. Possibly in a few years time they could work for you, but not now."

"Joel, this is ridiculous, we need the help now, not in a few years. Can't you see that this is a gift from Harry and me?"

"We don't need your gifts, Barney. You come back to London and throw your money around like a man with no arms, trying to buy everyone. Things may have changed for you, but our lives are much the same as they always were. We make a reasonable living running our pub, and the boys will find their own way in life without your help." I was stung by his words.

"I'm not just doing this to show off, you know. I'm doing this because we have a real need and I know that if you agree, you won't regret it! Please think about it for a few days, talk to your sons and see how they feel about it. In the meantime, we'll have dinner and we won't discuss this any further. What do you say?"

"I don't think so. Come on Joel, we have to go to work," Kate snapped.

"Kate, Joel please!"

"Barney, Kate and I will discuss this with the boys and we'll let you know."

"Thank you for that. Are you sure that you won't stay for a meal? You have only just got here."

"I know, but we really do have to go. It takes nearly an hour to get back to the pub."

"Let me call for a carriage to take you home."

"No, thank you, Barney."

Kate got up, kissed me lightly on the cheek, Joel shook my hand warmly and I opened the door for them. I watched them as they receded down the brightly lit corridor to the large, sweeping, central staircase.

I closed the door and slumped into a chair. I could not believe my sister could be so short-sighted about this. Perhaps I overdid it, staying in such an opulent hotel. It got up her nose. The amount I was paying for one night was probably more than they earned in six months or even a year. I decided that tomorrow, I would check out of the hotel and move to a more modest accommodation in the City of London.

I had to meet with a banker in the City this week and moving there, I would be closer to the family in the East End of London. Perhaps Kate would be more amenable to my idea, if she felt that I would not be a bad example to her sons. Yes, that's exactly what to do.

I met with Kate and Joel in their pub a week later. She had talked to Isaac, Woolf and Solly who were enthusiastic about sailing to the Cape Colony and joining Harry and I. However, Kate being Kate, decided that only one could go at this time and that would be Woolf.

"Why Woolf, he's what, sixteen?"

"Yes, he is, but he has a good head for figures and he is far more mature for his age than the other boys. I think he is exactly the man you're looking for."

"Great, I'm so happy you made this decision, you have my promise, you won't regret it."

"I certainly hope not. You must promise me that you will not allow him to go astray. You will be responsible for him. Do you understand what I am telling you?"

"Absolutely, you have nothing to worry about. I promise you that."

"A mother always worries, no matter what."

"I'll book his passage with me in the morning. In the meantime, I want to talk to him to let him know what is expected of him."

And that was it. I met with young Woolf, told him what his mother had said, explained what his job would be, that there was an awful lot to learn and the faster he learned it, the faster he would make money. He'd grown up a lot since I left England; he was taller than me and spoke well. He had been educated at the same school as I had, the Jews Free School. He had actually matriculated at fifteen, something I had not. Yes, I felt this was going to work out well and I have a good instinct for these things.

I arranged for a carriage to pick up my father and bring him to my new hotel, a modest affair on the edge of the City. Nevertheless he was impressed with the accommodation. It was wonderful to be able to tell him about Harry and my adventures. Of course I left out some of the scarier moments, not wishing to alarm him in any way. My father knew that, but that was alright.

When I broached the subject of buying him a new home, he did not want to admit that it was a dream come true. I asked him to look around, suggesting the area around Baker Street, close to Regents Park, which would be convenient for the Metropolitan Railway when he wanted to visit the family. The Metropolitan was an underground railroad and a network of lines that are being built to bring transport all over London.

I wrote down the name of my bank manager and told him I had made arrangements for the money he would need. I asked my father if he would like to retire or if he would prefer to have a shop. His preference was to continue working and he was delighted to be able to select a location that would be close to his new home. I did not want to insult him by giving him money that day. Instead I told him that I had made arrangements with the bank for a monthly allowance. The money was for him to spend however he wanted; new clothes, furniture and furnishings for the house. There was no need to tell father how to spend it. He'd been thrifty all his life and I knew that nothing would change. We had a very pleasant meal at a kosher restaurant in the Mile End Road and after that, he left for home.

Later that evening, I permitted myself a little indulgence, a visit to the theatre at the Old Vic, to see Othello. Life was good. Strangely, I now looked forward to returning to Kimberley, where many more challenges awaited me.

Chapter 18

On returning to Kimberley, Harry and Rachel called on me. Rachel was several months pregnant and looked very pale and tired. Apparently her pregnancy had been a difficult one. They wanted to hear all the news from London and, of course, to welcome Woolf to Kimberley. This seemed to lift her spirits. We talked till late in the evening, Rachel fell asleep on the sofa, which gave Harry a chance to bring me up to date. He was very worried about Rachel. The doctor had suggested that she go to Cape Town for the birth, but she could not face the journey across the Karoo and decided to have the baby in Kimberley. It was after midnight when they left for home.

Without wasting any time, I put Woolf to work early the next day. I took him out to our claim and showed him every job that my natives had to do: digging, hammering, sorting and sifting out the diamonds, overseeing the removal of the tailings. Every day before sunrise for the next month, I showed him diamonds, discussing the properties of each stone, made him examine the stones with a magnifier and access their values. I repeated this with stone after stone, watching his progress, listening to how he described what he saw and finally how he assessed the potential prices. He was a fast learner I only had to tell him something once and he got it.

It was about this time that the Government decided to make kopje wallopers illegal. An announcement appeared in the Government Gazette which read: "His Excellency the Administrator directs to be notified for general information that from and after this date the practice known as "kopje walloping" or otherwise the purchase of diamonds in places other than of Licensed Bankers or Diamond Dealers, will be strictly prosecuted by the police who have received orders etc. Offenses under the section relating thereto are liable to penalty upon conviction of not less than one hundred pounds and forfeiture of the license."

The reason for Government intervention was obvious. Illegal diamond buying had become a huge problem and it was being done at every level. Natives devised many ways to conceal diamonds, swallowing, inserting stones into cuts in the hard skin of their bare feet, hiding them in their thick matted hair and in rectal orifices. They could sell the stones, albeit at much lower than their real value. For the natives it was far in excess of what they could earn in a month. It brought them closer to their personal goal of returning to their villages with a gun, and possibly enough to purchase a few cattle, thus enabling them to marry.

A number of whites purchased diamonds from the natives and resold them making profits that rightfully belonged to another miner. Miners, finding very little and deciding to sell their claims, sometimes purchased these illicit diamonds and "salted" their mines. This was a practice where the diamonds were buried in and around the claim, enabling a potential buyer to find them easily, showing that the claim was productive and increasing the price that he would pay. This was the second most despicable action, and would often result in the new owner "losing his shirt".

The most despicable act was robbing miners of their finds. Everyday, men were "rolled" by prostitutes and their pimps. Drunks were a favorite of many thieves, as their faculties were impaired by the alcohol and the offer of another drink, often put them off their guard. Men could be vigilant all day, watching their backs, but with a few drinks inside them, they were the perfect victims. Without the support of the whites, who participated in these schemes, there would not be a problem, but the promise of riches brought many criminal elements to the area. Men and women too lazy to put in the hard work that was needed to be successful, resorted to illicit diamond trading. Additionally, there were the unsuccessful men who took advantage of this as a last resort before leaving the area.

One of the other problems with I.D.B., as this was known by everyone, was that it was easy to accuse someone of participating in this practice, which even if not true, ruined a man's reputation, resulting in his being shunned by other diamond dealers. A man's reputation in the diamond business was one of his greatest assets. Often the more successful miners were accused of wrongdoing through jealousy, envy and hatred or by a disgruntled employee.

Due to the excessive amounts of diamonds that were depressing the world markets, the government stepped in and added another level of regulation. Diamonds were now the number one source of income to the Cape Colony and the British Government was eager to protect this source.

Dr. Atherstone's theory regarding the hard blue ground holding many more diamonds proved to be right. Somehow, I felt that I had been given inside knowledge. Why was it that so many other miners hadn"t a clue about this? Our four claims were producing good size diamonds as we dug, hammered and scraped our way into the hard blue ground now known as Kimberlite after our town.

Our success was not unique by a long shot. Many other miners were now working the Kimberlite with varying success. The reality was that there were diamonds to be found there. The soft easy diggings were pretty much worked out. If anyone wanted to find diamonds, they had to work harder to get them.

Ultimately, the I.D.B. problem was leveled at me. There were those that could not believe that the worked out claims Harry and I had purchased, were now producing not just a few large stones, but quantities of large stones, in addition to quantities of smaller ones. I had to defend myself about this and on several occasions was forced to do so by calling out an accuser to either prove his slander or shut his damn mouth. I must admit to resorting to a couple of fistfights with a big mouth who just wouldn't shut up.

Woolf, as young as he was at the time, was fascinated with the way that diamonds had formed. I explained to him Dr. Atherstone's theory; how the diamond bearing ground was like vertical pipes that could conceivably go down thousands of feet or more. I had listened and learned from it. Woolf, in turn, thought that this whole area of Kimberley and De Beers mines must be separate pipes and that where no diamonds being found around the outer part, showed how wide the pipe was. That got me to thinking again about buying more, supposedly worked out claims that fell within the perimeter of the outer mined area.

I went to the claims office in Kimberley and looked at the map pinned on the wall that showed all the three and half thousand or so claims that made up the area of Kimberley. The official in charge said I could purchase a copy of the map, which I did. That evening after we had our supper, Harry, Woolf and I sat around and studied the map. The interesting thing was that the area of mining claims was more of an oval that a round, but certainly the pipe was at least two and half to three miles wide.

"In my opinion, we should be buying up any and every claim we can that sits within the boundaries that we see here." I said.

Harry gave me a look of disdain.

"Why are you never satisfied with what you have already, Barney?"

"Harry, it's not that I am never satisfied, it's because there are so many more opportunities now. All individual claims will eventually be consolidated into larger blocks. The government has already lifted the restrictions on the number of claims that one individual can own, and you know they will keep raising the number. There's talk of raising the limit from ten to fifty any day now. We could have ten claims right now. No, we could have thirty claims between us. Ten each."

Woolf looked at me enthusiastically.

"That would be fantastic, Barney."

"And where is the money going to come from?" Harry demanded.

I pushed on.

"We should be reinvesting seven or eight pounds for every ten pounds we make in sales, into purchasing claims. The same way as we did when we were just in diamond dealing. Putting the money back in the kitty to increase our inventory."

"I'm not comfortable with that." Harry persisted.

"Harry, you weren't comfortable when I wanted to buy our first claim. You're too cautious, if we don't gamble now, we will be too late. A number of big diamond dealers and existing mine owners are buying up claims right now, trying to consolidate. Rhodes I'm told has ten claims, Beit, and Wernher probably have the same. Even the big Parisian diamond dealer Porges has come here to buy claims, not diamonds. That tells us something and we should be listening."

"If you don't mind me saying so, Uncle Harry, I think that Barney is right. It makes sense that we should go all out to buy. If there are a lot of other buyers, the prices will rise and we could be shut out." Woolf was on my side.

It's funny how Woolf started calling me by my first name, but always called Harry uncle. The boy was more like a brother to me than a nephew. I could see that Harry was struggling with the concept of reinvestment. I knew he would think about it for a couple of days and come around. In the meantime, I would make it my business to see who wanted to sell.

As predicted, the government once again changed the rules on holding claims. There was no limit to the number that whites and corporations could own. Natives were no longer able to own any claims or even own diamonds. The fight for supremacy of the diamond mines was on. For my part I was going to be a player. The days of open-face mining in claims of thirty by thirty feet, were rapidly coming to an end. There were problems of the depth, reef collapse and flooding. Boundaries blurred as the rock collapsed into the holes. The extraction and removal of the tailings became ever more complex.

Modern up to date methods were called for and it would only be through consolidation that this would be possible. Syndicates were being formed, miners were banding together to increase the size of their block of claims and bringing in deep level mining, just like coal mining. Nobody would dream of mining coal using open-face methods, but here we were doing just that, digging ourselves into deeper and deeper holes.

Many more steam pumps were in use by now, Rhodes no longer had the monopoly. He had made a lot of money by being the first and, for a while, the only man with one.

There was a lot of action taking place over at the De Beers farm, especially with Rhodes, Beit, Wernher and Porges, so I decided to concentrate on Kimberley. We had more chance to buy where our claims are. That made sense. The real competition was coming from Jules Porges and his firm, Compagnie Française de Diamant du Cap de Bonne Espérance. What a mouthful that is. Porges purchased a large number of claims in Kimberley mine over a three-month period, resulting in a ten per cent holding. The patchwork quilt of claims was disappearing rapidly into large blocks. There was no doubt in my mind that the name Barnato Brothers was going to be on one of them, or my name isn't Barnato.

Harry reluctantly agreed to invest seventy-five per cent of our gross sales into purchasing more claims.

More of the diamond miners were convinced that gold was easier to find, especially alluvial gold near the rivers. The heavy winter rains washed the tiny flakes into dried up riverbeds, making them easier to see. Panning was a painstaking job, but not nearly as strenuous as the back-breaking work that was now needed to extract diamonds from the Kimberlite. Gold was being found in a number of areas in Northern Transvaal and this was working in our favor. Added to this, the worldwide diamond prices continued to tumble. After years of a dwindling supply from India and Brazil, there were now too many diamonds. All these factors put a lot of claims on the market.

I started marking those that were for sale on my map, now pinned up on our office wall. I penciled in the name of the owner and the asking price. Quite quickly, a pattern emerged. It pinpointed the madmen that were not at this point seriously interested in selling. It quickly showed me the men who were ready, reasonable and negotiable. My advantage, too, was that I had purchased stones from a number of the sellers. So I had a good idea of the quality and sizes of the stones that were being found. Not that this was fool proof, as some were still working the remaining yellow ground.

I heard that Rhodes was raising money from the Rothschilds, or at least trying to raise it. Every Jew in Europe knew the name of the most famous Jewish bankers. I was told that they had financed Napoleon as he swept through Europe. Whether it was true or not, they had been around hundreds of years and, without any doubt, had been the financiers of kings, governments and dictators.

For hundreds of years, Jews had been restricted to only a few professions and two of them were money lending and jewelers. So it was not surprising that Jews dominated the diamond industry here in the Cape Colony. I knew I had to learn more about the financial world, a subject that I was seriously lacking. I decided that on my next voyage to England I would meet with my banker and see if I could persuade him to work for us.

Chapter 19

Rachel died in giving birth to a baby girl. The baby was premature and small. It was a very difficult time for the family. Our little *shul* helped with the *shivah* at Harry's house, which was packed every night for a week with people paying their respects. The little girl was named Leah, after our mother. Harry somehow arranged for a wet nurse to look after the child. A young lady, who had recently arrived in Kimberley with her family, undertook the task of looking after the baby. Charlotte Gray took over the running of Harry's house, organized the servants, and made sure that everything was "ship-shape and Bristol fashion" as if she was the mistress of it. Before not too much time, she was.

Fanny helped as much as she could, but her father was got wind of it and told her she was forbidden to go to Harry's house in case I took advantage of her. This made me really angry and I wanted to go and sort him out, but I knew it would cause more problems with our relationship. I still had hopes of him changing his mind about me.

Fanny and I were able to meet regularly at the Dramatic Society. We managed to find a quiet corner where we could talk. I know that most of the members were aware of our courtship, but few if any, knew the difficulty we faced to get married. She wanted to know if I had spoken to my father about us. I tried to dodge the question, but I had to admit that I had only inferred that I had met a girl. She was disappointed that I hadn't the courage to discuss it, so I promised that I would write a letter to my father the next day. She insisted that I show her the letter before sending it and I agreed. I'm not much of a letter writer, so she said she would help me write it.

As a result of government restrictions, there was a lot of discontent by black and colored workers. Natives working in the area came from the Griquas, Korannas and Rolong areas. Coloreds were considered anyone who was not black but had skin other than white. This included the Indians who had been mining and cutting diamonds for hundreds of years.

Prejudice was rampant. The whites continually issued local regulations controlling everything that the natives and coloreds could do. Under the most recent ones, they could no longer own a claim or for that matter, own diamonds. Black workers were the backbone of the laborers in the diamond mines, especially the Griquas whose territory was recently annexed by the British government into the Cape Colony. Many of the whites considered the natives and coloreds to be non-citizens, but the annexation action of the British government meant that they could submit claims and own diamonds, under English law.

The fight between the diggers and this group of disenfranchised men had been going on now for several years. Things started to get ugly with racists often accusing them of I.D.B. and in a town where there was little police presence, men were flogged, beaten and sometimes killed by angry mobs. Law and order, was the responsibility of a volunteer force known as the Cape Colonial Force or CCF. These volunteers were made up all white men of various nationalities and the main purpose of the CCF was to defend the area in the event of a native uprising. There were a few Griquas in the CCF, but for the most part they were European settlers.

Things got out of hand in 1878, when the Griquas rebelled against their unjust treatment at the hands of the CCF. Men had been arrested and thrown into jail after a bar brawl in Kimberley. The Griquas were sentenced to ten years hard labor. The whites, the perpetrators of the fight, were let off with a fine or three months jail. The leader of the Griquas appealed to the Governor of the Cape, Sir Henry Barkly, who decided that the court had acted correctly and refused to intercede. The result was mass rioting in the streets of Kimberley. This was swiftly put down by the CCF and a number of the rioters were killed in the bloody skirmish. The effect of the riots was felt immediately in the diamond fields, when the miners were deprived of many of their workers and production ground to a halt for a short time. We were affected by this having lost a few of our natives.

Sadly, this unjust treatment of the Griquas did not help their cause and regulations and restrictions got more onerous. I felt really disgusted by the diggers and government action. All of us, regardless of the color of our skin, are entitled to the same opportunities, and I vowed to make sure, that any person in my employ had to be treated with respect.

The British government continued to expand it's influence in South Africa. After annexation of Griqualand, now called Griqualand West, the Secretary of State for the Colonies, Lord Carnarvon, put forward a proposal in the House of Lords, to create a South African Federation. A bold move considering the Boers, the Dutch settlers, had already formed their own republic. In a diplomatic move to appease the Boers, Carnarvon agreed to wage war against the powerful Zulu Kingdom that the Boers wanted for their own. The Zulus had fought the Boers early in their colonization of Natal and Transkei, massacring a large number of the early settlers.

African natives were ordered by the Cape government to give up their rifles under the Peace Preservation Act of 1878. The natives had purchased their rifles legitimately with money they earned working in the diamond diggings. Not only were these weapons their prize possessions, they represented years of backbreaking work. The order to give them up was unacceptable. They turned the rifles on the Cape police when they tried to take their guns by force. This act was the opening of a war that spread like wildfire across the Cape Colony and into Kimberley.

The Griquas, who had their territory annexed by the British a year earlier, also rebelled at the same time. Two Griqua chiefs were plundering and murdering whites in the Langeberg Mountain area near Griquatown. They were aggressively pursued by the volunteer Kimberley Light Horse, Kimberley Infantry and the Kimberley Artillery. The Griquas were overwhelmed and the rebellion was put down quickly and brutally.

The Zulu War that started in 1879, initially had minimal effect on our operations, as it was mostly taking place many miles from us. But it did increase the prejudice of the whites against the black workers and the animosity of the natives to the whites who they now distrusted.

I never had the patience to read a daily newspaper. Harry on the other hand, read all the newspapers without fail. He was my source of information about what was going on locally and in England. We were fortunate in Kimberley to have a number of newspapers, published both daily and weekly. I realized that I had to take more notice of news events as this affected diamond prices worldwide. From then on, I decided that after our evening meal, I would sit and read.

Chapter 20

I had not received any response from the letter I wrote to Mr. Bees. However, in anticipation of my wedding to Fanny, I purchased a large piece of land close to David's house in the new Kimberley suburb of Belgravia and had a beautiful, brick built house constructed. Fortunately, there were a number of builders who knew how a house should be built and I wanted our house to have all the latest features of a modern home.

One thing that I had to have was running water in the house, and we had large water tanks installed to enable daily bathing throughout the dry season. These tanks were filled and kept topped up by contract with the men who brought the water wagons into town. The local government was planning the installation of large community water tanks, which would enable water to be piped directly into homes, just as the big cities do. So I made sure that our new house had the necessary pipe work installed for that eventuality.

With our newfound wealth, Harry decided that he wanted to buy the London Hotel in the central part of Kimberley. The London was not fancy by a long shot, but Harry wanted an interest outside of diamond mining, This was his first venture in which I was not involved with him. He'd asked me if I wanted to partner with him, but I had no interest in doing so.

I planned an elaborate twenty-first birthday party for my darling Fanny at the Theatre Royal, our favorite place in town. The proprietor agreed to rent the whole of the first floor lobby for the evening and I had everything arranged; a cold buffet, wines and Champagne. The theatre's nine piece orchestra was to play for the whole evening. It was planned to be a night to remember. My hope of marrying as soon as she reached this milestone was dashed once again when I visited her father with an invitation to the party.

Mr. Bees greeted me with a withering stare.

"What do you want this time?"

"Mr. Bees, Sir, I really want us to be friends. Your daughter Fanny is very dear to me."

"How many times do I have to tell you, Barnato? I am not going to change my mind. I will never allow you to marry Fanny."

He was about to slam the door in my face, but I stuck my foot in the way.

"I have arranged a party for Fanny's twenty-first birthday, and want to invite you and your family to the celebration."

"We have our own celebration planned for her birthday and it does not include you. Get you and your foot out of the way, now!"

I could not believe that this man could be so stubborn. Once Fanny was of age, she would no longer have to be controlled by him. But deep down my fear was that she would always be under his influence.

There was no way I was going to cancel the party, even though I knew that Fanny would not be able to attend, but I was damned if I would allow this arrogant man to make me change my plans. So I called it an end of the war celebration.

It was time for another voyage back to England. I could not take Fanny with me as much as I wanted to do so, as we were not yet married. She did not have a problem with my leaving since she was busy adding furniture, drapes and all manner of things to the house. Fanny gave me a very long list of things that I had to bring back with me on the ship. I had no idea she was that organized, and I was sure that Harry's new wife, Charlotte, had a lot to do with it. I would find the two of them sitting in the drawing room with catalogs from Godey's showing the latest, most fashionable items to buy. It made me happy that my future wife and his new wife were becoming such good friends.

I sailed to England in April, arriving in the middle of a warm spell. The parks and squares of London thronged with people enjoying the weather. Fashionable ladies and gentlemen in open landaus were to be seen everywhere. There was something of a party atmosphere in the streets.

Kimberley was growing into a real town now, but it would never be a city like London. It would never have the grand buildings, it would never have the beautiful parks or garden squares. It was a town cobbled together around what was now, a huge, ugly, open-face mining operation. We had a nice little area with brick buildings and homes in Belgravia and Beaconsfield, the newly renamed Dutoitspan and Bultfontein part of Kimberley. The new name had been given officially in honor of British Prime Minister Disraeli who held the title of the Earl of Beaconsfield. No matter what though, Kimberley would always be an eyesore. You cannot make a silk purse out of a sow's ear.

Of course London had its share of ugliness, but it also had something that until now, I had never paid attention to, grand mansions. I wanted to own a house in a fashionable area, close to Hyde Park. I decided to give that some thought in the future.

My father had purchased a beautiful town house on the edge of Regents Park in an elegant Georgian terrace. He insisted that I stay with him and not at a hotel. I could hardly refuse, and I was happy to do so. I was delighted to see that my father had taken so well to his new lifestyle, and had a full time housekeeper and a cook. Father refused to have a manservant. That was not his way of life.

He had leased a shop on Oxford Street, a busy thoroughfare close to Regent Street. He was selling the latest fashions for ladies and gentlemen. It was a far cry from the used clothing of his earlier years. How his life had changed! How my life had changed in such a short time. I felt that I could achieve so much more now.

Our reunion was most enjoyable. I related all the things that Harry and I were doing, that his grandson Woolf had learned so much, so quickly. I expressed that I wanted Kate's two other sons to join me in the diamond business and hoped that he could influence Kate to agree. I never suggested at anytime that father should come and visit the Cape Colony for obvious reasons. There were probing questions about courtship and a letter I had written with Fanny's help. My father wanted to know who the girl was, how long we had been courting and of course, was she Jewish.

Why is it that parents always feel there is something missing if there is no immediate prospect of a wedding? I am sure that I will never be like that. I told him that Fanny was dear to me and that she was willing to convert and become Jewish, but it would take time. My response satisfied him, and I was relieved to have finally discussed it with him. I am my own man, but my father had always been my teacher, and I wanted his blessing.

Much to my surprise, the London newspapers were full of stories about the new Anglo-Zulu war going on in South Africa. I had no idea how the war affected the London Stock market, but it did and mining shares were taking a beating. Conversely, the diamond prices had spiked and this puzzled me even more. It was obvious to me that the British public had no idea of the size of South Africa or where the war was taking place.

A couple of days after my arrival I met with my bank manager, a Mr. Benham. He was a very distinguished gentleman who spoke with a refined English accent, probably a graduate of Oxford or Cambridge. In his mid fifties or so, I was told that he had a wealth of knowledge when it came to banking, and I needed to learn as much as I could from him.

"Mr. Barnato, thank you for selecting our bank in London for your business. How can I help you?"

"Mr. Benham, I am not an educated man. I know little of high finance. As you know, I have been successful in diamond dealing and mining in the Cape Colony. A lot of the success that my brother and I have had has to do with gut instinct and luck. What we need now is expertise in how to take us to the next level. There are huge opportunities to be had in consolidation of the myriad mining claims. We can see from the influential and wealthy men that are buying up claims left, right and centre that we have to be in there, competing with them."

"I am glad to be of assistance in that respect Mr. Barnato. My bank can definitely help and guide you." He was direct.

"How do you propose we compete? I was equally direct.

"Firstly, we have to put together a long-term plan laying out what funds are needed. How these funds will be spent. What period they will be needed for and calculate the return on the investment. You have to be realistic in this, not fanciful."

"How do I know how much I will need. The price that we have to pay for a claim is different every time we buy one."

"Yes. But you know how much you are prepared to pay to beat your competition. Regardless of the asking price or even how much each claim could be purchased for, is there is a higher price that you would go to, if you have to? That is how you must base the cost. If you are fortunate to conclude a deal at a lower cost, the difference will go to your reserves. At some point you may have to pay well in excess of your average to purchase some claims that are key to maintaining the continuity of your block holdings. Do you understand what I am saying?"

"Perfectly. What next?"

"You must estimate the yield of your mining operations based on historic numbers. You know how much your current holdings produce, what your overhead is, and how much you can expect in sales. Sales, minus cost, will give you the gross profit. Next, we must figure overheads, other than production costs, things like investment in equipment, interest payments on financing, etc."

"What you are saying is that we should borrow the money we need. Is that correct?"

"Not exactly. Simply put, Mr. Barnato, you do not have to borrow the funds to purchase the claims. You have to float a publicly traded company and sell shares to investors."

"But that would mean giving away a large portion of the company."

"Not at all. You are not giving it away. You and your family will still retain the majority shareholding. As the value of your shares increases, so will the amount of money you will have available to do the things that you plan to do. The City loves mining shares. The public will buy your shares if your prospectus is solid. The prospectus is your plan that we will write together. As you pay dividends to your shareholders, they will want to buy more. Your shares will be traded everyday on the London Stock Exchange. People have to invest their money, and I believe that they will be excited to invest in your success."

"What happens if the shares don't sell?"

"Our bank will look at the potential after you have put together your initial plan. We will then make recommendations on how to improve the public offering. The partners at the bank will consider what we call, underwriting. That is, we will guarantee to purchase any unsold shares and this will be for a fee. This fee is lower if we do not agree to underwrite."

"What is the fee?"

"That we will discuss with you after the partners have seen your plan. Please be assured Mr. Barnato, we have done this many times, floating new public companies and we have an excellent record of success. If this is done right, you will have more than enough funds to achieve your goal."

"As I have said to you before, I have no experience in finance, why should I select you bank and not say, Rothschild's Bank?" Benham smiled.

"I think that you already know that answer, but you could go to any City of London bank and receive the same advice. However, you have come to us by recommendation from your cousin, David Harris, I believe. Then of course you possibly know that a consortium of diamond dealers, headed by a Mr. Jules Porges and a Mr. Cecil Rhodes, have been doing the rounds of banks both here and in Paris, to secure financing to do exactly the same thing that we expect you will be doing."

"Did he come here?"

"I really am not at liberty to say so, but the reason I share this with you is that he has secured the services of the Rothschild Bank in Paris. You will need to move quickly on this, or he will be so far ahead of you that you will be unable to catch him."

"Will you help me with this?"

"Every step of the way."

"When do we start?"

"I would like to recommend a firm of accountants that our bank has used in the past and who do an excellent job. I suggest a meeting with them, one week from today. In the meantime, I would like you to put together some figures along the lines we have discussed today. Do not worry about how to lay this out. All the accountants will need initially are those figures that are easy for you to supply. They will of course need more information, but we will leave it up to them to discuss those details."

"Mr. Benham, I cannot thank you enough. I hope you were not offended by my questions. I'm good with numbers, but I lack the education in financial matters, something I intend to change as quickly as possible."

"Your questions are perfectly reasonable. Please be assured of our complete support."

With that, Mr. Benham escorted me personally to the large bronze doors of his bank, shook my hand and said goodbye. I met with the accountants the following week and for the next four weeks. Meetings followed meetings.

By March 1880, our prospectus for the Barnato Brothers, financiers and diamond dealers, was ready. The company was registered under the Companies Act with a nominal capital of £100 000 and I took the position of chairman of the board, with Harry and I as shareholders and the first board members. The bank agreed to a two per cent fee to underwrite the offering, which was over-subscribed by two hundred per cent within an hour. The next day the shares were trading at a high premium.

Before leaving London, Kate agreed to allow her oldest son, Jack, to accompany me to Kimberley. He was eighteen and enthusiastic to join his brother in the diamond business.

Chapter 21

To my dismay on my return to Kimberley, I found that Rhodes had just floated a public company in Kimberley, the De Beers Diamond Mining Company. Porges had been busy too, with the backing of the French Rothschild's bank. He floated his company Compagnie Française des Mines de Diamants du Cap de Bonne Espérance in Paris with a nominal capital of £560,000. Well, if Rhodes and Porges can do it in Kimberley, so can I. With the knowledge gained on my recent visit to England, I knew exactly what to do and how to do it. We immediately formed The Barnato Diamond Mining Company with a capital of £575,000. I said to myself, this is one battle that I intend to win. My war was on.

According to the newspapers, the Zulu war was not going well. Emperor Napoleon III and Empress Eugenie had been exiled to England in 1870. Their only son, Louis, the Prince Imperial, had been given a commission in the British Royal Artillery. At his urging, he had subsequently been sent to South Africa to fight in the Zulu war. Tragedy struck on the first of June,1879, when on a scouting mission, the Prince Imperial and his fellow officers were attacked by a war party of about forty Zulu warriors. Louis died from wounds sustained in the attack. To add insult to this, the Prince Imperial had been disemboweled by one of the warriors, a common Zulu practice to prevent a spirit seeking revenge on his killers in the afterlife.

This was a huge embarrassment for Queen Victoria and I am sure that she must have ordered her generals to finish this war and do so quickly. A month later, heavily reinforced British troops conquered the Zulu capital at Ulandi, defeating the warriors and the war was finally over.

I gave Woolf the job to show his brother what to do. Although he was younger, he really understood the diamond business and I was confident that Woolf had enough experience to teach Jack who would have to get used to the idea that his younger brother was in charge. I had too much to do now, especially looking at acquisitions of as many claims as I could readily buy. I acted swiftly.

"Woolf, I want you to show Jack around and teach him all you know about diamonds."

"Do I have to? I'm really busy at the moment."

"We're all busy and I wouldn't ask if I didn't think you capable. Jack can take over some of the jobs you're doing now. That will allow you more time for running the company."

"Whatever you say. You're the boss."

"That's right and don't you forget it. Anything happen while I was away that I should know about?" He thought about this for a few seconds.

"Well let me see. Elections are scheduled for the Cape Assembly next March. Any interest in running?"

"You have got to be joking; I have no interest in politics. Who's running?

"Frank Orpen, Dr. Matthews, George Bottomly and Cecil Rhodes."

"Cecil Rhodes! That man has his finger in every pie. What else?"

"Something really important that happened whilst you were gone. The Legislative Council has passed an ordinance that requires mine owners to search all employees of the diamond mines when they leave the workings. This is obviously to stop theft and crack down on illicit diamond buying."

"Are we enforcing this in our mines?

"Yes and no. We are searching the natives, but the white workers treat it as a bit of a joke. They don't think that it applies to them."

"Does the ordinance apply only to natives?"

"No, it applies to everyone, but the white workers refuse to be subjected to a search. They say it is degrading to treat them like the *kaffirs*."

"Don't use that word, you know I don't like it."

"I'm sorry, Barney, but those are the words the men use and a lot worse."

"What's happening in the other mines?"

"Same thing. There are pamphlets circulating that tell white workers not to submit to any kind of search, as it is undignified."

"I'm not going to push the ordinance; the last thing I want now is to create friction with my men. Sooner or later we will have to address the problem, but not now. If that is all, I am going to take a look at our mines."

The next day, I received a telegram from Mr. Benham in London to inform me that the Barnato Brothers Company had received five and a half million pounds in subscriptions in one day! When I showed this to Harry, he could not comprehend how much this was. He was staggered that we had that much money in our coffers. I couldn't be more pleased with myself.

That evening we had a celebration dinner at Harry's home with all of the family. We were millionaires. I have become a millionaire before the age of thirty, something that I could never have imagined.

Word spread quickly that the Barnato Brothers were buying. Every day I had a stream of men going through my office and deals were concluded swiftly and, in most cases, at my price. I never offered anyone a silly price, I wanted to be fair, and I was not interested in prolonged negotiations. The money was rolling into both the Barnato Diamond Mining Company and Barnato Brothers Diamond Dealers. A few of the miners wanted crazy prices, but when I showed them the stack of contracts that were now lying on my desk and the prices on them, they soon became realistic and deals were struck.

I purchased new offices on Stockdale Street to facilitate the transactions in the newly constructed building housing the Central Bank of Kimberley. We had the entire floor above the bank and our bank manager was happy to accommodate all the new business that was coming his way. Meanwhile across town, Rhodes was hard at it, buying as much of the De Beers claims that he could get his hands on. Around town, there were the other buyers; Beit, Wernher, Porges, all hard at it, accumulating and consolidating their holdings.

These were very exciting times. I loved the challenge. I really liked to wheel and deal with the miners, who by now were anxious to sell and move on to the gold mining areas to the west. I was also interested in acquiring properties in the Transvaal gold areas, but that would have to wait.

I cultivated a friendship with the Registrar of Claims who was giving me information about who was buying. I of course showed my gratitude with a number of modest diamonds for his personal collection. The map on my office wall showed our progress and that of the competition. There were more players in this game than I had originally thought possible. In addition to the obvious two powerful syndicates of headed by Rhodes, Porges, Beit and Wernher, there were a couple of others that I had not considered.

Russian Jews Sammy Marks and his brother-in-law Isaac Lewis had made a good living supplying miners with their everyday needs and equipment. They had branched out into diamond dealing and rumors had it that Jules Porges was a silent partner in their business. Now they were purchasing claims in Kimberley too.

Brothers George and Leopold Albu, German Jews, were attempting to buy claims, although they did not appear to have the funds to be serious competitors. These people really did not matter. We were flush with money and I could not see how they would adversely affect our consolidation plans.

In a nutshell, the problem that we all faced was the huge amount of diamonds that were flooding the market. Nobody was taking into account that we were depressing the world market with over-production. Prices had been falling for two years, and we were in danger of totally devaluing the price of diamonds altogether.

There had to be a way to control prices, even if it meant slowing our production, or even temporary closure of our best mines. Because there was so much competition buying up claims, it was impossible to approach the other producers of diamonds, to put together a plan that would be beneficial to all of us.

Chapter 22

Once the Zulu war was over, the Transvaal Boers, unhappy with the British Government annexation of their Territory in 1877, grew restive. Apparently, there were two Treaties that had been signed by the British Government and the Boers that guaranteed their homeland in the Transvaal. The Boers were self-governing and had their own elected parliament, the Volksraad. British Prime minister Disraeli had somehow ignored this when he decided that the Transvaal should be part of the Cape Colony.

The Governor of Natal and Transvaal, Major-General Sir George Pomeroy Colley, appointed an administrator to look into the Boer complaints. Unfortunately, the administrator had no understanding of the Boers mood or ability to put up a fight. The Boers declared independence from England and set up a volunteer force on the Natal border. If this wasn't enough to get the government's attention, they surrounded the British garrison in the Transvaal. Meanwhile, Paul Kruger, their leader, continued to negotiate to have the British Government rescind its annexation.

On December 16th, 1880, the Boers attacked a British column of the 94th Foot marching to reinforce Pretoria at Bronkhorstspruit. Most of the officers of the column were killed in the skirmish and within fifteen minutes, one hundred and fifty-six British soldiers were killed or wounded and more than one hundred others were taken prisoner.

Everyone was horrified by the losses reported in the newspapers. There were more battles in the following months that resulted in even more dead and wounded. Finally, the new Prime Minister, Gladstone and his government signed a peace treaty with the Boer leader, Paul Kruger, in March 1881. The war had lasted ten weeks, but cost hundreds of British lives. England agreed to Boer self-government in the Transvaal.

For the most part, the war, just like the Zulu war, really didn't affect life much in Kimberley. Diamonds were being mined at a rate as high as before, if not higher. The consolidation of mining claims was in full swing. Recognizing the need for modern underground mining methods, we wrote to an expert to advise us how to do this and arranged for him to come to Kimberley as soon as practical.

After the early spring rains, I met privately with Mr. Bees and asked him if I could marry Fanny. There was now no question in his mind that I wasn't going to give up on marrying her and that I could more than provide for the family. Not that he asked for money or anything, but whenever possible I lavished presents on the entire Bees clan whenever an occasion arose. We had to hide it from him or there was trouble. I could easily afford it and with seven children of varying ages in the family, other than Fanny, there was always an occasion.

I am not sure what Bees problem was with me. I believe he was an anti-Semite, although I would never say so to Fanny. She probably had the same opinion.

Once again he refused me. As far as he was concerned, I was not going to be part of his family at this time, regardless of how Fanny and I felt for each other. However, he was not going to stop us meeting and seeing each other, providing we were not alone. Fanny and I knew that we would marry sometime in the future and we felt able to wait till the time was right.

Our Friday night *Shabbos* dinners with David and Rose were easing Fanny into our Jewish traditions. I explained to her what she had to do to convert to Judaism. She was enthusiastic about it. Within a few months she was able to recite the Shabbat blessings with us all. Without the knowledge of her father, Fanny met with our rabbi from the West Hebrew Congregation each week to receive the education needed for conversion. He had met with us singly and together, each time asking if this is what we wanted. In Jewish law, the convertee has to want conversion and not have it forced upon them for any reason.

We celebrated my thirtieth birthday on February 21st 1881. We kept the occasion small with twenty-four guests at a dinner at Cousin David's home. He now had his own personal chef, who created a menu that everyone said was the best they had ever had in the Cape Colony. I liked the food although I found it a bit too rich for my taste, but I did enjoy a superb birthday cake. Fanny sat at my side and we held hands under the table. We both believed that it would not be long before her father would accept me.

My cousin Barney sat next to Rose's sister Martha and it was obvious that these two were romantically involved. Barney had his eye on Martha from the day he had met her five years ago. She had recently had her sixteenth birthday. This was considered a marriageable age. However, her father considered Martha a bit too young, but was not opposed to the marriage.

The year of 1881 turned out to be a banner year in so many ways. Business was booming. Our mines were producing diamonds well above the quantities we had projected. We were rapidly consolidating our holdings in Kimberley and we were able to purchase many small claims.

On the second of February, 1881, the Kimberley Royal Stock Exchange opened for business, the first Stock Exchange in South Africa. The only other exchange in Africa at this time was in Cairo, Egypt, more than seven thousand miles away. The few traders handled mining stocks almost exclusively. It was a great opportunity for those of us who had public companies on the London Stock Exchange, as we were now able to trade our stocks locally as well.

There were some dark clouds on the horizon. The London stock market was jittery. The wars in South Africa were creating a feeling that England would have to commit a larger military force for its protection. England was waging war in Afghanistan and the cost was too great to be fighting wars on two fronts. The English newspapers were full of it.

Mining stocks had soared due to large profits that had been made, but the drop in value of diamonds due to serious over-production, was having its toll on the ability of many companies to pay dividends. Over-speculation was rife, and there were, of course, the usual sham companies that were cashing in on the boom. Some were not even mining. They printed a fancy prospectus with the intent of defrauding investors. Sadly, these few companies hurt the legitimate ones like the Barnato Brothers.

It wasn't surprising that the bubble burst. The stock market took a plunge unlike anything that had been seen before. Prices were dropping in half and there were no buyers, only sellers. I received a telegram from Mr. Benham instructing me what to do in this situation. Buy all the shares in your own companies that come on the market. I was not sure about this at first, thinking that he was covering his bank with what they were possibly holding. When I thought about it some more, I realized the wisdom of this and immediately sent instructions to do just that.

Within a few months the market stabilized. Demand increased slowly at first and before long it was back to the levels we had seen before. The Barnato Diamond Company was able to weather the storm and emerge almost unscathed.

I wondered if Rhodes and his big plans had been seriously affected by the stock market crash. Did he know what to do in circumstances like this? My guess is he did. The amazing thing with Rhodes is that he always seemed to be doing something else other than mining. This year he got himself elected to the Cape parliament. If that was not enough distraction, he and Charles Rudd, his business partner and a number of local mucky-mucks had built themselves a gentleman's club.

The Kimberley Club was only open to members. It was a place where gentlemen could go to read the daily papers in the comfort of plush leather chairs, smoke their cigars and quaff Champagne. Apparently, I was told, membership was by invitation only and no females or dogs were allowed, I was not sure about Jews. The club was modeled on the gentlemen's clubs in London. Out of the original seventy-four members, none of them were my family. We were not invited to join.

Things seemed to have quieted down with the Boers, or at least for the time being. Perhaps with their demands being met, they will keep to themselves and stay away from our part of the country. As for the natives, that is another story altogether. Their loss of rights to own guns has certainly discouraged many to come and work in diamond mining.

It became obvious that it was a time for all of us to change the way we mine. I was told that underground mining was the way of the future and, if I was not mistaken, the future was fast approaching. It became imperative for us to find a good mining engineer, who knew how to do this. I sent another message to Mr. Benham to find such a man. I also made Benham an offer to work full time for Barnato Diamond Mining Company in London. He is a most valuable man.

It had been a while since I last visited my old haunt of the Pig and Whistle, and I decided to do so. Fanny said she did not mind, so I dressed in some old clothes, swapped my bowler hat for a cap and walked across town to the pub. The pub was packed with people, which was not surprising as it was early evening and the diggers had finished work for the day. Albert greeted me like a long lost relative.

"Barney, it is so good to see you. Where have you been?"

"Hi Albert, I've been busy, a little bit of travel, but mainly working hard."

"The usual?"

"Sure."

He poured me a good measure of Cape Smoke and slid it across the bar.

"Why don't you give me the whole bottle?"

"Hard day?"

"No, not really."

I looked around the bar and spotted a newcomer at the far end. You can always tell from the pale color of the skin and their clothes. He was explaining something to a man I recognized as a diamond miner by the name of Hall, who I had tried unsuccessfully to buy out of Kimberley.

I was most interested to overhear what they were talking about, so I picked up the bottle of Cape Smoke and squeezed my way close to their end of the bar, where the two men were in deep conversation. I hoped nobody would start talking to me, which would make eavesdropping difficult. The newcomer was talking about sinking a vertical shaft and then cutting horizontal galleries to be able to get to the Kimberlite underground. This would allow the diamonds to be removed without all the risks that open-face mining had, like reef cave-ins, which were happening at an ever more frequent rate now that the pits were so deep. I had to get to this man if possible and find out more.

I pushed between Hall and the newcomer and put the bottle on the counter in front of them.

"Good evening, Hall, I thought I would buy you a drink and see if you have changed your mind about selling."

Hall went silent and gave me an angry look.

"Sorry, Barney, if you don't mind, we're busy."

"Well at least introduce me to your friend, he might like to try our local brew."

Hall thought about this for a couple of seconds.

"This is Joseph Gouldie. Joseph meet Barney Barnato, one of our local personalities."

I held out my hand and grasped Gouldie's hand, pumping it hard.

"Good to meet you, Mr. Gouldie. Recently arrived?"

"Is it that easy to tell?"

"Have a drink; this is the best of the worst you can drink here in Kimberley. After a while, you'll get used to it."

I called Albert to give me two more glasses, which he slid expertly along the bar. Filled to the brim, I handed Gouldie and Hall a glass each. We clinked glasses and threw the fiery liquid down our throats.

Gouldie gasped and looked a bit flushed, so I filled all the glasses again and proposed a toast.

"*Le chaim*, to life. Tell me, Mr. Gouldie, what brings you to our beautiful town?

Before Hall could stop him he blurted out.

"I'm here to improve mining...."

Hall interrupted.

"If you don't mind, this is a personal matter between Mr. Gouldie and myself. Mr Barnato is a competitor of mine, Gouldie, and I prefer that you do not discuss anything in front of him."

"I'm terribly sorry."

"Don't worry, boys, I'm leaving. I just wanted to say hello. Welcome Mr. Gouldie, I am sure we will meet again."

With that, I took my leave.

Chapter 23

It was imperative for us to start underground mining now that we were able to consolidate a number of adjacent claims. This was on my mind for a number of weeks and we still had not found a suitable mining engineer to do the job. My competitors were ahead of me in this and that is something I had to change. I immediately cabled Benham in London. He had accepted my offer to run the financial side of our expanding company offices, and I was pleased to have such a seasoned professional doing the job. He wasn't family, but I trusted him.

A few days later, I received a return cable informing me, not only had he found the right man, but he already sailed from Southampton on the previous day and would arrive in the fastest possible time.

Early one morning, five weeks later a tall, thin man of indeterminable years, arrived at my office door, Mr. Herbert McLeland talked rapidly and got down to business straight away.

"I will need to reconnoiter the mining area and ascertain the best method to use. I understand that there are a number of competing mining operations going on simultaneously. This will affect how we shall proceed."

"That's no problem. I will have my nephew show you around. Once you have a better idea what we are facing here, then I will accompany you and you can show me what is needed. What is your experience in this type of mining, Mr. McLeland? "

"I have been running tin mines in Cornwall for the last twenty seven years. I know the problems of multiple competing mines undercutting each other. Mining tin is not much different from mining anything else using underground methods. Have you heard of the Gouldie system?"

"I can't say I have, but I believe I have actually met Gouldie recently in Kimberley."

"Is that so? Well his method works well enough, but I can improve on it."

"That pleases me. When would you like to start?"

"Now, this morning."

McLeland was thorough. He spent the next three days climbing in and out of holes, testing the compactness of the rock, boring test holes and much more. Woolf complained to me at the end of the third day that this man was like a mountain goat, and how did he do that at his age? McLeland was back in my office just after dawn on the fourth day, notebook in hand.

"Good day, Mr. Barnato. I am ready to give you my report detailing how we should progress to underground workings in your mines."

"Good morning, Mr. McLeland. My nephew has enjoyed working with you. I am sure he has learned a lot."

"Hopefully he has. He is bright and grasps concepts quickly. You have a good lad there.

Getting down to business, the disparate claims that you hold make it difficult to come up with a single solution. I understand that you are in an active acquisition stance, and it is your intention to purchase more claims, especially where these claims are contiguous to your current holdings."

"Yes, that is correct."

"It is most important that you purchase several claims that I have marked on your map of Kimberley mining claims. You may have to pay in excess of the true value for these, as they block the way for horizontal galleries that will be cut to access the Kimberlite. Let me explain to you how underground mining works in relationship to open face mining. First thing we do is to sink a vertical shaft or in your case several vertical shafts, into the ground as near to the workings as possible. The open face workings are getting close to three hundred or so feet deep. These shafts will go down to eight hundred feet. From the vertical shafts, we cut horizontal galleries thirty feet apart and toward the diamond bearing ground, inclining them sufficiently to access the next level. Do you understand this?"

I nodded.

McLeland drew a rough sketch to show me the relationship of the current workings to the shafts and where they should be positioned. He had numbered each of our claims and showed the direction that we would be moving underground. Once I saw the sketches, I knew exactly what he was talking about.

"Yes, I understand your plan clearly."

"Good! Work should start immediately on the vertical shafts. The horizontal galleries will have to wait until such time as you have acquired the keystone claims as indicated on your map. When that is completed, we can cut the galleries. For the time being, you can continue to work the open-face mining operations."

"Good, let's get this project organized. Mr. McLeland, I'm in your hands."

The second day of September 1882 was a day of celebration. Kimberley, now officially the second largest town in South Africa, was the first city in the Southern Hemisphere to have electric street lamps. Only a year ago, Godalming in Surrey, England, was the first town to have street lights in the entire world. We were beating most parts of London which were only just replacing gaslights and having them installed.

Our local newspaper ran a full page spread, crediting the invention to a Russian named Pavel Yablochkov. Where they got this information from is anybody's guess. Kimberley had reached a status as an important world center for diamonds and the new electric streetlights, were a show off our newly found wealth.

In the center of town, where the weekly farmer's market was regularly held, Rhodes and a large entourage from the Cape Parliament stood on a platform and in front of a crowd of thousands of people. At precisely 7 o'clock, Rhodes threw a lever and the lights went on. There was huge applause and cheers from the crowd. Rhodes tried to make a speech, something about the importance of uniting South Africa into one country, a United States of Africa. It was impossible to hear him over the din and excitement of the event unless you were up close. I guessed the speech was more for the ears of the attending members of the Cape Parliament rather than for the uneducated residents of Kimberley.

Over the next three months, McLeland worked the laborers constructing the first shafts like a madman. He had them start work as soon as it was light. He even tried to get them to work after six in the evening, the traditional end of the day. I ignored the complaints, as I knew that it was critical to complete the main shafts before the winter rains came. We ordered two steam pumps from England and delivery was expected to be on time. At a depth of eight hundred feet, our shafts were going to need to be pumped throughout the winter rains.

Meanwhile, I was busy with my acquisitions of the remaining claims. Knowing what I did, I made offers for claims well in excess of their value, but some of the miners were turning down my offers. I was not the only one buying and these rogues were not going to miss out on taking a huge profit, knowing full well that they had me.

This needed a new strategy or we could miss out. After much thought, I came up with the idea of offering shares in the Barnato Diamond Mines instead of cash. That way, if sellers considered that we would be more successful than they had been, they would be able to share in the profits. Our local Stock Exchange had a large chalkboard on the wall with the daily prices of all the mining stocks in our area, so it was easy for anyone to see if they wanted to buy, sell or hold.

As usual, Harry didn't like the idea. After I explained it to him for the third or fourth time, he came to his senses. He agreed that we should at least try it and see if it worked. It worked like a charm. The remaining holdouts felt they were getting a better deal and, in fact, they were. We were getting a better deal too, as our shares continued their meteoric climb.

Solly, Kate's youngest son was now eighteen. He had nagged his parents continually for months about coming to South Africa since his brothers had joined the company. Finally, Kate and Joel relented. He arrived in Kimberley whilst we were in the middle of shaft construction. It was a good opportunity to have one of the boys learn about mining methods from McLeland, so I made sure that he was with him every day. That allowed Woolf to come back to the office. His expertise in sorting and selling diamonds was more valuable to me, than having him out in the mines.

Woolf had grown up quickly in Kimberley, but he had some traits that worried me. He loved to stay up late, drinking and gambling. For all I knew, he was carousing with the local women, even though I had given him and his brothers, the same talk my father had given me about the risks. Still, it really was none of my business, but I also worried about some of the company he was keeping. We Barnatos had earned a good reputation, and I did not want it damaged for any reason. In this business, it was not only important to be fair and honest, it was absolutely essential. I also wanted to make sure that he was not a bad influence on his brothers.

Sinking a shaft through solid rock was a tremendously difficult task. It was obvious the length of the horizontal galleries was such that it would be impossible to dig them out without the use of explosives. McLeland showed me, using the recently invented Nobel's Blasting Powder. It was called dynamite. It helped break up the rock before the men could get in with picks and shovels to remove the debris. The sticks of dynamite were about eight inches long and one and a half inches thick.

"These little sticks of dynamite pack one hell of a blast, Mr. Barnato. I experimented with this explosive in England. Initially we did not know how to direct the blast for maximum effect. That was critical as one mistake can be fatal. An adequate length of fuse has to be attached to the dynamite to allow enough time for men to clear the area. Close attention is needed to see where each man is when the explosion goes off."

"How many men he have you killed with it?

"Only two."

I looked at his face and I knew he wasn't joking. I warned Solly to be extra careful when McLeland was setting the dynamite. The last thing I wanted was anyone killed, especially one of my family.

The first shaft was reaching the eight hundred foot level when something went horribly wrong. Dynamite had been set in a bore hole and the fuse had been lit. The men waited for the blast and nothing happened. After a few minutes two men were lowered down in a rough wooden cage, to reset the dynamite. One man pulled out the stick of dynamite to attach another fuse. As he did so it exploded. The cage holding the men disintegrated and blood and body parts were splattered around the walls of the shaft.

McLeland sent one of the natives to the office to tell us what had happened. We all rushed over to the shaft to see if we could do anything. There was little to be seen from the top of the shaft and nothing that could be done.

McLeland was in a state, badly shaken and distraught. It was impossible to pacify him. We had to continue with our excavations and everyone knew the risks. Today was one of those days that you never forget. I decided that McLeland should take a few days off to get over the tragedy, but he wouldn't hear of it. The next day he was back working as soon as the sun came up, but Solly was back working in the office again.

I paid for their burial and sent money to the men's families.

Chapter 24

"It id not in the stars to hold our destiny but in ourselves." William Shakespeare (1564 – 1616).

Diamonds continued to flood the market from the South African mines, further depressing the prices. There was a real danger that production would eventually outstrip demand, which would be disastrous for all of us here. Production from Brazil and India is now almost down to nothing. Our production was up twenty-five percent at our existing mining operations. We were required by law to work every claim, so we decided that the newly acquired claims should be worked with a small token number of laborers to keep unauthorized people out and maintain the condition of the reef to stop it collapsing.

The number of owners in Kimberley dropped to less than one hundred. This was a huge reduction from the original three thousand, six hundred owners. At this time, we were gradually completing, or negotiating the purchase of more than twenty or so claims. My biggest worry was the French Company that owned a large L shape, swath of claims that divided Kimberley Mines into two. For all intents and purposes, they could not be purchased at any price, but we would see. Two other large holdings presented a challenge, the Standard Company and Kimberley Central Diamond Mining. Both were public companies with their shares trading on our local Stock Exchange. That meant we could purchase shares at the going daily price, and we did every working day. Our holdings increased substantially. The French Company's shares were still controlled from Paris, mainly closely held by the Rothschild family.

I had this idea. If we could only get to the point where there were four companies running the four diamond pipes at Kimberley and De Beers, and the two lesser mines at Bultfontein and Wesselton, we could then regulate the volume of diamonds reaching the market. This would stabilize prices; even create shortages from time to time to increase prices. Profits could be staggering!

By the time the winter rains were over, we had completed our north shaft and the first of the horizontal galleries at our mine. Our equipment was impressive. Our company has imported rolling stock from England and installed a rail system so we could easily remove the Kimberlite from the galleries, haul it to the surface and from there out onto flat fields, where the Kimberlite is laid out, flattened and left to decompose. At that point, it is sieved and the diamonds are extracted. It is a fantastic sight to see, fields producing not vegetables but diamonds. We completely stopped open-face mining in our section of Kimberley, switching exclusively to underground mining.

Over the course of 1883 shafts were sunk by a few of the other diamond companies. Even so, there were men working in open face claims, which had become extremely dangerous due to the depth and continual reef collapses. I decided to call a meeting of all the mine owners in Kimberley. I felt that it was up to Barnato Brothers to lead the way.

The meeting, held in our offices, was well attended by mine owners and representatives. I think they were curious to see what we had in mind. Joseph Robinson who owned the Standard Company and even Francis Baring-Gould the owner of Kimberley Central turned up. To my disappointment, there was nobody representing the French Company. So be it.

I began,

"Good evening, gentlemen, thank you all for coming. Of great concern to all of us is the world price of diamonds. It is in all our interests to get our over-production under control. If we fail to do something, diamonds will either be so low in price that it will be impossible for us to make a profit. Or worse still, the market will be unable to absorb the sheer volume of diamonds."

I looked around the room and tried to get a feel for the mood of my audience. A man who I did not recognize standing at the back of the room, perked up.

"Do you mean that you are worried that you will be unable to pay a dividend to your shareholders?"

"I am concerned that people who have put their trust in me and my companies will suffer, yes of course. Let me be clear about this. Prices in Europe for one to three carat size rough stones have dropped to ten shillings per carat. Our costs and your costs, if you have calculated correctly, are fifteen shillings per carat. How long do you think we can afford to lose money on ninety per cent of what we are mining?

"So this is all about your shareholders then."

"Not at all. This is about the future. What we need to do is to join forces, bring all mining operations under one management. Not only will we save a bundle on overhead and equipment costs, we can control the quantities of diamonds that move into the market."

Robinson chimed in.

"How do you propose to do that? We are not the only mining area here. What about De Beers?"

"Well I'm glad you brought that up, because that is exactly what Mr. Rhodes is doing over there."

The man continued.

"What's the point of this, you can never control the price of diamonds in a world market, nobody can."

"I have to disagree with you, Mr. Robinson, I countered, "We can if we are united in our purpose. Look at it this way. When the market is sluggish and the economy is weak, we hold back on selling our diamonds to say, sixty per cent of what we are selling presently. What happens then, when there are not enough diamonds to satisfy demand? The price rises because the jewelers will pay more to keep their business going. As the price rises, we increase the quantities to seventy-five per cent. The immediate reaction is that there will not be a shortage, but the reality is that we are creating the shortage because we control the volume. Do you understand that?"

"I think it is a ridiculous idea."

"Wait a minute, I'm not finished. I have only talked about when the economy is weak. What happens when the economy is strong? That is when we sell the accumulation of the poor years, at much higher prices than if we had sold earlier. Think about it. We have the opportunity to control the entire production of diamonds worldwide."

Robinson got up and walked to the door. Looking back at me. He had to have one more dig.

"Seems to me this is all about Barney Barnato taking control of the whole of Kimberley for himself."

With that he left and everyone started talking and shouting. Some men left, others just stood and argued. I tried to quiet them down, but realized that it was hopeless. I knew my audience.

"I want you all to think about this and then we can meet again to discuss it further."

The meeting broke up, but I was well satisfied. I knew that there were a number of miners that liked the idea. In addition, there were more sellers who would be knocking at my door. In all, it was a good evening's work.

My relationship with my brother Harry has always been very good. I think, traditionally, younger brothers are expected to defer to their older brother. With us it was quite different. I'm not saying that I am cleverer than Harry, or for that matter, that he is cleverer than me. After all, we both had the same education. There is a difference though. I am a quick thinker, I can assess a situation and come to a conclusion quickly. Generally, it turns out to be the right one. Harry is a thinker and takes much longer to reach an opinion. So I have to constantly nudge him in the right direction. This caused some friction between us as he saw me as the decision maker, often making decisions without consulting him first. This rubbed him up the wrong way.

"That was a bit of a failure. Did you think you would be able to persuade them that your plan would benefit all of them?" Harry chided me.

"I think the meeting, short as it was, went well. I don't expect the miners to immediately agree with me. They have to mull it over, but if they have half a brain they will see that there is really no choice if we are all to stay in diamond mining."

"The smaller claim holders are hanging on by the skin of their teeth. They know that your plan will not include them, so why would they agree with you?"

"Opportunity is the answer to your question. Opportunity."

"I'm not sure I am with you on that." Harry pushed on.

"Think about it, Harry. At this time they can sell out for a decent price. We are buying and paying well, others are buying too. That means they can sell out before the price of diamonds drops so low, they will just walk away from their claims because they will not be able to afford to keep going. Keep on flooding the market and it will collapse."

"I am not sure that I agree with you. There will always be a market."

"Not if you make diamonds as common as coal," Harry laughed.

"That's an exaggeration and you know it."

"Maybe. If these men sell out now, they can go and stake claims in the gold mining areas in the Transvaal. There's plenty of money to be made in mining gold and there is always a market. You cannot devalue the price of gold by over production because the world money markets rely on the stuff to back their currencies."

"So why aren't we concentrating on gold mining?" He asked.

"We will, but not until we have diamond mining under control. I know my idea is good. You wait and see. Within a couple of years, everyone will look back and say this was the defining moment in diamond mining history."

"Within a few weeks, I heard my plan coming from many sources in our community, large and small. Cecil Rhodes was claiming it to be his idea, something he had known from the start. As much as that angered me that somebody else would claim it as theirs, I was pleased that it was gaining momentum at every level. Proving to me and Harry especially, that this would be a reality in the not too distant future.

Chapter 25

Kimberley racecourse got started when a few gambling men decided to have a horse race. It started as nothing more than a field that had been fenced in when it was used as a farm. There were plenty of gamblers in the area. In fact every day was a gamble for all of us. The first stand was built in 1872 when the Jockey Club of South Africa came into being. My cousin David is fond of horses and decided to build his own stud, importing horses from England and Europe to race at the Kimberley racecourse. It amazes me how a man who, like me, didn't have two halfpennys to rub together, can now afford to have his own stud farm. My nephews, particularly Jack, spent what little spare time they had, at the farm and the racecourse. I feel to some degree, it has kept them out of mischief. They only told me about the wins they had. Like most gamblers they never had any losses, or certainly none they talked about.

For my part, I like to have a wager. I have a certain fondness for horses since I purchased the old nag from Jack Saunders that had been so valuable a buy. Of course, the nag, who never had a name that I knew of, is long dead. I have purchased many fine horses since then, but that old nag will be the one I'll always remember.

The racecourse was not much of a course, an oval roughly half a mile around with a covered stand that could seat about a hundred people. The horses were often men's personal riding horses, although a few of the richer owners, like David, were breeding horses for racing. The regular meets were fun events and well attended.

Fanny still occupied all my leisure hours, which sadly were dwindling rapidly. It seemed that every day was filled with meetings with miners wanting to sell their claims, dealing with stockbrokers as well as overseeing the diamond sales. Harry was taking less interest in the day to day workings of the companies, so I was glad to have Woolf keeping a watchful eye on things and reporting back to me. Our office staff had increased to twenty. We employed more than one hundred and twenty whites and a thousand natives. Harry spent a lot of time with Lily, his daughter, and I suggested that he take a voyage to England with his wife and daughter so the family there could get to know them.

Harry agreed and plans were made.

My old partner, Louis Cohen, had landed a job writing a regular column in the local daily newspaper. Thanks to him, my name appeared regularly. Every time I purchased another claim, I was in the paper. The day-to-day movement of the publicly traded shares in Barnato Diamond Mining was reported, as were the dividends paid. It seemed that I had become newsworthy.

On the other hand, there was a lot more reported about Cecil Rhodes, who as a member of the Cape Assembly was responsible for the political side of our community and the region. Rhodes had grand ideas for the British Empire, which was to colonize the entire continent from Cape Town to Cairo. He proposed the formation of the United States of South Africa to start with, linking all the various territories into one.

Of course the Boers would never agree to that, especially under British sovereignty. It was hard for me to understand his vision when there was so much at stake here in Kimberley. Yet he had these grand aspirations. My first thought was that he might give up on trying to monopolize the De Beers mine, but then I realized that he needed a fortune to be able to achieve his goal.

Rhodes managed to tie together the entire holdings in the De Beers field by March of 1883. He proved that it was possible to do it, initially by amalgamating with C.D. Rudd as early as 1874. A year later, he partnered with three more claim holders: Runchamn, Hoskyns and Puzey and together they acquired Baxter's holdings. Now they were united under one company, the De Beers Mining Company with a share capital of more than eight hundred thousand pounds. Rhodes was the largest shareholder. It was a blow to me that he had achieved it and I had not. On the other hand, it gave me hope that we could do it in Kimberley under Barnato Diamond Mining, providing we were able to purchase the French company.

By this time, reef collapse had become so commonplace that it was obvious to some of us, that open face mining could no longer continue. The Kimberley Mining Board implemented a new rule that the reef had to be completely removed and the working area terraced to prevent further cave-ins. This proved to be much more difficult than expected.

Only forty percent or so of Kimberley was being worked, the rest was considered unproductive, or had difficult access. A series of roadways that had been constructed a few years ago had almost disappeared as diggers undermined the roadway in an effort to reach what they considered prime spots for diamonds. In some cases, they were right, but it made access to many claims much more difficult. The diggers did not want to spend their time removing the reef, as it was a losing proposition. A few years earlier, it was necessary to remove one load of reef for every seven loads of blue ground. But now it was necessary to remove five loads of reef for only one load of blue ground. So the result was catastrophic and uneconomical.

Cave-ins were a common daily occurrence as diggers took risks that cost lives. The reef would crack at first before a collapse and the diggers would access how much time they had to keep working. When it did collapse, it would sweep men and equipment away in a wave. Apart from the loss of human lives, hauling the debris away after a collapse could prevent further digging for several months.

Underground mining for diamonds was still in its infancy and, as a result, had its own set of problems. Two or even three groups of miners might be working the same diamond pipe but coming from different directions, creating horizontal galleries that ran into each other. The resulting cave-in took lives, resulting in an accident rate that wasn't much better underground than it was above. Galleries collapsed onto each other where there was insufficient depth between the upper and lower levels. There was careless handling of the underground rolling stock that often hit the sides of the galleries, ultimately undermining the supporting timbers.

More problematic was the heat underground. Men were finding it difficult to work the long hours they had done so in the past without taking more breaks to cool off and drink something. The lack of water further exacerbated the problem. As a result, there was a considerable amount of discontent among the miners. Many of the natives were disappearing off the job and going back to their tribal lands. At the same time, worldwide prices for diamonds were still falling. So the vicious circle continued.

The news on Old Year's Day in 1883 was not good. The Zulu King Cetshwayo, who had been deposed by the British and his kingdom broken up, was fighting Zulu chiefs who governed what remained of his territory. The Fengu, who were the sworn enemies of the Zulu, joined in the fight. It looked like we were going to go through another series of Zulu wars that would drive down the value of our shares.

We were hoping for better things in the New Year 1884.

Chapter 26

On January 1st, I received an unexpected visitor. Cecil Rhodes strode into my office with his gangly gait.

"Good morning, Barnato, I think it is time that you and I had a talk."

"Good morning to you, Mr. Rhodes and a Happy New Year."

"Is it the new year already? I seem to have lost count of the days recently. It is said by many a man. So much to do and so little time to do it."

"Why don't you take a seat. I'll close the door and we can talk in private."

It had been several months since I had seen him last . He appeared thinner than I remembered. His complexion was sallow; he was clean-shaven, and his hair neatly parted. His clothes looked like he had slept in them, which he probably had. He sat in the easy chair I placed in front of my desk. I offered him a cigar which he refused and a glass of Cape Smoke, and this he accepted even though it was before seven in the morning.

"So what can I do for you today?"

"Well, I have heard your idea about amalgamating all the diamond mines into one organization. You know that this is nothing new to me, I came up with this long before you did."

"I'm not so sure about that."

"No matter. The point is that we agree on this plan, and we have to work together to make it happen. I have pretty much consolidated the holdings in the De Beers field with the help of Alfred Beit.

Now we have to do the same in the Kimberley mine. Your holding is large, but you do not have the ability to consolidate all the remaining claims."

"I'm afraid I have to disagree with you. Barnato Brothers will prevail. We will control Kimberley within a short period of time."

"I'm not saying you won't, but I think you will need my help to do so."

"Without appearing to be rude, let us just say that we both have our goals and we will continue to pursue them to their conclusion." Rhodes took a sip of his drink.

"Agreed, but there is much more at stake here than just the accumulation of wealth. For me wealth is a means to an end. That end is the creation of a confederation of states here in Africa under England's rule. I contend that we British are the first race in the world, and that the more of the world we inhabit, the better it is for the human race. If there be a God, I think what he would like me to do is paint as much of the map of Africa, British red, white and blue, as possible."

I sat there for a few moments contemplating this statement. I had heard that Rhodes was the son of a vicar of the Church of England, but had no idea that he felt that he had been chosen by God to colonize the black masses of Africa.

"In a short period of time, a railway line, currently being built from Cape Town to Kimberley, will be extended to Port Elizabeth and eventually will be constructed northward into the heart of Africa. This is our opportunity to bring civilization to the Dark Continent," Rhodes went on.

"Mr. Rhodes, this is all well and good, but I don't see how it relates to diamond mining. I know that as representative in the Cape Assembly you are charged with many duties and that you have great aspirations for our country, but you came here today, to do what, buy me out?"

"If need be, Barnato."

"I don't want to disappoint you, but the answer is never. How about I buy you out?"

"Look here. We both agree what needs to be done. We need to control the world market price of diamonds; we can only do it if we consolidate our holdings. You must see that."

"Yes, I do, but not if it means that Barnato Brothers is out of the game."

"Well let's think upon how we can help each other. I admire you Barnato. You have done extremely well. In my opinion, you are the only other man outside of Beit and possibly Wernher, that really understands the concept we have discussed. Why don't we meet later in the week at the Kimberley Club and we can discuss it further?"

"I'm afraid that I'm not a member of the club, nor accepted by the club members if I recall."

"No matter, you will be my guest. Perhaps if we come to a satisfactory arrangement I could influence the membership committee to grant you membership."

"It is not important, I am a member of a much larger club."

"Oh really, I had no idea. Which one would that be?"

"I am a member of the tribe!"

"Zulu, Sosha, which one?

"I am a Jew."

Fortunately for us, Zulu chief Cetshwayo died in early February, five weeks after the start of the new tribal war. Apparently he was poisoned by a member of his own inner circle. The war was over and the stock market rebounded quickly.

My nephew Jack was in charge of entering our daily diamond production into the ledgers. Different sizes of diamonds were in different ledgers; stones of up to three carat, from three carat to seven and a third ledger for seven and up. It was not unusual to have several hundred diamonds produced in a single day, with sales at a similar or slightly lower level. The only day of the week when sales were almost zero was on Saturday, the Jewish Sabbath. The majority of diamond dealers and cutters were religious Jews and did not work on the Sabbath. Hundreds of entries were made every day to ensure that our business was conducted correctly.

Early in March, a law enforcement officer named John Larkin Fry, authorized by the Diamond Mining Protection Association to stamp out illicit buying, entered our offices in Kimberley. He demanded to see the ledgers and the stones that were currently in our inventory. Jack took Fry into one of the buying offices and returned with a number of boxes of diamonds, each one folded into a traditional flute. A flute is a piece of paper folded in a special order five times. The weight and other details can be written on the paper and it makes them easy to store in long boxes that went into our safes.

Fry asked Jack about the system we use to match the diamond with the ledger entries. He then proceeded to check every single stone in our stock. Late in the afternoon, after several hours of examination, Fry came across one diamond of 8.20 carats and could not find it in the ledger. Jack was at a loss as to why it was not found. Checking the weight, he found that it is 8.30 carats and showed Fry there was an error and an appropriate entry for it.

"This is not good enough, Mr. Joel. This diamond appears to be from an illicit purchase."

"Absolute rubbish! I have shown you that there was a human error and that it had been incorrectly weighed, and there is an entry for it."

"You have come up with an explanation, but in my capacity as an investigator I've seen all this before. I have long suspected your company's wealth has come from I. D. B. "

"That is a complete outrage. This company has thrived on being ethical and I resent your remarks."

"Personally, I don't care what you resent. I am arresting you on the charge of Illicit Diamond Buying."

With that he called to two of his men that were standing around outside by their wagon to come and help him make the arrest. They manacled Jack and unceremoniously took him outside, locked him in the back of the wagon and drove off.

Solly witnessed the whole event and came looking for me.

I was at Kimberley talking with the foreman of the mine when a Solly ran up and told me what had happened. I was fuming, how dare they accuse us of I.D.B. We had never dealt in illicit diamonds but have been verbally accused of it by jealous competitors, but never to my face without me calling the person out with no hesitation.

I got on my horse and went to see this zealous policeman. Fry was strutting around and looked really pleased with himself when I arrived at the police station.

"What do you want?"

"To obtain the release of my nephew Jack Joel."

"He has been arrested on a very serious charge of Illicit Diamond Buying."

"He may have made a human error, but he is definitely not guilty of I.D.B. My company does not have to buy illicit goods, our mines produce vast quantities of diamonds, more than we can sell. So I ask you, why would you think that this diamond was purchased illegally?"

"You may think you're above the law, Barnato, but I know your type."

"And what might that be?"

"You Jew boys are all the same. You did not make your fortune without doing a bit of illegal dealing."

It was very hard for me not to flatten this anti-semite, but that was what he was waiting for, the chance to nail me for assault, but I wasn't going to give him the chance.

"How about we come to some agreement here?"

"Are you trying to bribe an officer of the court?"

"Absolutely not. I just suggested that you agree to drop the charge and I will be forever grateful."

"That sounds like you are trying to bribe me. Penalties for bribery are severe."

"You are mistaken. I only asked that given the lack of evidence you reconsider the charge. Perhaps a fine would appropriate for the error?"

"No fucking way."

With that I left, there was absolutely no point in trying to reason with the bigot. I've seen it too many times before, especially in London.

The next day Jack was charged in court with Illicit Diamond Buying. Our solicitor appealed to the magistrate for bail. Fry objected, stating that he felt the crime was too serious to allow his prisoner to be released. Fortunately, the judge did not agree and Jack was released on bail of four hundred pounds.

The penalty for this crime is five years hard labor, building a breakwater in the dangerous waters of the harbor in Cape Town. Not something that I would want any member of my family to be sentenced to, especially as it appeared that Mr. Fry had a grudge against us.

I went to see Rhodes at the Kimberley Club that very day. Rhodes thought that I had come to talk about amalgamation, which at this time was the furthest from my thoughts. We sat in a private salon that was elegantly furnished, the smell of leather, cigar smoke and cognac in the air.

"Mr. Rhodes, I am sure you have heard about the outrageous conduct of an I.D.B. enforcement officer at my offices this week."

"Of course I have. Everyone has, and I was deeply surprised."

"The charges are ridiculous; a human error in weighing a single stone was the basis for this charge. This man Fry appears to have decided that we are guilty and remained examining our inventory and records for many hours, well beyond the norm."

"He does appear to be over zealous. But I don't see what that has to do with me."

"Quite simply, I want this man squashed like a fly. I want his job and I want an apology."

"Oh, I see. I am not sure that there is anything I can do about it. You know that illicit trading in diamonds is a serious problem."

"Of course I know it, and you know it. But I am one of the driving forces that is trying to stamp it out and I always have been. This is a trumped up charge, Fry would not accept Jack Joel's explanation. He had already made up his mind that he was going to arrest someone in my office. I have no doubt that had I been there, he would have arrested me too."

Rhodes sat there for a few moments, took a cigar from a humidor on the table at his side. A native servant immediately rushed over and struck a match to light the cigar. He took a couple of puffs whilst he contemplated how to answer.

"I am not making any promises. I have no doubt that this case will come to trial within three weeks or so. But I will do what I can. You understand that?"

"Yes, of course. I am grateful for your help. But remember, I want this man squashed."

"I've got the picture."

With that I got up, shook Rhodes hand, and went back to my office.

Jack Joel looked visibly shaken; the prospect of a trial and incarceration was weighing heavily on him.

"What am I going to do, Barney? I cannot face five years hard labor. I've heard that conditions are appalling and that a large number of men have drowned trying to complete the breakwater."

"Don't worry. I have spoken to Rhodes and he is going to see if there is anything he can do about this piece of shit, Fry."

"But what happens if they find me guilty? Honestly, I am diligent at what I do, but I can make mistakes just like anyone else."

"I know this is what you do. You will book passage on the next ship out of Cape Town and go back to England. Go home and start packing, you will not be coming back to the Cape again."

"That's it? I'm being fired."

"No Jack, you are not being fired; you are going back to England and will be part of the London office. We don't want to wait to see what Rhodes will do. No matter what, you will be safe and I will have my revenge on Mr. John Larkin Fry.

Two days before Jack was to appear in court, I received a telegraph from London informing me that he was home in England. Our solicitor appeared before the magistrate to inform him that Jack Joel had failed to surrender to the court and had apparently skipped bail. The magistrate issued a bench warrant, and bail was forfeited. The best thing of all was the look on the face of Fry. He looked like he was going to have a fit. As he stepped outside of the court, Fry was surprised to find Solomon Rathbone, the chairman of the Diamond Mining Protection Association waiting for him.

"Mr. Fry, I wonder if I might have a word with you in my office."

"Of course sir. When would you like me to come?"

"Now."

They walked across the street from the courthouse to Rathbone"s office.

"I am not going to beat about the bush, Fry. The members of the board are terminating your services as of today."

"I don't understand why, sir. I've always done my job to the best of my ability."

"That I fear is the problem. Your abilities seem to be somewhat lacking."

"Lacking! Are you kidding me? I'm trying to stop criminals in their tracks. You know what happens when they cross the Vaal River into the Boer's Orange Free State, they're free to trade in illicit stones."

"Fry, I am fully aware of the facts, nevertheless, your methods and heavy handed approach, are not what is needed. We have decided that we will pay for you return passage to England, second class of course."

"This has to do with Barnato, I know it."

"No, Mr. Fry, it has to do with you. I don't think we need to discuss this any further. See my clerk on the way out and turn in your credentials. Good day to you."

It was true that the Boer Orange Free State did not share in the diamond bonanza and cared little about the British laws regarding trading in illicit diamonds. In fact they openly rejected it. As far as I was concerned, pressure had been applied in the right place and Fry had been sacked. I had no doubt that there would be others like Fry. So I approved a new system for logging our daily production. Put forward by Woolf, it would require double entries and would be checked by our accounting team. There would be no repeat of the fiasco that had befallen Jack.

More trouble in April 1884. Both white and black workers in all the diamond mines; Kimberley, De Beers, Dutoitspan and Bultfontein went out on strike. We had not seen anything like this before. For the first time since diamonds had been discovered here absolutely nothing was being mined. It was a complete shutout.

Still rankling the white workers was the searches that were now being forced on them by the mine owners. No more special treatment for the whites. The rule applied to all diamond workers. At first they had laughed it off; this was for the *kaffirs*. They insisted that they were above such indignities. The men tasked with the job of searching were intimidated and easily backed down in a confrontation. Things had changed. The mines were in the hands of large companies. The estimated losses due to theft had grown to more than twenty five per cent of all diamonds mined. This had to stop. Bigger and better security was now in place and full body searches had begun.

The native workers already had full strip searches carried out by native security men. They put up little resistance to it and had mainly accepted that as a fact of their employment. Their pay was eight times higher working in the mines than working on a plantation, twenty to thirty shillings a week on average, which at this time, was more than laborers earned in England. They could also earn a huge bonus of £20 if they found a large diamond and handed to their overseer instead of smuggling it out.

The biggest problem we were having with native workers was that every time there was a tribal skirmish, their chiefs would call the men back to fight. These men would quietly slip away at night. The next day we would have to scramble to find more workers. Fortunately, the chiefs sent many of their young men to work in the mines. This was how they were able to equip their armies with guns to fight other tribes. Brokers contracted with the chiefs for so many men at a time. Selling guns to the natives had been illegal for quite a while, but there was always someone willing to trade for diamonds and it continued to be the driving force that encouraged the natives to steal. I was told that before coming to work in the mines they were taught how to conceal diamonds around and in their body.

The reason that the natives were on strike, a concept that they could little understand, was that the large mine owners were instituting closed compounds for the men. This was a barracks like set up where the men would be housed, fed and spend their off duty time. They could not leave during the term of their employment without a pass. The term was now extended to a two-month period.

The communal bunk houses were very basic with hard wooden bunks and a single blanket for the cold nights. A communal mess hall provided their basic food of mealie and dried meats. A latrine was dug on the far side of the compound with urinals alongside. A large bathing pool was the only relief from the hot weather and a place to wash off the dust and dirt. The natives had an infirmary and a hospital wing. In fact this system was much more efficiently run than the underground mining. The natives worked a twelve-hour shift, with an hour break for dinner in the middle of the shift. A pass was required if they wanted to go into town. It was issued for a set number of hours and if they did not return on time they were arrested and charged. The penalty was one month hard labor, Guess where? In the diamond mines. Ultimately, this meant that additional convict quarters were built in the closed compounds to house the prisoners.

The closed compound became the model for all mine owners. Once again the white workers did not see how this applied to them. White workers could take advantage of relatively comfortable quarters on the far side of the compound, away from the natives. They had the choice of living in these quarters, or living in the town, but everyone was searched before leaving.

The strike didn't last long. The organizers, both black and white were dismissed and everyone went back to work.

Chapter 27

In England, the railway system links up every city and most towns in the country. So the idea of a railroad linking Cape Town and Port Elizabeth through Kimberley was an exciting concept. John Molteno, the prime minister of the Cape Colony, made it a priority of his government to link the coastal cities and ports to the interior of the colony. The diamond boom in Kimberley was part of the impetus to develop the system.

Due to the ready supply of native laborers, the construction of the Cape Government Railway, Cape Western Line, progressed quite rapidly. The lines had to climb a substantial coastal mountain range and then cross the inhospitable Karoo desert. After more than twelve years of construction, the lines reached Kimberley in 1885 causing much excitement from the locals. Cape Town was now only a day and half away. What a contrast to the twenty-seven days it took me to get here when I arrived.

Kimberley had become an important town in the region with more than fifty thousand residents. Development of new buildings and houses, solidly built out of stone and brick, could be seen everywhere. These were a far cry from the humble beginnings of a tent city. Construction of an electric tram service for the town was beginning, linking up the outlying areas of our community. The Town Council had big plans for Kimberley.

It was inevitable that with all the changes that were taking place in the diamond mines, many of the prospectors who had come to Kimberley would ultimately be displaced. These were men that had mining fever, men that had occasionally struck it rich, or had at least made some money at prospecting. Now they were selling up, or had gone bankrupt. But the fever was still there.

The earlier finds of alluvial gold in 1871 and 1873 in the Northern Transvaal had attracted fairly large numbers of the unsuccessful prospectors who were looking to get rich quick. Sadly, for them, the gold deposits were small and were worked out quickly. Men who had lasted in the diamond fields for the last dozen years were a different breed. They worked hard at mining and were persistent beyond belief. Now they were on the move, looking for the next big find. And that is what they did, day after day.

George Harrison, an Australian prospector, and his partner were working in the Transvaal and had obtained permission from a farmer to work a rocky outcrop on a farm in Langlaagte in the Witwatersrand. It is impossible to know if they were looking for diamonds or gold, but they were certainly prospecting for anything of value. Who knows if it was by chance or from previous experience of gold mining in Australia, that on this beautiful March day in 1886 the men found gold? The previous discovery of gold in the area had played out rapidly. The mining towns that formed around these areas, had been quickly abandoned. From all reports, this discovery looked different.

The Transvaal was a Boer Republic and mainly consisted of farms eking out a hard-scrabble living. The prospectors had probably offered the farmer a cut in anything they would find and he was happy to allow them to work on a non-productive part of his land. The gold was close to the surface, which meant that it could be worked with picks and shovels, much like the beginnings of diamond mining in Dutoitspan and De Beers.

The news of the gold find, like others before, spread like wildfire. Headlines in newspapers around the world proclaimed "An endless treasure of gold that runs for miles underground." The result was another gold rush and a huge influx of men of many nationalities. In addition, the displaced miners of the diamond fields flocked to the region as they were much closer. The men had the equipment and knowhow to stake their claims and start mining gold. Very quickly, a tent mining camp grew up. Ferrira's Camp as it was initially known, was named after the leader of the first group of miners that settled in the area after the Harrison find. Harrison apparently felt that this claim would play out quickly, so he sold his stake for a few measly pounds.

We lost some of our best men to this gold rush. Close professional examination showed that this was a huge find. Possibly running for miles underground.

Woolf was convinced that the news was really big. He wanted us to stake claims in the Witwatersrand and start a gold mining company.

"Barney, this is a great opportunity for us to expand our operations into gold mining. We have the expertise, the manpower and the money to do it. This could turn out to be bigger than diamond mining."

"That is something I doubt very much." I responded.

"What have we got to lose?"

"Control of the Kimberley Mine!"

"How is it going to affect our operations here? It could be a totally separate company with its headquarters in the Witwatersrand." I stood my ground.

"I don't want to deviate from my goal. If we start another operation, it will have to be on a large scale. That would take money away from purchasing more claims here in Kimberley.

"Barney, listen to me, every major country in the world has to have enough gold to cover their currencies. This is called the Gold Standard. There will always be large buyers of gold. The price is pretty much fixed by governments, so there is not the fluctuation in price that we see every day with diamonds. Why don't you let me be the judge of what is good for the company once in a while?"

"I'm sorry, Woolf; I know you are probably right about gold mining, but not now. Let's see how things work out here. Once we have control of Kimberley Mine, then we will invest in gold mining. I'll even make you the managing director of the new company when we do it."

"Have it your way, but I think you are making a big mistake."

Woolf certainly had a good head for business and I knew he was possibly right about the opportunity. I could not risk taking a chance at this juncture. This new find could be just like all the others before it. I knew that if it turned out that the gold deposits were as huge as the newspapers claim, we could invest. There are always those small prospectors that sell out rather than work their claims. I've seen it in Kimberley a dozen times. I knew how to turn it to my advantage.

The next day it was Harry who wanted to know why we were not investing in gold mining.

"What are you thinking? There is a ton of money to be made in gold mining and we're not even looking at it. Why?"

"I don't think we should deviate from our current plan. That's all."

"That's all! Are you nuts? This new discovery is going to be so big, it will make the diamond business look like petty cash."

"You don't know that. It could easily turn out to be a dud like the previous finds."

"It could, but if it does turn out to be a big as everyone says we'll have missed the boat. I don't think we can afford to take that chance. Our competitors are already setting up shop in Witwatersrand."

"Who do you know for sure?

"John Hayes Hamilton has gone to Witwatersrand to stake out or purchase claims on behalf of Rhodes."

"How do you know this?"

"Because our wives are friends and they talk."

"Both you and Woolf are driving me crazy on this matter. Neither of you can see that it will dilute our funds and may ultimately stop us from controlling the Kimberley diamond mines."

"You know Barney, you are not always right, but you think your ideas are the only ones that are important. It's about time you got it into your thick skull that your partners aren't idiots."

"Alright, if you're so keen on this, you go to Witwatersrand and check it out. Buy or do whatever you have to do and stay out of my hair while I do what I have to do here.

"I will and I'm going to take Woolf with me."

"Good, 'cause I've had enough of all this. We still have a way to go to gain full control here."

A week later Harry, Woolf and a couple of our knowledgeable mining crew set off for Witwatersrand.

Bad news arrived the next day, Fanny's mother died. I immediately went round to see her and offer my condolences to the family. For the first time I wasn't shown the door by Mr. Bees. He was one tough nut to crack. He sat stolidly in a high back chair in the bedroom that he had shared with his wife. Mrs. Bees was laid out in an open coffin for the family to see and pay their respects. I found this really strange for I had never seen it before. In the Jewish religion we don't have open coffins and we bury the dead within twenty-four hours, unless it is the Sabbath.

Fanny and her sisters were crying and her two brothers were trying to comfort them. I really didn't know how to handle this situation. I went up to Mr. Bees, told him how sorry I was. He said nothing. He just stared ahead as if I didn't exist. I went and talked to Fanny, I wanted to put my arms around her, but knew that this would not be the place. I stayed only a short time before making a hurried departure. I went to the funeral several days later, but felt totally out of place in the Bees family. I had never had a chance to get to know the family, or even speak to Fanny's mother, other than to say hello if I saw her on the street in town.

Chapter 28

Shares in Barnato Diamond Mining Company were selling at higher and higher prices every day. It was apparent that we were under threat of being taken over. I found out that Jules Porges, who had come to Kimberley for the first time only three years earlier and formed the Compagnie Française des Mines de Diamant du Cap, was now trying to purchase as many of our shares as he could. Hermann Eckstein, a very bright and talented manager of the Phoenix Diamond Mine, was now part of a new Porges company with Wernher and Beit. These men were the biggest threat to my completing the consolidation of Kimberley Mine.

I gave instructions to purchase any of our shares that were put on the market. The bidding war was on. I had to not only defend myself, but continue to purchase any and all claims in Kimberley that I could.

It was really no surprise that Porges and company were buying up our shares. We in turn had been purchasing shares in the French Company for months in an effort to gain control of the whole of the Kimberley Mine. The central location of the French Company holding splits the mine in two. I knew that unless we control it we would never be able to consolidate the entire mine.

Early one morning, my chief accountant pointed out to me that a number of my local competitors were purchasing shares in Barnato Diamond Mining. A list of shareholders was produced by the company each month, Beit, Rudd and Rhodes names stood out on the list, each with a large percentage of holdings. This was disturbing to me as it represented a possible threat to my control of the Kimberley Mine. I had stockbrokers in both London and here in Kimberley, purchasing any and all shares that came to the market. So it meant that some shareholders were either getting a higher price, which I doubted, or they were deliberately selling to my competitors to stop me getting control.

What was the matter with these people? Didn't they understand that the costs of production can be kept at a reasonable level, and we could control the amount of diamonds that are released into the market? Diamonds rely on their scarcity to maintain value, and scarcity can only be achieved with a balance of availability relative to demand.

I immediately sent a telegraph to Mr. Benham in London to ask his advice. His response was even more disturbing. Rhodes was in London seeking funds from Rothschilds Bank and that he had several meetings with them. Subsequently, he left for Paris, where he was at that time.

Damn him I knew exactly what he was up to. He had got his funds from Rothschilds and was making an offer to Porges for the French Company. Well, he wasn't going to beat me. I immediately sent another telegraph, this time to Mr. Jules Porges of the French Company. I requested that if there was a sale imminent for his company that he would allow me to make a counter offer.

The next twenty-four hours was spent in a marathon session with my accountants and senior financial men. We had to make sure that we were in a position to outbid all competitors by a substantial amount. We knew there was a high probability that Rhodes had the financial backing he needed, but he is not a business man like me. His offer would be for the full amount that he had obtained, keeping nothing back in reserve for a counter offer. Now it was wait and see who would be the winner.

It was another three days before the response came. The short telegraph read:

"Compagnie Française des Mines de Diamants du Cap de Bonne Espérance has an offer of £1,400,000 sterling. What is your offer?"

They had taken their time to respond, probably to talk with the Rothschilds, who had substantial control of the French Company. So I decided to wait before sending my response. We had the funds so I was not worried that we could beat the offer and I wanted Rhodes to sweat.

In the meantime, I took a break and went to see Fanny. She had been very patient with me, considering the long hours I was spending at the office and the many evenings meeting with men wanting to talk about selling their claims. I had hardly seen her in the past few weeks since her mother died and I really missed her. Still no word from her father when he would allow me to marry his daughter.

Three days later, I sent a telegraph to Mr. Porges in Paris. My offer for his company, £1,750,000 sterling, an increase on Rhodes offer by twenty-five per cent. I had no doubt that Rhodes was astonished by this huge offer. It did not take long before there was another telegraph; we were certainly keeping our telegraph office busy. To my surprise, it was from Rhodes, not Porges.

Rhodes asked me to withdraw my offer before it was accepted by the board of the French company. I couldn't believe that he would ask that. However, there was more to this request. If I agreed to withdraw he would purchase the company for his original offer. On a back-to-back contract, he offered to sell the French company to Barnato Diamond Mining for £300,000 plus a twenty per cent interest in my company.

This was indeed a great offer on the surface, but was it?

Saving £1,450,000 is a huge saving and acquiring the French company, something that I have long awaited and could never be sure to own, was now in my grasp. It meant that the Barnatos had almost complete control over Kimberley Mine, certainly more than 90% of it and the rest could be had for the right price.

The snag was Rhodes himself. He wanted control of all diamond mining, as did I. But his reasons were very different from mine. I wanted to do this for my shareholders; Rhodes wanted to do this to finance his expansion of the British Empire in Africa. It worried me that this is not what business is about. He was a highly intelligent man and had a great deal of influence in the Cape Colony, which was an advantage to both of us.

The only real objection that I could come up with in my mind was if the Barnatos and our close associates held enough shares to still have the controlling interest in our own company. After a long session with the best men in my financial department, I decided that I would agree to Rhodes' deal. I telegraphed Porges withdrawing my offer with no reason stated. Next, I sent Rhodes my reply. Another telegraph went to Mr. Benham in London, instructing him to draw up a contract immediately and proceed to Paris for the necessary signatures.

One month later, we were the owners of the French Company properties in Kimberley and Rhodes and I were in partnership. There was one extra stipulation that was not in the contract. Rhodes would make sure that I was invited to become a member of the Kimberley Club. His positive response to the request was that he would make a gentleman out of me yet.

Chapter 29

Without any doubt, I enjoyed the shareholders meetings. It was a time when I was able to detail our many achievements. It was a time when I could be a showman, no different from when I am on stage in a Shakespearean play with the exception that I get to not only act the lines, but write them too. Not that I actually wrote anything down, it was not necessary, I knew exactly what I wanted to say.

The Barnato Diamond Mining Company was now in control of the more than 90% of Kimberley Mine. We could go ahead with sinking new shafts for underground mining of the diamondiferous blueground. Up to this point, our horizontal galleries were quite short, but with the acquisition of the French company, it was my intent to lengthen all existing galleries so to transverse the entire area. I told the shareholders that we would continue to remove loads of sixteen cubic feet of broken blue ground for an average yield of 1.2 carats per load.

This was well in excess of any other diamond mines and a full twenty-five per cent better than the De Beers Mine. Once again, we would be paying a nine per cent dividend for the quarter, thirty-six per cent for the year.

Rhodes had returned to Kimberley although I had not seen him. For the first time he sat in the audience. He owned a substantial block of our shares, so it was no surprise to see him at the shareholders meeting. I couldn't help feel that he was more interested in seeing who was at the meeting than to hear what I had to say.

There is no point in listing the big name investors who attended the meeting. That is a matter of public record. It appeared that every important diamond dealer and mining company was now represented. I could not help but laugh to myself when I thought that in a dozen years I had become the king of diamonds. In fact, that was what the newspapers were calling me.

I quickly came to the recognition that Rhodes wanted to control all diamond mines in the area, including Kimberley. I knew he was buying into the two poorer mines, Bultfontein and Dutoitspan Mines. The yield on the latter was poor, but the quality of the diamonds found there was far superior to all the other mines. It was a gamble that underground mining could make both of these mines more productive.

There was a lot of competition between all the players. The demands on my time were becoming more than I could manage some days. I was working sixteen or seventeen hours a day; in meetings, with my financial people, with sellers of claims and with stockbrokers. There was no time to hesitate when an offer to buy came in. I had to make a decision on the spot or the seller was out my office and over to my competitors. Fortunately, our production had continued to increase month over month, and we were selling a high percentage of our diamonds on the European markets, outstripping the American market. How long this was going to last, was anybody's guess.

Rhodes and other mine owners were doing the same. Between us we were flooding the market in an effort to gain control of it. What could anyone do to stop the inevitable? I had already tried to reign in the competition. Now it was a race against time to monopolize the diamond mines before the end product became worthless. We were all responsible for the glut in the market, and we all stood to lose everything. This worried me immensely as we were getting closer to a complete overproduction that would cause a world market crash.

My worst fears were quickly realized. The price of diamonds in London and Amsterdam fell to their lowest point we had ever seen. I received a telegraph from Benham in London telling me that Rhodes companies were selling off huge quantities of diamonds. What on earth was he playing at?

Newspapers reported the huge oversupply of diamonds by De Beers had flooded the market and it was speculated that it was possible that diamonds had no intrinsic value because such huge quantities were being found. Within days our share prices took a beating in a sharp downward spiral. I continued to purchase shares in our companies in an effort to maintain prices.

Suddenly, things swung the other way. There was obviously another buyer snapping up our shares at their lowest price ever.

What the hell was going on? Discreet inquiries showed that Rhodes and Porges were buying up our shares, Rhodes sought complete control of Barnato Mines. Of that there was no doubt, but he wasn't going to get it without a fight. I put out buy orders that brought our share price up almost to the level that they were before. In three months the price of Barnato shares had tripled. The shares soared from £14 to £49. In my mind, I was sure we were going to beat Rhodes. What I did not consider is how much backing he was getting from the European bankers.

By early March, Rhodes announced that he had control of more than fifty per cent of the shares in Barnato Mines and proposed a merger between De Beers DMC and Barnato DMC. This was a huge blow to me, as I had fought like a madman to keep control. Rhodes had got his foothold in my company by taking a twenty per cent share in it with the acquisition of the French company. That had given him a firm base to start with and now he had the controlling interest.

It was arranged that we would meet for lunch at the Kimberley Club to discuss matters. My membership in the club had just been approved. This was my first visit, so I had mixed emotions about my meeting with Rhodes. Could I refuse the merger? What would it mean to the shareholders? So many questions that I knew had to be answered at our meeting.

The Kimberley Club was quite elegant. It smelled of cigar smoke and well oiled leather. The many comfortable armchairs and imported English furniture, gave an atmosphere of calm. Outside was a verandah with tables and chairs, where one could dine, or just enjoy the pristine garden that extended to a line of trees, planted to give the members privacy. It was a bit of old England in the heart of the Cape Colony.

"You know your membership here was not easy to obtain. I had to submit to a little subterfuge when the members voted, I'm afraid that the voting box was accidentally dropped and it is possible that a number of black balls were inadvertently lost. However, I can confirm that it was indeed a close affirmative vote."

"Thank you for your efforts, Rhodes, I hope that it turns out to be worth it."

"Oh. I am sure it will."

A uniformed waiter came and took our order for drinks and lunch. I ordered a Scotch and soda Rhodes ordered a gin and tonic.

"You know, Barnato, you and I share the same dream. We both recognize the need to control the flow of diamonds into the market. Now we have the opportunity to do so. With our two companies merged into one, we will put that into practice. I hope you don't feel too badly about the my gaining control of Barnato DMC. You put up one hell of a fight."

"I should have questioned your generous offer when you gave me the opportunity to get the French company for a great price in exchange for twenty per cent of my company. If something looks too good to be true, it generally is. But I have no regrets. Explain to me your proposal, how do you want to do this merger?"

"We will form a new company called De Beers Consolidated Mines. You will exchange your stock in the Kimberley Central Mine for stock in the new company. This in fact will make you the largest single shareholder in the new company. However, my colleagues and I, that is the Rothschilds, Beit and Porges, will have the controlling interest."

I sat for a few seconds contemplating this information. How did I feel about losing control? What were my choices? Rhodes broke my thoughts,

"I propose to appoint four life governors to the new company; you will be one with Alfred Beit, Frederic Philipson-Stow and myself. You will hold this position for the rest of your life. I feel, with a company that will be worth as much as the balance of Africa, you must have four or five men for whom it is worth their while to devote a great portion of their time to it. "

"That is a very interesting proposition."

"Would you like to think about it?"

"No, we will have to work out the finer details later on. I agree to merge my company with yours. I am not sure how the shareholders will react, but that is something we will have to wait and see."

"You evidently have a fancy for building an empire in the north, and I suppose we must give you the means to do so."

We shook hands and the deal was done. No paper work, no solicitors involved, at least not at this stage. We had a gentleman's agreement.

Chapter 30

I went back to my office and held a meeting with Harry and Woolf to let them know what had happened and my decision to agree to the merger. Harry, as usual, was not at all pleased with my decision.

"We don't have to merge with Rhodes, you could have refused. I'm sure we can buy enough shares to regain control of our own company."

"I'm sorry, Harry, I don't agree. It's my understanding that Rhodes has plenty of financial backing to buy more shares if they became available. Having achieved a majority shareholding, he is not going to give us the opportunity to rebalance."

"I think you're giving up too easily."

"No I'm not! We were coming out of this deal millionaires. With this kind of money we can invest in other mining projects. We can buy property. We can start new businesses. Can't you see that?"

Woolf cut in,

"I agree with Barney, Uncle Harry, I know I am only a small shareholder, but this will give our family a lot of clout."

"Woolf, you always agree with Barney. How much are we talking about?" Harry asked.

"I don't know at this point, we still have to sort out the details." Harry was plainly irritated.

"I've expressed my opinion, but I know that you have given your word and you won't rescind it. Go ahead and sort out the details with Rhodes, I'm going home."

The meeting broke up and I could not help feeling a bit sad about losing control of Barnato DMC. But it was time to think about investing the proceeds. It was time to consider buying into the Witwatersrand gold fields.

We had been successful in diamonds and could do it again in gold.

Rhodes and I met at his little cottage a few days later to discuss the details of the merger of our companies. We sat down with a bottle of French Cognac in Rhodes living room, a sparsely furnished room with well worn but comfortable furniture. Rhodes invited Alfred Beit and I brought Woolf Joel with me. It was just the two of us that were really involved in the discussion that followed. Beit and Woolf were there only in a consultation capacity and that suited me just fine.

"De Beers Consolidated Mines will not be limited to diamond mining, even though that is our principal business. Our trust deed will allow us to own anything: buildings, mines, farms, even tracts of land. These can be in Africa or anywhere, there will be no restrictions. These can be held with rights transferred to the company by indigenous rulers. We will be able to use our resources for the pacification and administration of such estates. De Beers Consolidated Mines can trade in all manner of precious stones, minerals, machinery, patents, inventions and products in Africa and elsewhere. We can construct and operate canals, railways, gasworks, reservoirs, factories, and so on and so on. And we can engage in banking." I stopped him.

"Just a minute, Cecil, this sounds to me more like an imperialist manifesto, rather than a company trust deed. What are you thinking here? I am not interested in using the new company to help British colonialism."

"I am sure you know that my ambition is to help expand the British Empire throughout Africa. I see our new company as a vehicle that will help our colonization of these primitive peoples, bringing civilization to stone-age natives."

"What if they don't want to be colonized?" Rhodes shot me a patronizing look,

"Barney, you must understand that it is our duty to civilize all primitive peoples. It will bring them prosperity within the sphere of the British Empire."

"I'm certainly not sure about that. But please continue."

De Beers Consolidated Mines will control the world price of diamonds by restricting the quantities that flow into the market. Currently, as you and I both know, there is a huge overproduction which is depressing the prices continually. That will stop once we complete our merger. Between us we control sixty percent of Kimberley Mine, one hundred per cent of De Beers mine and I might add we have a controlling interest in both Bultfontein and Dutoitspan mines. The remaining interests will fall in with us. Of that I am sure. If they don't we will buy them out, or squeeze them out."

"So who will be running this new company?"

"I propose that we have four life governors who will make all the decisions regarding the running of the company. The governors will be you and I, with Alfred Beit and Frederick Philipson Stow. We represent the highest echelons of the diamond mining industry, we have the experience, business acumen and foresight to make De Beers Consolidated into the largest mining company the world has ever seen."

"And who will be the chairman of the board?"

"Beit and Stow agree that I should be the first chairman."

"I see. What if I want to be the chairman?" Rhodes lit a cigar, eyeing me before speaking.

"That would present some problem, as the majority has the consensus. Please let me continue, I think you will like what you hear."

"Go ahead, I need to know the entire proposal."

"The capitalization of the new company will be in excess of twenty million pounds."

"I presume you have run the figures through your accountants and financial people."

"Absolutely. That number is very conservative; it may well be higher by two or three million pounds. As life governors, we will be entitled to special participation in the profits of the company. After annual distributions of dividends of thirty-six per cent are paid to the shareholders, we will split all remaining net profits between the four of us. That is profits in excess of £1,440,000 made in any one year."

"My word that is a tidy sum."

"You will receive 6,658 De Beers Consolidated Mines shares, Beit, Stow and myself will receive 4,439 shares each." Rhodes paused held up his hand and puffed on his cigar.

"I'm not quite finished. Each of us will receive compensation of shares valued at three million pounds at formation. These shares are intended to be held long term for us and our families."

"These are more than generous terms," I commented.

"I don't think I have forgotten anything. We will have to talk about who will be the recipients of our production, but first we need to have agreement on the initial proposal."

"It is a pretty impressive proposal, Cecil, but what about my shares in Kimberley Central Mine?

"I think you are probably going to have some problem shareholders who will be unhappy with the merger and they will sue. In fact you can count on it. I have spoken to my solicitors who assure me that in this event all you and I have to do is to sell the shares to De Beers Consolidated and liquidate Kimberley Central." I perceived a gap in his presentation and spoke out.

"Tell me how you see the distribution."

"Obviously, there has to a single channel of distribution. The days of selling directly to small diamond dealers are over. If we are to maintain prices, we have to strictly control all sales of rough diamonds. When times are good, we can allow a larger volume into the market. In times of recession and a slump in prices, we will restrict the volume to keep it close or even slightly less than demand. By doing so, world prices can be maintained at a steady level. In truth, that is what consolidation is all about. This single channel is of course our new company, De Beers Consolidated Mines.

"Who are the dealers you have in mind that will form the syndicate?" I pushed further.

"I have put together a list, I am sure you know all of the diamond dealers on the list. They are all substantial companies. They will be responsible to coordinate distribution for Europe and the diamond centers in London and Amsterdam. There are ten firms; Wernher, Beit & Company, Barnato Brothers, Mosenthal Sons & Company, A. Dunkelsbuhler, Joseph Brothers, I. Cohen & Company, Martin Lilienfeld & Company, F. F. Gervers, S. Neumann, and Feldheimer & Company."

"I'm glad to see that you have included the Barnato Brothers on your list."

"Well, what do you say, is it yes or no?" I hesitated,

"Much of your proposal I can agree with. I absolutely do not agree with the trust agreement that includes colonial expansion, it does not belong there. The rest we have to negotiate."

"Go ahead, tell me what you want to change."

We spent the next few hours hashing out an agreement and finished a second bottle of cognac in the process. Just as day was breaking with the light creeping into the eastern sky and one of the most beautiful early morning sunrises that only can be seen in Africa, we reached an agreement.

Rhodes conceded little and I felt that even though I wanted to be the chairman, he had been most generous in his dealings with me. One thing that had been a sticking point was the appointment of David Harris as my alternate life governor in the event of my incapacity, for whatever reason. Finally, I managed to get Rhodes to agree to this stipulation. I am not sure why I felt that this was very important to me, but I wasn't going to let it go.

"Well, Cecil, some people have a fancy for one thing, some for another. You want the means to go north, and I think we must give it to you."

"Barney, you and I are from very different backgrounds, but we both understand what needs to be done and how to do it. You amaze me with your ability to comprehend the most complex of deals and without hesitation, make a decision. I admire you for that."

"Thank you, Cecil. We will take our leave of you now for I have much to do in preparation for our merger."

Chapter 31

Extracting gold from the quartz veins utilizes a lot of heavy machinery. Different machinery from that needed for diamond mining. Yet there are similarities in the mining methods. Mining is mining, whether it is tin or coal or gold. Reports coming back from the Witwatersrand appeared promising, but I was still skeptical.

A number of the wealthier mining companies from Kimberley were now involved in gold. We decided to send our principal engineer, Neville Abrahams, to do extensive research on our behalf. I had been against getting into earlier gold finds, as it was necessary to continue our expansion of our diamond mining holdings. I must say that Woolf kept up the pressure on me to do something.

Now that Harry was spending much of his time in other pursuits, Woolf had become my right hand man. So I promised him that if Abrahams' research was positive, we would invest in the Rand as it was being called.

As a principal shareholder of the De Beers Diamond Mining Company, Limited, the predecessor of De Beers Consolidated Mines, I was present for the first time at the annual meeting held in Kimberley on May 12th 1888. Rhodes chaired the meeting. As is my way, I felt it was time for me to propose a vote of thanks to the chairman and directors for their past services.

I was recognized by the chairman and stood up.
"Before the meeting breaks up I should like to say a few words concerning the chairman and the directors for their past services. I am unaccustomed to eulogizing any one; criticism is more in my line; but, after the various remarks as to the position of our industry and the cutting notes printed in various journals in England, it behooves us to pass an extra vote of confidence in the directors. Particularly to Mr. Rhodes for his services rendered to the De Beers Diamond Mining Company." I paused and took a look around the crowded room.
"No person knows better than myself the labour that Mr. Rhodes has had to convert me to the De Beers Mining Company. I may say that day after day and night after night Mr. Rhodes has been working to get me to take De Beers shares for Centrals. I gave way when I saw diamonds down to eighteen shillings a carat, for I then saw no alternative but to consolidate the interests of the companies, and on those terms I came in. Another condition I made a *sine quâ non*. I have devoted a lifetime to furthering the

interests of the diamond mining industry; and with the interests I hold in these mines, amounting now to nearly two millions of money, I should be a fool indeed to allow my interests to drift into the hands of any particular body of men. One never knows what may happen, especially what may happen here in Kimberley; and if this property should get into the hands of a London or any other syndicate, they might knock it about as they liked. Therefore I determined to protect my own interests by acting as a life governor." I could see the shareholders were in agreement with me.

"It has, moreover, been arranged that the life governors shall keep an interest of not less than a million of money in the company. If ever there was a safeguard in any company, the holdings of the life governors are a guarantee to the shareholders that their property will be carefully and judiciously managed." I sat down to muted applause.

I knew that this meeting would be fully reported in the newspapers in London, Kimberley and in the Cape Colony, and it was important to make it clear the reasons that we were merging. The proposal to create life governors had caused quite a stir. We received criticism from a minority of shareholders and the newspapers who had verbally attacked both Rhodes and myself. We had both received letters from disgruntled shareholders assailing us. We responded by buying out all the dissatisfied shareholders.

After the meeting a young man named Harry Raymond, representing a prominent newspaper, approached me.

"Mr. Barnato, I'm Harry Raymond and I work for the Argus. May I have a word with you?"

"What is it you want, Mr. Raymond?"

"I would like to interview you for my newspaper."

"I'm sorry, it was not really my style to give interviews."

"I promise that I will quote you correctly and not change any of your words."

"I am very busy at this time, what with the merger of the companies and other commitments. Perhaps you could come to my office after the special board meeting being held in August for Kimberley Central shareholders."

"That would be most kind."

I shook his hand and made for the door.

Chapter 32

Wednesday July 11th 1888, started like many others at the De Beers Mine. With underground mining it was possible to continue twenty-four hours a day. This day was no different. At around 6:20 in the evening, the day shift was switching over to the night shift. Ten white workers were drawn to the surface from the 700 ft level. Everything appeared normal.

The white workers were the only ones that rode the skip to the surface; the native workers had to climb up by a series of ladders. As the next skip ascended at 6:30, something happened and the wire rope broke, sending the skip and the men crashing down to the bottom. Within a few minutes of the fatal descent of the skip, smoke was seen billowing from the shaft. A fire was raging and workers were trapped.

The fire bell was rung, warning everyone working in the mine to find a way out. This bell rings so sonorously it can be heard all over the area of the mine, both on the surface and below. The fire brigade and volunteer rescuers rushed to the scene. I ran out of my office and over to the mine to see if there was anything I could do. The mine director was busily ordering men and organizing rescue equipment.

"There's anywhere from six hundred to seven hundred men in the mine at this time/ We were changing shifts when the accident happened."

"Can we get the men out?"

"It's hard to say, but we'll do our best, Mr. Barnato, sir."

This was a terrible disaster that we had tried to be prepared for, but you never know if preparations are adequate until it happens. Fire damp that is experienced in coal mines is not the threat here, but we store large amounts of dynamite and use oil lamps in the mine, not a good combination!

The fire in the wooden casing of the number one shaft, spread rapidly and around ten o'clock that evening, there was a noisy ground shift as the shaft caved in, blocking it completely. Smoke billowing from the number two shaft, increased tremendously. Rescuers risked their lives and went into the mine through the old workings at the 380 foot level, trying to find survivors. They worked tirelessly all through the night and the following day. They managed to rescue more than four hundred natives and forty-three white men.

Gardner Williams, the American born superintendant of the De Beers Mine worked alongside of the rescuers. I gave him much praise for keeping a cool head and organizing his workforce in an effort to save as many as possible.

There were many stories told about the horrors that faced the men in the smoke filled galleries; of those that had suffocated from the smoke and fumes. Dead natives were literally piled up trying to climb over those who had succumbed to the fumes and heat, blocking the passageways that the rescuers managed to enter. After the fire was extinguished, an examination of the plaited wire rope of the skip that crashed at the bottom of the shaft, showed that it had been badly burnt, reducing it to half of its normal thickness. On further inquiries, it was found that the rope had only been in use for eight days. The possibility of sabotage was strong in my mind, but by who and why? I immediately instigated added security measures to make sure that this could not happen again.

In the final count of the dead, twenty-four white men and two hundred natives perished in the fire. A dreadful waste of life.

I called a special meeting of the shareholders of the Kimberley Central Diamond Mining Company in August to confirm the merger with De Beers. I expected there would be some that would be critical of my handling of it.

Woolf Joel chaired the meeting; I sat in the front row. As expected, there were objections from a few shareholders who were unhappy with the terms of the merger, particularly the price offered for the shares. However, more than seventy-five per cent of the voting power approved the merger and as a result the amalgamation was approved.

Rhodes was right about the lawsuit. It only took a few days before the disgruntled shareholders went before the Supreme Court of the Cape on August 20th, 1888, in an effort to stop the merger. In support of his argument, their counsel J. Rose Innes Esq. read from the trust deed of De Beers Consolidated Mines the objects of the company that these were dissimilar companies and therefore their amalgamation was not valid. The judge, Mr. Justice Smith, interrupted.

"It would be far shorter to tell us what the company may not do." Mr. Innes continued,

"They can do anything and everything, my lord. I suppose, since the time of the East India Company, no company has had as much power as this. They are not confined to Africa, and they are even authorized to take steps for the good government of any territory; so that, if they obtain a Charter in accordance with their trust deed from the Secretary of State, they would be empowered to annex a portion of territory in Central Africa, raise and maintain a standing army, and undertake warlike operations. Yet, it is said that this company is formed for the same purposes as the Central Company, which digs for diamonds in the Kimberley Mine."

The Chief Justice rendered his judgment.

"The applicants in this case seek to prevent the carrying out of certain resolutions arrived at by a majority of the shareholders of the Central Diamond Mining Company, at a special meeting, convened on August 7, 1888, with reference to the amalgamation of that company with the De Beers Consolidated Mines. The applicants are shareholders in the Central Company, and they now seek to interdict the carrying out of the agreement of amalgamation, on the ground that such agreement is *ultra vires* of the powers of the company; and the question to be decided by the Court is, what construction is to be put upon the 83rd article of association of the Kimberley Central Diamond Mining Company."

The judge rattled on for some time. Even before he reached his conclusion it was obvious we had lost our case for amalgamation of Kimberley Central and De Beers Consolidated. Based on my own objections to Rhodes, about the sweeping powers that the new company would have.

In the end, Rhodes and I liquidated Kimberley Central Mine and sold the assets to De Beers Consolidated for the grand sum of £5,338,650 sterling. I personally received a cheque for my shares which amounted to more than two million pounds sterling. Not bad for a poor Jewish boy who started with nothing. The proceedings and the purchase of the shares made national headlines.

In the British newspapers, the story was relegated to the inside pages because of some murderer they were calling Jack the Ripper, who was on a killing spree in my old part of London. My sister Kate sent me a copy of the paper, along with a letter telling me that she and Joel had sold the King of Prussia public house and were moving to a new home in the western suburbs of London.

Chapter 33

Due to my busy schedule and commitments, my meeting with Harry Raymond had been postponed several times. I had spotted him in the crowd at the Supreme Court hearing, busy scribbling notes and listening intently to the proceedings. He came to my office early on a Monday morning, looking smartly dressed and ready for action. As he sat across the desk from me, I could not help but wonder what must be going through his mind.

"Mr. Barnato, I really want to thank you for taking the time to meet with me and I am eternally grateful for this opportunity"

"I'm sorry it has taken so long to get together with you, as I am sure you are aware, things have been most hectic and demands on my time are huge. Anyway you're here now. What is it that you want from me?"

"I represent the Cape Argus and would like to ask you a few questions for the newspaper. The Argus is a prestigious publication. Our readers are interested in what happens in the diamond mining business and the important members in it. I have been following your progress for some time."

"Who else have you interviewed?"

"Well, actually, you will be my first."

"That sort of puts me on the spot doesn't it?"

"How so?"

"If I deny you the interview, you will have to find somebody else. To my knowledge, you have spent some many days following my progress. Furthermore, if I say no, then I may be guilty of delaying a budding career in journalism."

"That is a fair assessment of the position."
"You know the press has not been kind to me in the past. I have had many things said about me that are patently untrue. I have not challenged these lies, as I am not prepared to be drawn into this kind of fight, which ultimately only the newspapers win by selling more."

"That is all the more reason to allow me to report your words faithfully."

Somehow I trusted him, and what did I have to lose at this stage of my life? We spent several hours talking. Actually, I did most of the talking and Raymond asked short questions about my life and successes that allowed me to elaborate in my own way. It was a good experience and at the end of the interview I asked him to show me a proof of the article before publication. This he refused to do, telling me that I would have to contact the editor if I wished to see a proof.

"I trust you Mr. Raymond to report my words faithfully as you have promised to do so."

"Sir, your answers will be published exactly in your own words with such few of my questions as are necessary to make the whole plain."

"I want what I said published and not what you may think I intended to convey. I say to you as I say to men who try to tell my stories: either tell 'em as I do, or else tell 'em as your own and nobody will care."

"You have my word, Mr. Barnato. Thank you. At some later time I may like to revisit you and perhaps write your biography, with your kind permission."

"I don't know about that, Mr. Raymond. Let's see how well you write this first.

With that he took his leave and I got back to the work in hand. Write my biography indeed. The man is ambitious I'll give him that. It had never occurred to me that someone might be remotely interested in my life story. It got me thinking, so much so, I started to write my story myself. I have never written much in my life, other than essays we were forced to write at school. My handwriting isn't bad, in fact I think it is rather neat and easy to read. My meeting with Harry Raymond started something that I could not have imagined.

Harry Raymond kept his promise. He wrote about the interview in the Argus, which I read with satisfaction. He didn't change a word I said.

Chapter 34

Our Kimberley and De Beers mines were removing vast quantities of rock from the underground workings. It meant that we needed to improve our recovery practice. In the past, the removal of the diamonds from the ore involved crudely pulverizing the ore with hand tools. Then passing it through fine wire sieves to separate the dust from the larger pieces and pebbles. This was risky as larger diamond crystals could be damaged. In the next step it was laid out on tables, where it was laboriously sorted, removing the diamond crystals one by one.

As the volume of ore increased, the blue-ground was weathered in fields dotted around the mines. These fields were called floors. Over a period of nine to eighteen months the blue-ground decomposed after repeated harrowing and watering. It was just like farming, only nothing grew. This practice eliminated the need to pulverize the ore. With the advent of water to the mines and the development of rotary pans to wash the concentrate, yields improved. This was still a very slow process allowing only thirteen loads of ore per day. A load represents approximately sixteen cubic feet of broken ore.

Our consolidation of the mines meant that we could centralize the operations to one area for each mine. We acquired larger acreage for our floors and added a series of pans that enabled us to treat three hundred loads per day, a huge increase. The concentrate produced by these pans was then delivered to our new Pulsator Plant, where a series of Harz jigs reduced the concentrate by forty per cent. It was this residue that went to the sorting tables, where the diamonds were picked out by hand.

The white workers sorted through it first and then it was re-sorted by the native workers. Finally, it was picked over a third time by African convicts who were assigned to us by the government. This cut down on the problem of theft and increased our productivity immensely. Large numbers of workers were needed for hand sorting. I went to see the new Pulsator Plant and was very impressed with what I saw. I knew that there had to be a better way of separating the diamonds from the other minerals and we had to find it.

The year 1888 was turning out to be my busiest year ever. With huge amounts of money sitting in the bank, it was essential to invest in new projects. The amalgamation of the mines was almost complete, but I was still busy tying up the loose ends and finalizing our marketing plans. In a way I was at a point in my life where I had to decide what I wanted to do next.

I had been asked to run as a candidate for Kimberley in the Cape Colony House of Assembly by a number of local officials, including Rhodes. I am not a political person by nature and had rejected the idea some years ago. I was going to reject it again, but something happened that made me change my mind.

Even before I had made my decision, a group of local merchants formed the Citizens Political Association to oppose my candidacy. The C.P.A. as they were known, were dead against me representing the town. They considered that anyone else would do, even if it were someone who was totally ignorant of what mattered to Kimberley. Their argument was based on my representation of the diamond mining industry, which they felt, was interested in not only controlling the mines, but on controlling all trade in Kimberley. Why they did this was obvious to me. We had introduced compounds for our workers, which restricted their movements and had definitely affected their buying in the town. This we did out of necessity, but the merchants saw it as encroaching on their livelihood. I can't say I blamed them. It was how they went about their opposition to me that really got me rattled.

In my time in Kimberley, I had made a few enemies. Some because they were jealous of my success, others because they felt that I had got the better of them in a deal, be it for the sale of their claims, or because of the profit I had made from diamonds I purchased from them. Knowledge is king when it comes to buying and selling. I made sure that I acquired as much knowledge as I could. Many men were too lazy to learn. Anyway, I had my detractors, not that it matters; no successful man is without any.

The C.P.A. decided that I should be driven from the contest, dishonored and in disgrace. One of the two daily newspapers, the Independent, immediately attacked me in their leading article on September 27th. I remember the date with great clarity. I was outraged. They stated that I was not a fit and proper person to represent this constituency in Parliament. That my election would be detrimental to the mining interest, to the general interests of the place, and for the credit and welfare of the Diamond Fields.

I am not going to detail every word, but they went on to say that I was dishonorable and using my wealth to further my ends. In their opinion, the people of Kimberley knew me well and would never elect me. The newspaper hinted that there were too many skeletons in my closet so I should immediately withdraw.

Withdraw! I hadn't even decided to run! My nomination had come from the Miner's Union and had been endorsed by the Licensed Victuallers Association, the only two organizations that existed in Kimberley at that time before the C.P.A. came on the scene. Never one to back down in a fight, I wasn't going to allow this kind of character assassination from anyone. I would accept the nomination and to hell with these cowards. My instructions to my solicitor were to proceed with high court action against anyone who in any way libels me in the election. In fact, I hoped that I would be able to take some of my detractors to court to make an example of them. The solicitor was not sure the article in the Independent was actually libelous; certainly it was full of innuendo, but not a clear case of libel. As if I was not busy enough, I now had to concentrate on my election campaign.

Rhodes chaired a special meeting held to inform the employees of De Beers of my position in the election.

"In reference to Mr. Baranto there has been a great and organized opposition in the camp, and I shall put to you the case clearly and distinctly from our point of view as directors of your company. Mr. Barnato has been accused of being devoid of honor. Various other terms have been applied to him, and he has been subjected to intense and great ill-feeling."

Rhodes once started was a great orator, although a bit long-winded. Rhodes went on.

"Our policy has been to keep the company in South Africa with a colonial directorate, and the directors are unanimous on that point. Mr. Barnato has supported me earnestly in that. But people say 'Oh yes, you have got Mr. Barnato under your thumb and make him do just as you like.' Now I conceal nothing, and say that the gentleman to whom we refer, owns no less than one-tenth of the De Beers and Kimberley mines, and he is supporting me on all points I have mentioned. But I go a great deal further, and I hope you will not disagree with the next point I am going to make: if he is good enough to be a co-director with me, he is good enough to represent us in Parliament, holding as he does one-tenth of the mines."

Rhodes at that time of course, was a Member of Parliament and told me that he expected to become Prime Minister in the next session. I told him I had no experience in politics, to which he replied that running a country was little different to running a large company like ours. He was convinced that I was well qualified in both.

My first public speech prior to the election was calendared for the evening of nomination day, October 30th, held at the Kimberley Town Hall, a new and imposing edifice in the center of town.

"I ask you to give me a fair hearing." I began, "I am here for the first time in my life on a political platform. I must say that this is a new position for me I therefore ask you to listen to me patiently and when I have done, if you disagree with me I shall like you just the same. No doubt you are aware I was nominated today. My object in going down to Parliament is not to satisfy my personal vanity; neither am I anxious to represent the diamond fields on general grounds of ambition; I desire to go down to protect the interests of Kimberley. As many of you are no doubt aware, I was asked to stand for Parliament in 1881, when Mr. J. B. Robinson stood; but I was a young man then, and I declined to accept the responsibility. Now, what with the experience I have gained, and with my large interest in the most important industry in the colony, I do not think I am presuming if I take it upon myself to come forward as your candidate.

I spoke at length for more than two hours. Relating how I had been instrumental in keeping control of the diamond mines in South Africa and not allowing the financiers in London to take control. That was my great strength when it came to convincing the audience that I was the right man for the job. I continued.

"Back in 1880, when I was a member of the Kimberley Town Council, I had been instrumental in bringing the water supply to Kimberley and, together with Rhodes, we purchased the water concession thus guaranteeing a plentiful supply to the town and the mining industry. We then gave the water concession to the town.

There was a lot of criticism when De Beers took over the mines over the possibility that we were going to shut down Dutoitspan and Bultfontein mines, throwing men out of work. This was far from the truth. We had no intention of doing so then or now."

I explained that the consolidation of the mines was to protect the diamond trade from the price undercutting like that we had seen in 1881 and the following two or three years, when one company was fighting against another. This had caused panic and put many men out of work, not only affecting those in Kimberley, but in the whole of the Cape Colony. I had their attention and I was enjoying myself.

"Another question I would like to say a word about is the compounding of natives. The compound system was introduced while I was in England, but I think you will all admit it has been a very good thing for the moral and social well-being of Kimberley. You need only refer back a few years ago, when we used to see natives walking about the principal streets in all stages of drunkenness on Saturdays and Sundays. Respectable people were afraid to make their way through the thoroughfares to church on Sundays. On one day the streets were filled with drunken *Kaffirs*; the next morning the police court was occupied all day with the cases arising from the lack of control over them. But now, with the compound system generally adopted, no such disgraceful scenes occur."

I knew that this was the possible key to getting the support of the voters and I was not going to let the opportunity pass.

"I have referred to the Miner's Union and the Licensed Victuallers Association, but now there is another association in the field – the Citizens Political Association. Well, gentlemen, that simply means the anti-Barnato League. I must confess I have always thought a lot of myself, but I never did think, until the work for this election commenced, that I was so important as to necessitate the establishment of an association to keep me out of Parliament."

This caused a murmur to run through the crowd, for it was obvious that there were a number of members of this group in my audience.

"This anti-Barnato League has no politics. They do not care what the electors do, or whom they return, so long as they keep Barnato out. Let me, however, refer to an advertisement which you may have seen, and which says, 'Electors of Kimberley and Beaconsfield, if you wish to successfully oppose the election of Mr. B. I. Barnato, then vote for Messrs. Lange, O'Leary, Cornwall and Lynch.' You see, it is just as I have said; they have no politics. You can put six members into a bag, shake them up, and take any four out as your representatives, only do not let Barnato be one of the six." There was laughter in the crowd and some looking uncomfortable.

"I am aware that candidates who stand for Parliament have many a various charges leveled against them, but I make bold to say that no man who was ever in my position was attacked in the gross and unseemly manner which has been my fortune during the last week or so. I say it is unprecedented in the history of the diamond fields, for they have not attacked me as a politician, they have unmercifully assailed me in my private and individual capacity."

I made the point to my satisfaction; I knew I had to get the majority of these men on my side. I went on to give them all a brief biography of myself, from my poor beginnings to my current success. This was my opportunity to correct some of the misinformation that had grown around my persona. Next, I talked about a proposed diamond tax that John Merriman had proposed in Parliament, a tax that the diamond mining community of Kimberley could ill-afford, one that would reduce outside investment in our companies.

I had already cabled the Prime Minister in Cape Town that we strongly opposed this tax. Mr. Merriman, who represented copper mining interests, was successful in having a copper tax thrown out, but strongly advocated for this diamond tax. I made a point of this.

Finally, I brought up the extension of the railway to Kimberley that had cost our town excessively; I outlined how the current government had sent men to London who had no experience in financial matters to negotiate terms of a loan for this extension. As a result, they had cost us many thousands of pounds that we should never have had to pay.

Without doubt, I felt comfortable that I had achieved my goal of convincing the majority of the audience to vote for me. The audience listened with respect, stayed to the very end as I held their attention for the entire speech. A unanimous vote of confidence was given to me and I was chaired round the building by a cheering crowd.

In a society where gambling is an everyday occurrence, the odds on me the day before my speech, were two to one against my being elected. The day after my speech, the odds were not only three to one on my being elected, but would be the top candidate out of the list of those being returned. Men were even betting on how many votes I would lead the other candidates.

For the next two weeks, I campaigned vigorously, hardly stopping to eat and with very little sleep. Fortunately, I don't need a lot of sleep; four or five hours is quiet enough for me. Anywhere that men congregated, I took the opportunity to speak to them; street corners, pubs, the corner store, it made no difference. I wanted to meet as many men as I could before the election in November.

But not all of the crowd was friendly and on more than one

occasion I was shouted down by men who opposed me. Experienced as I am on the stage and the music halls, this didn't bother me one bit. When someone asked a difficult question, or accused me of something that they felt they knew about, I quickly challenged them, and for the most part, was able to use it to my benefit.

However, on one occasion I was with Woolf and two of my political team, John Lawrence and Dr. Rutherford Harris. A bunch of drunken hooligans wanted to beat us up. I am not one that backs down from a fight, but in this instance, it wasn't just me. So we prudently made our escape out of a back window and ran like the blazes.

Another notable event was in the Theatre Royal in Beaconsfield. I turned up to find that the opposition had organized the crowd. For more than an hour, they shouted and heckled me, not allowing any opportunity to speak. Things got out of hand when a group of my supporters decided to eject the rowdies. It ended up looking like a barroom brawl. Sadly, there was quite a bit of damage to the Theatre, which I immediately offered to pay for. They rowdies either were thrown out or decided that they had had enough. I was able to speak at length and received a vote of confidence at the end.

The Saturday night before the election I was back at the Kimberley Town Hall to give my last speech to a packed house. Many people, who really had little interest in politics, had got caught up in the events of the weeks running up to the election. There were many who had never before shown any interest, for some it had become entertainment.

I talked at length about my opponents, their lack of understanding of the issues, and their unscrupulous attacks on me. It still rattled me, but I was going to get my revenge by being elected to the Cape Assembly. Of that, there was no doubt in my mind.

"I have been for two months the target for every kind of abuse. There has been time and opportunity for my enemies to rake from their own heaps all possible filth. I have challenged them all, and asked and demanded that they tell me, if possible, of anything that has been alleged against me or whether the first assertions have been justified? No, not one of you can tell me of anything that has been brought forward in the least to my discredit. But I can tell you why my enemies have not succeeded because there is nothing in my life that I am ashamed of. The best sign of proof as to whether I am a fit and proper person to represent you, the people of Kimberley, and your great industry, will be shown on Tuesday next, November 13, when I will be placed by you at the head of the poll."

I went on to repeat my life story from the time I arrived in Kimberley till the present. I had to have one more go at Mr. Merriman.

"Only a few weeks back Mr. Merriman called the people of Kimberley 'peripatetic adventurers and wandering thieves!' I could tell you a good deal about how Mr. Merriman tried years ago to consolidate the mines here with a capital of twenty million pounds, and to transfer the management to the hands of foreign capitalists. But I am going to keep that shot for use at a proper time."

Not to bore you with the rest of the speech, it came to a satisfactory conclusion with cheers and applause.

By noon on Election Day it was obvious that I had not only won election, but had beaten the rest of the candidates. This gave me the opportunity to go to Barkley West where Rhodes was a candidate once again and offer him my support. Rhodes was easily re-elected. No surprise there.

I must say that I really enjoyed electioneering, it agreed with me and I was looking forward to the challenges that I knew I would find in the Cape Assembly.

Chapter 35

Solly and I decided to go the Witwatersrand to take a look at gold mining opportunities. Rhodes, Beit and Robinson were investing huge amounts into mining in the Rand. Even my cousin David was getting into gold mining. I felt that maybe I had misjudged the opportunities there when I had visited briefly a few months earlier. At the time I was not impressed.

It was the first time that Solly had travelled to the Transvaal. We headed for Langlaagte, the area where two years earlier gold had been found.

After riding for several days in a north-easterly direction across the Orange Free State, we arrived at the border of the Dutch Colony of the Transvaal. It was quite an uncomfortable ride over rough track, riding in my new carriage. I would have preferred to ride on horseback, but I had to keep up appearances now.

It was interesting to me to see how fertile the land was and the extensive farming in the Free State. Much of the produce that we get in Kimberley comes from this land. The land itself is pretty flat, dotted with native dome shape huts that are made out of wooden struts and covered with matted grass. The Hottentots build square houses of stones and there were many of these as we travelled the rutted roadway.

We saw the camps of the men working on the new railway line that was under construction. I knew this would open up huge areas previously difficult to reach.

There were some formalities at the border, but we were welcomed and allowed to go on our way without delay. Once we were in the Transvaal, there was a wide, well travelled road, the route to the capital Pretoria and the center of government.

We arrived at the farm that was known as Langlaate to find a small township where shops and offices had sprung up. There were the canvas and wood buildings that housed the saloons, brothels and tradesmen. Tents dotted the area, and already there were a few brick houses. The township of Johannesburg, as it was now being called, was growing rapidly around the goldmines.

It reminded me very much of how Kimberley had looked when I first arrived there. Only at this stage it was much smaller. The population appeared to be similar too. The exception was the large number of Jewish

Lithuanians who had recently migrated here to avoid pogroms in Lithuania. The miners, some I even recognized from the diamond fields, were for the most part Europeans with a few Australians and Americans in the mix, and there were a large number of native tribesmen at a ratio of ten to one.

I was pleasantly surprised to find that there were even enough Jews here to start a congregation. The Witwatersrand Hebrew Congregation had been formed a year ago. On *Rosh Hashana,* they had taken over the Rand Club, located in the center of town, for the Holiday services. Ironically, the Rand Club did not allow Jews to be members. The congregation was in the process of building it's first synagogue. I went visited the rabbi and gave him a large donation to help finish the building.

Our first task was to seek out a knowledgeable mining engineer. After a few inquiries, we were directed to Cousin Jacks Corner, where we were told the Cornish miners met most evenings. The Cornishmen had extensive knowledge of tin mining and had arrived in the Witwatersrand almost as soon as gold had been discovered in 1886. At the time, the tin mining industry in England was going through a slump and hundreds of men had been thrown out of work.

We met with a group of them and bought them all a round of beer. These men had broad Cornish accents that for us Londoners were quite hard to understand. But we managed. They told us that gold had been found in a wide area across nine Boer farms in Langlaate, Doornfontein, Turffontein and Vogelstruisfontein. In September of 1886, the Transvaal government declared all nine farms as public land and open to anyone for digging. By December, they subdivided the farms into lots, similar to Kimberley, thirty by thirty Cape feet each, and sold them off. Thousands of men travelled to the area to try their luck at gold mining.

One of the Cornishmen named Bailey seemed very knowledgeable. He told us that in his opinion the gold veins extended twenty or thirty miles across the region. His mates argued with him as they did not agree. It had been assumed by the early prospectors and the Boer government, that this area would be like Barberton a few hundred miles away that had played out quickly. The town planners were obviously of the same opinion and pegged out a small town that did not encroach on the mining area. Furthermore, Bailey told me that these veins of gold went really deep and that underground mining would be essential. He and his Cornishmen were the men that understood how to do the work. I took him aside to talk to him privately.

"Mr. Bailey, I would like to offer you a job."

"I don't wish to be rude, Mr. Barnato, but I have a big investment in my own claim here."

"How much do you think it is worth?"

"Well, I'd say it's worth more than three hundred pounds."

"And how much would it cost you to start underground mining?"

"Ah, that would be much more than I could afford, but I think I can possibly make as much as one thousand pounds out of it before I return home."

"I'll tell you what I'll do. I'll give you one thousand pounds for the claim now and I will pay you five hundred pounds per annum for the next two years to work it and to run it. Do you think you could do that?"

"I don't know what to say, sir but thank you. There is one thing that you should know. The gold found here is poor in quantity, tiny flecks of gold in large amounts of quartz. Extraction will take heavy and expensive machinery to do the job properly."

"So what are you telling me?"

"It will take a lot of money to do it right."

"That is not a problem, Bailey. By the way, where is this mine that I'm buying?"

"It's in Germiston. I should tell you that two doctors, MacArthur and Forrest, discovered a new process for extracting gold from the ore using cyanide. I'm told that you can extract ninety-six per cent of the gold from the ore using this process."

"Find out more about it. We will incorporate that in our mines." Bailey scratched his head.

"I will. Well, this has been quite a day for me. When do you want me to start?

"We'll find a solicitor in the morning and draw up the papers. In the meantime we'll shake hands on the deal. I'm going to need you to scout out properties that you consider will be productive using underground techniques, preferably adjacent to the first mine. When you find them, I will have my bank send you the funds to purchase. Tomorrow, when we meet with the solicitor, I will give you all the necessary authority to do it. You will be compensated at a much higher level once you get things underway. Do you think you can do it?"

"Without any doubt, sir, but you don't know me, and you're willing to trust me with all this?"

"Yes. I like a man who speaks his mind. Your mates don't agree with your assessment, but you stuck to your ground. I trust that gut instinct, I've had it myself and it's worked for me."

"Thank you. I don't know what else to say now."

"We'll meet here in the morning, and if you have any questions, ask me then."

We said our goodbyes and I left to find some accommodation. The next morning we were in the gold mining business.

We spent the next few days meeting with the mining board, town officials and geologists. Gold was very different to diamonds in the marketing aspect. Most civilized nations pegged their currency to a gold standard. That is they printed paper money that was backed pound for pound, with gold at an agreed value. Because of this, every ounce of gold produced could be sold at the internationally recognized fixed price. The Bank of England purchased the entire production of gold from South Africa at £4. 2s. 4d pounds per ounce. The United States Treasury was at that time proposing to demonetize silver as the backing for the dollar in favor of gold at a price of $20.67 per ounce. In addition, the Treasury proposed to maintain a minimum of $150 million in its gold reserves to back up its currency. There had been a lot of speculation in gold in the United States for the last fifteen years and it was selling at a premium.

The Gold Standard was highly likely to become law as it was de facto at this time. According to our consultants, we could sell all the gold we can produce to the Bank of England at £4. 2s. 4d per ounce. It was much easier to sell gold than diamonds, as there was no market fluctuation.

Efficient mining methods and extraction were the order of the day. It was obvious to me that only the large wealthier companies were going to be the ultimate players in this endeavour. A few of the major Kimberley diamond companies had already set up in Johannesburg. I knew that Rhodes had set up a company with Charles Rudd, Gold Fields of South Africa. Hermann Eckstein had already built an impressive block in the center of the town, set on the corner of two streets. It was known as the Corner House, located across the street from the recently opened

Johannesburg Stock Exchange. George and Leopold Albu had set up their company, General Mining and Finance Company, as well as J. B. Robinson. We were late coming here. Perhaps that was a mistake on my part, but we would out-do them all if I had my way.

We found ourselves the best solicitor in town. After a long meeting with him, our company was formed; the Johannesburg Consolidated Investment Company. We also formed four more companies that would eventually be used for various projects.

Cables were sent to England to purchase the latest and most efficient equipment we needed to get started. I sent Solly back to Kimberley to arrange for a few of our best engineers and managers to come to Johannesburg to help get our mining operation organized.

There were plenty of skilled men in the town and more were arriving daily, but the town needed organization, it needed men I trusted. I went to look for a suitable location to build our offices in town and found a sizeable lot on the corner of Fox and Harrison streets. I instructed our solicitor to draw up the contracts for it. Our building was going to be the biggest in town when it was finished. A Lithuanian architect was recommended by the solicitor and after a detailed meeting with him, he accepted the commission and promised sketches for my perusal before the end of the week.

It was obvious that one of us would have to spend a lot of time in Johannesburg. That meant that it would probably be me, as I was yet unmarried. That was something that I planned to change as soon as our gold mining projects got underway. So the next thing was to find somewhere to live, and I was not going to stop till I found what I wanted. It didn't take long to find the perfect location in the Doornfontein area, along Saratoga Avenue. It was a quiet street, away from the noise and squalor of the town. Eckstein had already built a sizeable house there, and I would be his neighbor. I went back to the solicitor, had him draw up the contract, and from there I went to visit my architect again.

The architect was surprised to see me so soon; I think he thought I'd changed my mind. So I told him what I wanted and that this house had to be built and finished within three months. I now had a timetable in my mind and it included getting married to Fanny regardless of what her father wanted. She was of age and could make her own choices. As far as I was concerned, we were in love with each other and there was no reason to delay. We shouldn't have to wait till her father dies. I wanted to have children and a family life. For that, we both had waited too long.

Chapter 36

Before returning to Kimberley, I wrote to Harry and Jack Joel in London to tell them that I was going to invest heavily in gold mining on the Rand. I was satisfied that we had made a good start on our new venture into gold mining. I felt exhilarated and Solly was really excited that we were going ahead with this new project. Solly, Woolf and I had a meeting to summarize what we had done and worked out a twelve month plan of action. Buying up claims and land to develop our extraction plant was the order of the day.

Woolf suggested that we look at purchasing properties that could be developed into supplying the mines. He liked the idea of constructing a stone building in the center of town, where we could house a large stock exchange and something like one hundred indoor market stalls. He suggested that we should be buying suitable farmland to produce vegetables and fruits, which were currently being brought in by ox wagons as far as a hundred miles away, all good ideas, which I immediately agreed to.

He thought we might be able to grow grapes for wine production, something that I had not thought about. So we set our priorities and worked out which of us would be spending time in Johannesburg. Our house had to be large enough to accommodate all of us.

Harry telegraphed me that he was going to spend most of his time in London, but would be willing to spend part of his time there, but only if necessary. He also told me he had purchased new offices in Draper's Gardens close to Throgmorton Street in the City of London, to handle the expected increase in business. I telegraphed my approval. Woolf, Solly and I were going to be the mainstay of our development on the Rand.

It was hard for me to realize that my world was changing. It wasn't so much the wealth, it was my preoccupation with diamond mining that had filled my every waking hour. The exception was my time spent with Fanny. Dear Fanny was most patient with me; she needed to be as I could forget everything when I was working, often not getting home well after midnight and rising before the sun to be out at work. She was an angel who put up with my moods and my eccentricities. I would go days without seeing her and she never objected. Her brothers and sisters kept her busy and her father, still the awkward, stubborn man he had ever been, was more demanding of his uncontrollable, independent daughter. So I planned to see him again, this time to give him my ultimatum.

Over the next few weeks, I was incredibly busy with the new acquisitions on the Rand. Solly was in Johannesburg full time, as I was. We made deals to purchase all manner of properties, particularly around the Market Square that was the *de facto* center of town. Up till now almost all the buildings were tin shacks, but I had my construction people tear them down and start work on proper stone buildings.

As I recall, this was the only time that Solly argued about something I purchased. In reality, it was the price I paid for a property that made him angry. On the far corner of the square was a lot that had a few tin shacks standing on it. What he and others had failed to see was that there was an abundance of red clay on the property. When I brought to his attention that this would be perfect for making bricks, he apologized to me. Bricks and mortar were going to be needed in huge quantities.

The foundations were laid for the Barnato Building where we planned to house a new Stock Exchange. The existing one story building was far too small and much of the dealing was happening on the street. There were so many deals in mining stocks every day, even on weekends, that the price of newly floated shares were doubling and tripling as soon as they were issued. I could see that this was a formula for disaster. The shysters were floating new companies almost every day on worthless bits of land. Many had no intentions to mine anything, but the profits they could reel in from a fancy prospectus were huge.

Within two or three months, we had purchased a large number of claims with auriferous reefs of proven value in the best part of the Rand. Our geologists and engineers were able to pick and choose the best available. It could be said that I was the cause of a lot of the speculation; people thought I literally had the Midas touch. What made the difference was that my engineers were already sinking deep shafts into the reef and our geologists had discovered that the gold was much deeper than anyone could have imagined. Most of the newly formed companies were not equipped to mine at these levels, nor did they have the financial means to do so.

On New Year's Day 1889, I held a party in Johannesburg for my nephew Woolf, who was now my principal partner and running the diamond side of our business in Kimberley. He had come to Johannesburg to see for himself what we had achieved in a very short time. Woolf had quietly married Olive Desmond, an English actress whom he had met and fallen in love with. She was not Jewish, but had converted to Judaism before the wedding. Woolf was incredibly happy and wanted to share his joy with me. I was delighted to hear this news. Once again it made me look to my own stalled wedding. Fanny was thirty now and I was thirty-eight.

I toured with him around the mines and told him my vision for the future of this town. On the last day of the old year, we completed the purchase of all the claims and property of the Moss Rose and Primrose Companies. Woolf and I were about to float the New Primrose Gold Mining Company, our first gold mining company on the Stock Exchange. It was as exciting for me as the time I floated my first diamond mining company. It was like starting again, only this time I had the money to do it without the need to go to a bank for help. At the same time, we floated the Johannesburg Estate Company that had nothing to do directly with gold mining, just real estate holdings in the new town of Johannesburg.

My beautiful new house on Saratoga Avenue was completed on time. It had a magnificent garden set in five acres of land. I planned to put in a tennis court, not that I have ever played tennis, but it seemed that everyone living on Saratoga Avenue had one. There was even a suggestion by the architect that I should put in a swimming pool, but I did not care for the idea. I cannot swim. In February, Fanny came to Johannesburg with Eliza, one of her sisters, and they spent their time furnishing and decorating the twelve-room house. This gave me the opportunity to spend some precious time with my fiancée. She was in agreement with me that we should not wait any longer to marry. If her father, or for that matter any of the family decided that they were not going to attend our wedding, that was their loss. We had waited too long and we both wanted to start a family. We decided to get married in the new synagogue that was a few weeks away from completion.

Johannesburg was really good for me and people liked me. There was none of the animosity here that I experienced in Kimberley, and I was grateful for that. The difference between the two towns was that in Johannesburg, I was someone to look up to. I was promoting the town in every possible way, I attracted investors who wanted a share of the wealth that I predicted would surely come. Of course, I had come here with huge amounts of money to spread around, I had already made my money and even though I expected to make much more, people did not criticize me for doing so. In Kimberley, I had come with nothing and made a fortune that made competitors resentful, and those less fortunate than I really very jealous.

Johannesburg offered more than any other town in South Africa. It's potential was like no other town. I could see it as the financial Gibraltar of South Africa. My hope was that the Transvaal government, under complete Boer control, would understand its importance and not pass laws to stifle its expansion.

Our biggest problem was water; 1889 had the most severe drought in living memory. This was causing all sorts of problems and shortages. The provision wagons, when they arrived, were only half full. Many wagons just didn't make it across the Karoo. I was told there were carcasses of dead oxen feeding the vultures every day. Even a few of the wagoneers didn't make it. This combination of lack of water and provisions was causing problems with the natives in the mines. Many of them left going back to their kraals where they felt they could do better hunting their own food. Certainly, many were right about that. Prices of basic foods soared out of reach for the majority of the miners and that was bad.

A couple of years back, I had invested a small amount of money with Sir James Sivewright, an engineer who had decided to buy a few acres of land to build a reservoir to supply water to the mines and townsfolk. His syndicate was woefully underfunded. There was not enough money to pay for the infrastructure of pipe work and machinery that was necessary to bring the water into the town. I bailed him out at a cost of £30,000 to pay off his creditors and to save the project. Without water this town was not going to survive. This gave me a controlling interest in the new Johannesburg Waterworks, and I pushed like a crazy man to get the water flowing to where it was needed.

After the formation of our Johannesburg Consolidated Investment Company that year, we went on a major acquisition plan investing in multiple businesses; building materials, transport, food wagons and liquor. We even acquired the Argus Printing and Publishing Company which published the local newspapers.

Meanwhile, with the persistent drought and huge speculation in the share market, it did not take long before the economy took a nosedive. Nobody knows where the rumor started, but there was talk that the gold had given out. The smaller surface miners were hitting a bad area in the reef and coming up with a lot of pyrite, fool's gold, and they were abandoning claims or selling them off for a few shillings on the pound.

These things start small, but it doesn't take long before the panic sets in. The stockbrokers were immediately marking down shares by forty and fifty per cent. By the next day, they were marking the shares down by even more. I tried to convince them that this was temporary and that with patience, things would improve, but nobody was listening. We were committed, and I knew that this was going to happen sooner or later. Of course, it was good and bad. The good thing was we could take advantage and buy prime properties for incredibly low prices. The bad thing was that our shares were worth hundreds of thousands of pounds less.

Once the panic starts, there is little anyone can do. Several banks went belly-up. Diggers left town, going back to Kimberley and other towns. Some went as far as the Klondike in Alaska, half a world away, where gold had recently been discovered. Both Solly and Woolf were nagging me to slow down on buying new claims and properties, but I could see the future. If I slowed down, then shareholders would sell off thinking that Johannesburg was just another flash in the pan. That it was finished almost before it got started. I didn't want that to happen. Besides we were picking up prime properties for a fraction of their cost. Our geologists were excited about the amount of gold that they estimated was just waiting to be mined.

I was getting reports that gold in our New Primrose Mine went down not just hundreds of feet, but thousands of feet. We had bore holes that reached down three thousand feet and there was plenty of gold at that level. Still, it was going to be hugely expensive to extract the gold from the deep mines.

Alfred Beit told me that he had calculated that it would cost one million pounds to make a profit for each mine that reached that depth. There was little doubt about that, but we had the knowhow and the men to do it. We had the equipment arriving daily that we needed for underground mining, including installing railcars to bring the ore from the mines to our stamping and extraction plants. Finally our first cyanide extraction materials had arrived and the extraction plant was being set up. Once we got that operational and proved its viability we would get a jump on our competitors.

Chapter 37

In April 1889, Fanny laid the foundation stone for the Barnato Buildings in the center of Johannesburg. Construction on the new synagogue was going well except that funds were being depleted at a rapid rate. Most building materials had to be brought in by wagon and the cost was much higher than had been expected. I was asked if I would perform at a fund raiser at the new Globe Theatre in town. Never one to pass up an opportunity to play to a crowd, I gladly accepted. *Ticket of Leave Man* was one of my favorite plays and I had played the part several times in Kimberley. My old partner Lou Cohen was to play opposite me, which made the experience all the more fun.

It was a great success and we raised enough to be able to finish the building. Unfortunately, I got really ill for the first time in my life. I never get sick, so this was a shock to me. Woolf wanted to have Dr. Jameson examine me, but I wanted Dr. Joseph Matthews, my old friend from Kimberley who had done an admirable job when there was a smallpox epidemic there. He had recently moved to Johannesburg, setting up a practice quite close to my house. Dr. Matthews was not very positive about my chances of recovery. I told him he was mistaken and that I had no intention of dying till my work was finished. He got quite cross with me and told me that I was to rest. I thanked him for coming and as soon as he was out the door, I called Woolf and Solly to my bedroom and gave them instructions on what I wanted done until I recovered. It took a couple of weeks and I felt half dead, but I wasn't going to let a bout of pneumonia beat me.

In early May, the stock market was making a slight recovery. I felt the worst was over. It was also time for me to take my seat in the Cape Assembly in Cape Town. Fanny, her sister and I took the carriage back to Kimberley where my first business was to visit Mr. Bees.

"Like it or not, I am going to marry your daughter. I have fixed a date for the wedding, which will be in the Jewish faith, for my birthday on February 21st."

"My family are Huguenots, we have fought and died for that right. I certainly don't want Jews in my family. I will never speak to Fanny again." He tried hard to argue with me, but I was having none of it.

"We don't need your consent or your blessing, Fanny is of age. It will be better if you accept this and be part of our family, or if you prefer otherwise, then so be it."

With that I left his house not looking back at him. He had been duly informed. Now it was up to Fanny and I to plan a lavish event for all the family.

Having got that out of the way and feeling very pleased with myself, I spent a few days to check on things at De Beers. Fortunately we had an excellent and competent staff. Rhodes had already left for Cape Town so I met with Philipson-Stow, Beit and our general manager to find out what had been going on in my absence. Since the amalgamation, our production figures had increased, as had the price of diamonds. We were controlling production to the point where the supply that we allowed into the market was slightly less than the immediate demand. This had stabilized the prices and had given us a small percentage increase in the price per carat, exactly as I had envisioned it and as we had planned.

Yes, we were stockpiling diamonds, but that was what we wanted: mine it today and hold on for higher prices when world markets improved. I have a good head for figures and I never write them down. The revenue numbers given me by our general manager were almost exactly as I had calculated before our meeting. I was very pleased.

After a few days, I was off to Cape Town by railway. This was a much different mode of travel, a most comfortable and enjoyable journey.

The House of Parliament in Cape Town had magnificent Palladian style portico made of white stone with contrasting red sandstone façade. It is very impressive. Walking through the portico into the building for the first time made me quite nervous. What did I know about how things were done here? How was I going handle myself as a politician? I certainly did not want to make a fool of myself. After standing looking around for what felt like many minutes, I was addressed by a liveried footman who asked my name, consulted a list and escorted me in the right direction to the Lower House.

Taking my seat in the back row on the right side, I looked around at my colleagues hoping to see Rhodes somewhere. Never one for punctuality, he was nowhere to be seen, I found out later the he was in England, drumming up support for his northern expansion of the British Empire into Basutoland and Matabeleland. Before making my maiden speech, I decided to keep my head down for the first few weeks to learn the ropes. I nodded to other members of the Assembly and they nodded back to me. Several were looking in my direction and, I assumed, talking about me. Let them look, if I'm all they had to talk about, the colony was in bad shape. It was like being the new boy in school, having arrived in mid-term. I'm a friendly sort of chap, so I guessed it wouldn't be too long before I made a few friends and probably some enemies too. It was challenging for me, and I did like a challenge.

About six weeks had gone by. During that time I studied the daily proceeding diligently, even though some days it was hard to sit for hours on end and listen to men who liked the sound of their voices too much. The opportunity came for me to speak on a bill before the house, and I caught the eye of the speaker, who announced that the representative from Kimberley be recognized. All eyes turned toward me and the house went deathly quiet. I'm not going to go into the details of the bill other than to say I was quite nervous. I've played to enough theatre audiences to know how to present myself, but this was not quite the same. I felt that every gesture I made was being watched, digested and analyzed. I know my voice carries well, and I don't think there was any hint of nervousness. I made my point and was about to sit down when I decided to bring up a different subject.

The police force in Kimberley was woefully undermanned and it needed to be strengthened. So I brought this item before the House and appealed for a substantial increase in funding and an expansion of the number of police. Having finished, I sat down and was surprised how subdued was my reception. I didn't expect a round of applause, but I thought that I had done really well. Discussion ensued on the bill and a modified version was passed. Then they discussed my proposal on the police. It ended in increased funding and enlarged recruitment for the Kimberley police department. I had made my maiden speech and had my first success in the Cape Assembly! It was exciting.

As soon as the first session of Parliament was finished, I hurried back to Johannesburg, stopping first in Kimberley for a few days for the annual general meeting of De Beers scheduled to coincide with my visit. Rhodes, who would normally have chaired the meeting, was busy with his push northwards in the acquisition of territories for the British Crown. He had a mandate given to him by the British Prime Minister, which meant that almost all his efforts were to continue the policies that he had personally drafted and convinced the politicians in both England and the Cape Colony, to accept.

He had written to me, asking that I chair the meeting in his place and I had accepted the task, which turned out to be very crowded with many investors, stockbrokers and mining executives in attendance. Did everyone own shares in De Beers these days?

I had been given hundreds of sheets of financial information prior to the meeting which I hardly needed to glance at. I knew the numbers and the facts. It didn't matter if I am hundreds of miles away in Cape Town, or Johannesburg; I knew exactly what was going on and how much we produced in output or income. But rather than rattle these numbers off without any notes, I had the financial statements in front of me.

Our dividend for the first year since the amalgamation was nine per cent, considerably lower than the thirty-six per cent that we had been paying through Barnato Diamond Mining Company. This prompted me to give a full explanation, which I gave clearly and without equivocation. There had been huge expenses for the amalgamation, not withstanding the over five million, three hundred thousand pounds paid out for the shares in Kimberley Mine. As we were now mining underground completely, there had been a large expenditure for equipment.

I had to spend more than an hour detailing this and then a further hour on our reserves and prospects for the future. Lastly, I paid tribute to Mr. Williams and the brave volunteers who risked their lives, working through the night and the following day to rescue the trapped miners after the fire. Whereas the loss of life was more than two hundred men, more than five hundred men were rescued.

By the time I had finished and answered numerous questions, I was please to receive applause from the assembled crowd.

The newspapers the next day were very complimentary of my handling of the General Meeting and noted that "B. I. Barnato was without doubt a financial force to be reckoned with." What had they thought of me before? I was especially pleased with the report in the Financial News on August 13, 1889:

"Mr. B. I. Barnato, the chairman on this occasion, is well known as the founder of a firm of diamond merchants and dealers in stock, which has recently assumed importance on account of its immense wealth. Although the Hon. Cecil Rhodes, who is at present conducting negotiations on behalf of these mines, has been credited with being the chief mover in all that has been done hitherto in the carrying out of the amalgamation, yet it is well known here that behind Mr. Rhodes was a greater power, who controlled his movements and from whose fertile brain emanated most of the ideas which were finally adopted and carried out by the founders of the amalgamated company. Mr. Rhodes has hitherto been *facile princeps* as the expounder of the policy of the company, because of the modesty of the other, who preferred to remain in the background in deference to the superior culture of his leader. But the absence of the chief gave Mr. Barnato the opportunity, which was all that was required to establish his reputation in the eyes of the world as a master of finance."

The biggest diamond ever found in the De Beers Mine, weighing 428.50 carat, was discovered soon after this meeting. It was big news and was reported in newspapers around the world. Almost immediately we received a telegraph request from the French government to exhibit the stone at the Paris Exhibition that was to open in the summer. I considered taking it to Paris personally, but was talked out of it by Woolf and my security manager. This diamond was so valuable that it was dangerous for one person to carry even with a bodyguard. I had thought that it would be exciting to visit Paris at that time and then travel on to England so that Fanny could meet the family, but that would have to wait.

Noting the financial opportunities in Johannesburg, a number of the wealthier people living in Kimberley were considering moving there, or at least buying a home in the new town. Unfortunately, there were a lot of problems that made it difficult for families to relocate. Johannesburg was like most mining towns in the infancy stage. It was rough. The bars and gambling dens made up the majority of the businesses in the town and there were hundreds of brothels. Drunkenness, fights, and thefts were common everyday events and the local constabulary was hard pressed to contain them. The inhabitants of the town were from many walks of life, but the atmosphere of any mining town breeds the worst in human instincts.

As part of the mine owners group planning the layout of the new city, we understood it takes time to create the right balance between the roughness of one way of life and the respectable, genteel lifestyle that we all wanted from our new town.

I purchased the rest of the Doornfontein farm for the development of family houses. There were already a number of mansions that I and other members of the community had constructed. More modest dwellings were springing up. Schools, a hospital, places of worship, a cemetery, shops and business buildings were being constructed and the town was growing. I wrote to President Kruger, asking if we could form a municipality, but to my disappointment he replied in the negative. Kruger did not like the growth of a mining town filled with *uitlanders* that might one day want self-government.

I was popular with the large number of stockbrokers. After all, I had made them a lot of money in my various ventures. However, there was one particular broker, who will remain nameless for this record, who was a flagrant anti-Semite. On a visit to the Exchange on day, I heard him refer to me as "that little yid who should go back to where he came from". It was obvious to me that he wanted me to hear the remark. Without hesitation, I swiftly crossed the room to where he stood and flattened him. He was bleeding from a broken nose and had a shocked look on his face. He immediately called the director of the exchange who demanded an apology from me, which I refused to do. The director told us both that we were suspended from dealing for three months and asked for my resignation. I was forced to point out that he could not throw me out as I owned the building. For my sins, I became the chairman of the Stock Exchange and was responsible for building the new exchange on land which I already owned. I'm not sure what happened to the anti-Semitic broker, but he was not seen in Johannesburg again.

Meanwhile, Fanny was preparing to accompany me to Johannesburg, once again with her sister Eliza. As soon as she was ready we left Kimberley. Fanny and I decided that she would not return to Kimberley until she and I were married.

Barney Barnato and Fanny Bees Wedding - Johannesburg 1889

Chapter 38

Our wedding took place in Johannesburg in November 1889. Fanny looked radiant in a beautiful Thule dress that had been made for her by a Cape Town dressmaker. She had found the dressmaker during one of my many parliamentary sessions, and I had no idea of what she had in mind. There were dozens of dress designs from Godey that she had considered before meeting the dressmaker, but abandoned all of them.

It was a formal occasion attended by all my close family living in South Africa. Harry and Rebecca came from England accompanied by Lily, their daughter. She was growing into a beautiful young woman and looked a lot like her late mother. The Harris family was well represented with David and Rose, Barney and his wife Gladys accompanied by their children who made up the compliment of bridesmaids and pageboys. Woolf was with Olive, Solly was accompanied by a friend of Olive's. All had come to Johannesburg to celebrate with us.

Sadly, Fanny's family was poorly represented. Her father refused to answer our invitation. Only one sister and her older brother and their respective spouses decided to be a part of celebration. I felt really bad for Fanny, as I knew she was hurt by the rejection by her father. But she was resigned to it after so many years of waiting to marry. Deep down, she really wanted his acceptance.

The family gathered at my house for a wedding breakfast earlier in the day and we had Mr. Davies, our local photographer make a family photograph for the attendees.

I invited Rhodes, now the Prime Minister of the Cape Colony and the other life governors of De Beers, all the upper managers of the Kimberley and Johannesburg companies and various dignitaries from the towns, to a banquet at the new town hall.

The food was catered by my own cook working with David's chef and a gang of helpers in the kitchen at my home. We had ordered a vast array of foods from both Port Elizabeth and Cape Town that were sent by train and then by horse to Johannesburg to ensure that it all arrived in the freshest condition. Harry had arranged for Fortnum and Mason in Piccadilly to ship out some of the things that were impossible for us to find in the Cape. The seven-course meal was extravagant, but having waited so long for this day, it was part of finally marrying the lady of my love.

As a courtesy, having invited the Prime Minister of the Cape

Colony, I also sent an invitation to the President of the Transvaal. It would have been interesting if they both had decided to come, but both made their apologies that due to pressing engagements they were unable to do so. President Kruger was most courteous and invited Fanny and I to come and visit him in Pretoria. I was flattered by his invitation. After all, he was a most important man who controlled, and to a great degree, legislated everything that went on in Johannesburg. So I graciously accepted his invitation, telling him that I would come and visit at the earliest convenient time for both of us. This was a great opportunity to speak to him about the extension of the railway to Johannesburg, which was important to the growth of my new city and for the Boer Republic.

Four weeks later, Fanny and I made the short journey from Johannesburg to Pretoria. Paul Kruger, the president of the Transvaal, obviously knew all about me, or at least about my mining ventures and the land I was developing in his Boer Republic. He was an impressive bull of a man, easily eight or ten inches taller than me. With his rather wild profusion of chin whiskers, and large rounded proportions, he was not at all how I had imagined a president would look like.

He welcomed us at his modest, whitewashed bungalow home and the seat of power of the Boers. He was charmed by Fanny and insisted that we both call him Oom Paul, an affectionate name given to him by his loyal citizens. He laid out a simple dinner for us and after the President's wife and Fanny withdrew, we entered a comfortable but sparse parlor to talk. I was surprised that the most powerful man in the Transvaal lived in such modest surroundings, as he was reportedly a very wealthy man.

Through an ever present interpreter, Oom Paul chewed on his pipe and asked many questions about Johannesburg.

"I have never visited Johannesburg and I have no desire to see it," He said.

"Why not? I am sure you realize how important it is to the Transvaal Republic."

"It is full of uitlanders; it is a dirty and disgusting place, ungodly."

"Sir, there are churches in the town including the Dutch Reform Church."

"Please call me Oom Paul, Mr. Barnato."

"Oom Paul, we have places of worship for many religions. I'm

Jewish and we have a small temporary synagogue and are building a much larger one. It would be a great honor to us if you could attend the opening ceremony next year".

"You will have to send the details to my secretary at the Raad, and he will put it on my calendar."

"Johannesburg will take a little time to grow, but it definitely has a great future." I assured him. "The wealth of gold and other minerals is immeasurable. The people living in the town will clean it up quickly, we saw the same thing in Kimberley in the early days, and now it is a safe town with families and children everywhere. I see the huge changes every month. You will see, in no time at all, Johannesburg will be transformed."

"I will come and see for myself in the near future. Unfortunately, the reports I get from my people are not encouraging." I kept on.

"If we build the railway from the Cape into the Transvaal and on to Johannesburg, it will make a huge difference. We will be able to bring raw materials and food to the town in sufficient quantities for the growing population. As it is now, everything has to be brought in by ox wagon, hundreds of them every week. The roads are poor and when the rains come, they are almost impassable, and with the summer heat, many don't make it."

Oom Paul knew that the extension of the railway to Johannesburg was important, but his main concern was who would pay for it. However, I didn't realize that he had his own railway project to run from Pretoria to Delagoa Bay, and that would take precedence. I outlined several ways that I could see would be workable, including a public unsecured bond. He listened but did not offer any opinion on the merits of my ideas. The president understood the need for the connection to the second largest town in the Republic, but felt that the cost should be paid for by the gold mining industry.

Paul Kruger wanted to get my opinion on a variety of things; water problems, gold mining, workers in the mines, expansion and construction. His questions were probing and well thought out. I was sure that he understood my English and I tried to talk slowly, something that I find difficult when I speak about things that I am passionate about.

I could see that Oom Paul was getting tired, so I told him that I was tired and should take my wife to our hotel. The ladies came in on cue and we said our goodbyes.

"Mr. Barnato, would you consider becoming a citizen of the Zuid-Afrikaansche Republiek, the Boer Republic and give up your British citizenship?"

The question threw me for a few seconds.

"Under no circumstances would I give up the citizenship of my country."

I watched his face for a reaction. He smiled and said goodnight. I think we liked each other, partly because we both lacked much education and have made something of ourselves in spite of it. Many British newspapers have reported that Kruger hated all British. Perhaps they saw the Boer Republic as a stumbling block to the colonization of the African continent. But as far as I was concerned, the President and I saw eye to eye.

Chapter 39

On January 27th 1890, Fanny and I, accompanied by Woolf Joel, left on a voyage to England. I was anxious for all my family and particularly for my father to meet Fanny. Due to an unspecified health problem, he had been unable to make the journey to South Africa for the wedding. I nagged Harry about it wanting to know more. All he would say was that our father was just getting on in years and could not face the long sea voyage. He had seen the best doctors in Harley Street and they had found nothing wrong. That worried me even more as my father had always enjoyed good health. And I prayed that he would not die before we arrived back in England.

My reputation for being the man with the Midas touch preceded me everywhere now. Personally I found this a bit pretentious as I feel many a man can do what I do by paying attention to the details. My education is basic, but I have a good head for figures and I can see the end result in most situations. You could say that I could figure the odds, just like a bookie. I was able to make as much money by understanding the balance sheets and reports of many companies, as I have from mining. Every day I took risks in investing and buying into companies, never before knowing what the company was currently worth and its unrealized potential. If need be, I took a majority position, so that I was able to gain the full potential.

My father was excited to meet his new daughter-in-law Fanny. I was delighted to find him quite spritely and in apparent good health. When I asked him about his health, he told me he was fine. Just a shortness of breath occasionally. His personal doctor told him there was nothing to worry about. I considered contacting his doctor, as my father was not one to ever complain about his health, but thought better of it.

In the course of telling my father about my business I could see in his face that he was proud of my accomplishments.

He had retired and spent his time walking in Regents Park and going to his synagogue everyday. He liked it that Harry, Rebecca and Leah lived quite nearby on Hamilton Terrace, visiting every Friday night for *Shabbos*. Harry and Rebecca would take him out for a ride in their carriage once or twice each week, at which time they would visit my sisters Kate and Lizzie and their families. My father still liked to visit his old friends in Whitechapel. When he did so, he would take the Metropolitan Line train instead of his own carriage. He did not want them to feel he had risen above them.

Only a day after we arrived, Harry asked me to come to the office as soon as I could. He wanted to have a discussion with me about our companies. It sounded like there was a problem, or he had a problem. He seemed anxious.

We took his carriage to our new offices in Draper's Gardens. This was the first time I had seen them. He showed me around before taking me to a large well-appointed room. The tall picture windows looked out onto views of the busy street, two stories below.

"This is your office, Barney," he began.

"I'm not sure that I need my own office, Harry, I could easily share yours."

"I don't agree. You will undoubtedly spend more time in London in the future, so you should have your own private office."

"Well, get rid of that abominable desk and get me a long table instead. I cannot stand those things."

"I will have that taken care of, I should have remembered that you hardly ever sit down. Look, Barney, I am concerned about the huge expenditure that is going into the gold mining business, particularly the land speculation in Johannesburg."

"Why would that be of concern? Gold mining is the future. Johannesburg is the future. If I am not mistaken, we are incredibly fortunate to be in at the beginning of development of a town that will one day become one of the most important cities in the world."

"It's a shithole and you know it. I'm not one of your glib investors, I know what Johannesburg is and so do you. Spending millions of pounds is not going to turn a sow's ear into a silk purse!"

Harry was fuming. I had never seen him in such a mood. It was so unlike him.

"That is where I cannot agree with you. There are beautiful suburbs springing up all over the town. We are constructing stone buildings. We're going to have a tramway to connect the outer areas to the center."

"Yes, and that is all because we are paying for it. In the meantime, the buildings are empty and there is a depression that is driving men out of the town. Look at your Waterworks Company, it has never shown a profit and is unlikely to do so in the near future."

"It has a considerable amount of valuable land," I countered.

Harry's fury increased.

"By my calculation, it is worth less than one tenth of what we paid for it. Then there is the Barnato Buildings where we are the only occupants. What do we have? Forty, fifty rooms available? Plus the forty market places on the street level with not a single tenant!"

Harry's face was red with rage, I had to do something to cool him down or he might drop dead of a heart attack.

"What do you want me to do, Harry?"

"What I want is for you to stop spending money like a man with no arms. Stick to what we know, diamonds. Our profits from diamonds this year will easily exceed one million pounds."

"Alright, Harry, I won't invest any more of our money in Johannesburg until some of our investments show dividends. After that, I will be investing once again. Will that satisfy you?"

"I'm sorry, Barney, I don't mean to have a go at you, but we are so far apart, and it's difficult to convey my feelings in cables and letters. I wanted you to know how I feel. So yes, I accept your concession."

"Good, let's go and have drink."

Chapter 40

My arrival in England caused a bit of a sensation in the financial newspapers. There was much speculation as to what and where I would be investing during my time in the country. This sparked all sorts of rumors that I would be transferring control of my Johannesburg mining and property interests to London. Something I had no intention of doing.

In all likelihood this rumor was prompted by my negotiation for a piece of land on Park Lane at Stanhope Gate for our London home. It was necessary for me to come to England each year as my financial interests and family were there. So we wanted to have a home in London. But I was now a senior member of the Cape Assembly for Kimberley, and I could not shirk that responsibility. That said, I was still trying to balance my time between London, Cape Town, Kimberley, and of course, Johannesburg, where there was still much more to do.

According to the Financial Times, I was the most important operator of *Kaffirs*, a term being given to South African stocks. It was said that no one could float a new company in these instruments without consulting me first. That was not entirely true, as there were some outrageous floatations of entirely worthless stocks. I did my utmost to show my disapproval of these worthless companies whose quick demise left shareholders with shares that weren't worth the paper they were written on. It made British stockbrokers and investors very cautious, as it should have. However, this was at the time when De Beers Consolidated finally had a quotation on the London Stock Exchange.

The horse races at Ascot, Newmarket, and Sandown Park were my favorite pastimes in England. I took Fanny to the Newmarket races. It is a spectacular event where the finest horses in the world race in the most prestigious outings of the year. I hired the best coach with four white horses that I could find for the journey. We arrived a few minutes before the Prince and Princess of Wales, who were accompanied by the Duke of Connaught.

People thought we were royalty and the men raised their hats and the ladies curtsied. Our seats were in the Tattersall's Paddock, where the owners and trainers showed off their magnificent horses. I had one of my coachmen place bets on the horses that Fanny and I liked. Fanny picked two winners by their names I only picked one after studying the form of the horses I fancied. It did not matter; we enjoyed a picnic, fine Champagne, strawberries and cream, which were the order of the day.

We spent an enjoyable sunny afternoon. I decided that it was time to start my own stable here in England. I had a few horses back home in Kimberley, but they were nags by comparison to the fine thoroughbreds that we watched this day. I supported every race meeting I could in South Africa, as it is difficult to get enough horses to race. Sometimes, I even put up the prize money.

Lord Marcus Beresford had a winner that day, and I walked over to congratulate him on his success. We chatted for a while. I told him my name and that I would like to buy a few thoroughbreds. I don't think he had any idea of who I was, but he graciously invited Fanny and I to dine with him at his country home nearby. We were delighted to accept his invitation. As a result, we had a most pleasant evening with him and a number of racehorse owners and their wives.

After the ladies had withdrawn, I was able to get advice from them all. It was suggested that I purchase horses that already had won or placed second in this year's events. The preference was for three-year olds, although there was a lot of discussion about yearlings. The trouble with seeking advice from so many experienced men was that you get too many opinions. As I was the guest of Lord Beresford and he had a winner that day, as well as many others during the season, I decided to take his advice and go with his trainer, Joe Cannon, who had his stables at the Heath in Newmarket. Beresford said he would arrange a meeting with Mr. Cannon and even offered to sell me the winner of the day. We did not discuss price, but I felt that I would like to see the horses available from various stables. It was far too late to travel back to our hotel, so we accepted our host's invitation to stay overnight.

Over the next few weeks, I purchased a few horses and started my own stables.

Our circle of acquaintances in England was growing fast. The landed gentry liked to throw extravagant weekend parties in their country estates. Invitations arrived almost daily asking us to join one party or another. Shooting, hunting and gaming were the pursuits on these weekends, along with elaborate seven and eight course dinners. These were followed by musical entertainment and balls at night, often going on into the early hours of the morning.

Personally, I had no interest in the outdoor sporting parties, but I did enjoy a card game and the opportunity to entertain with a quote from my large repertoire of Shakespearean soliloquies. It was hard for me to imagine myself in this position twenty years earlier. In fact, I found it incredibly amusing that these titled people would want a cockney boy and a Jew as well, to come and stay in their opulent homes.

Of course, we were rich and for the most part, accepted by our hosts without question. Most did not care how we made our money and very few of this crowd ever discussed money. It was beneath them. However, men would corner me at most of these weekend parties, and ask my advice on which shares to invest in. Was this a good buy? Should I sell or wait? My reputation as the golden boy was too tempting for them to ignore, and they were pleased to invite us as houseguests.

Fanny loved to wear some of the most beautiful diamonds I had given her. Her shopping sprees before each party were a great delight to her. She looked wonderful, and I was proud to show her off. She and I danced beautifully together, something that we had little chance to do back in South Africa.

We spent several months in England on this trip, but after a while I got bored with the lifestyle. I was impatient to get back to the Transvaal to continue building our financial empire and attending the Cape Parliament. I missed the daily excitement. That is not to say there was nothing for me to do in London. There certainly was.

My racing stable of thoroughbred horses was building nicely, although I had no winners yet. Jack Joel, my nephew, got interested and decided that he too would start a racing stable. Horseracing from an owner's point of view is very different from just being a punter. I often placed bets on horses that I didn't own, even when I had a horse in the same race. There is something about backing the winner that has nothing to do with how much I could win.

We sponsored a number of charities. Begging letters came in daily and I kept a staff just to handle them. The charities ran the gamut of deserving needs. Many were Jewish charities, but not all. Some wanted our attendance, others just money. We laid cornerstones for new buildings; we visited hospitals, wounded soldiers, and the poor in the East End of London, where I had grown up.

My old school, the Jews Free School, asked me if I do a benefit performance for their building fund. The Octoroon was being held at the Novelty Theatre. I couldn't refuse and it was a great success. The school raised enough to add a whole new wing with a bit of extra support from the

Barnato family, of course.

No matter how much these pursuits occupied our time, my favorite pastime was still the Music Halls and we would visit them all during our stay. Every week we would go to the theatre, especially to see my favorite actors Henry Irving and Ellen Terry playing a role. We saw plays by George Bernard Shaw and Oscar Wilde, the most important playwrights of the day. The West End of London had wonderful theatres.

Harry and Jack took care of the diamond business from our offices in Draper's Gardens. I would go there every weekday when I was in London. Things had changed so much. I found that I was overseeing much of our business, but I could no longer be a worker, pulling my weight with my men. I was surrounded by a huge and competent staff, which hardly let me do anything for myself. At least back in Johannesburg, I could still get down and dirty with my men.

We rented a delightful house on Park Lane with large windows overlooking Hyde Park. The large four-story house had everything we needed. From time to time, we would look at houses that we could purchase. Each time I felt that it wasn't exactly what I wanted. Obviously, we would have to build our own mansion, just as we had done in Kimberley and Johannesburg. The problem was finding a suitable property in Mayfair. We decided that if we purchased a house it had to face Hyde Park, which offered the finest views in London.

The Duke of Westminster owned all the properties in Mayfair. His family had held them for hundreds of years. I was told he never sold any of his properties. At best one could purchase a long lease. I was in no rush, as it was not my intention to spend too much time in London.

Fanny and I decided that we should have a second wedding in England for all the family who had been unable to travel to South Africa for our first wedding. It would be a celebration for us all.

The New West End Synagogue's Rabbi Singer, refused to marry us as Fanny had not taken sufficient instruction in Judaism. I argued with him on this, pointing out that our rabbi in Johannesburg, whom he knew, had no problem with our marriage. He had received a letter from him, outlining the instruction that was given to Fanny over quite a long period of time. Rabbi Singer was adamant that unless Fanny was instructed by him, he would be unable to perform the marriage. I could see that I was not going to be able to change his mind. We were both disappointed as the New West End Synagogue was one of the most beautiful in London.

After much discussion, Fanny and I decided that on our next visit to England, we would have a civil ceremony followed by a grand ball afterwards.

On September 26th 1890, we left for Cape Town. The new Union Line Dunnottar Castle has reduced the voyage from twenty-four days to a little less than eighteen days. Unfortunately, we were unable to get a booking on this ship, so we settled for the smaller and comfortable Roslin Castle. I couldn't wait to get home!

Chapter 41

In my opinion, the six months spent in England was far too long. Unfortunately, just the journey alone takes six weeks or so. I was delighted that my entire family had now met Fanny and loved her. I enjoyed the theatre and the horse racing events, but there were many days when I was antsy. The pursuits of the wealthy can be quite trivial, and I longed for action like in the old days.

De Beers continued to expand. We just purchased the newly discovered Wesselton Mine for half of a million pounds, something of a high price, but we had little choice but to pay it. Wesselton was the latest diamond mine discovered in Kimberley and it was imperative that we held control.

Meanwhile, labor trouble was brewing at De Beers again. When we consolidated Kimberley and De Beers Mines, we created a certain amount of unemployment. This was to be expected. Of course it was very unpopular with those men, both whites and natives who joined the ranks of the unemployed and unable to find work. White workers earned four to five times that of non-whites, which included Indians and men of mixed race. The white workers lived in company houses, in an attractive purpose built suburb that had a clubhouse with parks and recreational areas, all built at company expense. No work meant no home and abject poverty.

Rhodes, the Prime Minister, created a select committee to look into the problems. He appointed Merriman and I to the committee. Not the best association, in the light of Merrimen's attempt to have the diamond industry taxed, but we got on well enough. We established that we were in fact employing more men now than before the amalgamation, that unemployment was the natural result of market conditions. However, we were soundly criticized and I will admit that we failed to take into account the amount of poverty that existed in Kimberley at that time.

A group of men, calling themselves the Knights of Labour, was demanding that we open up the Wesselton Mine to the public, to allow anyone to dig for diamonds as they had done in the early days of Kimberley. Furthermore, they demanded that we work the poorer mines of Dutoitspan and Bultfontein, which were for all intents and purposes, closed as they were unprofitable at the current price of diamonds.

In their manifesto, the Knights of Labour called for impeachment of Rhodes and me for "abuse of their public power and place, to further and promote their private interest." This doctrine was simple enough, but dangerous. Furthermore, the organizers declared "Perpetual war and opposition to the encroachment of monopoly and organized capital." It wasn't just the whites that were part of this. It included quite a large number of natives and Indians as well. It was surprising to all of us at De Beers. The natives were not that educated to be part of this organization. We knew that there were a few agitators in the white population that were behind it. Some suspected missionaries, certainly the Dutch Reformed Church were involved. Others seemed to think this action was orchestrated by a few of the disgruntled shareholders, who had taken us to court over the amalgamation of the diamond mines. Whoever was behind it mattered little. We had to put an immediate stop to it, which was easier said than done.

On the brighter side of things, over a two-year period De Beers had been able to increase the price of rough diamonds by fifty per cent. Now that we had a monopoly we were making sure that we only sold diamonds to meet the current demand. There was no excess entering the market as there had been for the last dozen years. Unfortunately, this had affected the markets in Europe. The higher prices and smaller amount of diamonds had put hundreds of Dutch diamond workers out of a job. This brought us severe criticism from the brokers in Paris and London, but they were also taking advantage by doubling their profit margins.

Fanny and I spent a week in Kimberley, visiting our relatives and bringing gifts from the family in England. Woolf had returned from England ahead of us. With his new wife Nellie, they moved to Johannesburg to take charge of our business there. I could always rely on Woolf and Solly to look out for our best interests. I did not have to worry when I was travelling whether things would be handled well. Woolf loved the rough and tumble of the life on the Rand.

Solly was fascinated by diamonds and was much happier spending his time in Kimberley. One hates to have favorites, but I always felt closer to Solly than to his brothers. He and I loved to do the same things; we liked horse racing, poker and an evening of drinking. I think his wife was happy that I spent most of my time away from Kimberley.

Off to Johannesburg once again, this time we were travelling with a considerable number of trunks, containing accessories that Fanny had found in London for our new house. We had an extra carriage just for her 'cargo'. She confided in me that she missed all the fine shops of Regent Street and Bond Street, especially Fortnum and Masons and couldn't wait to get back there again. It had been her first visit to England and she enjoyed every waking moment of it. I promised her that we would go back before the end of 1891.

We were stopped at the border of the Boer Republic of the Transvaal for several hours. A new customs office had been erected on the main road leading from Kimberley. After an exhaustive search of our trunks and boxes, we were charged what I considered, an excessive amount of duty. I was outraged by this and the way that the search was conducted. I vowed to write to Oom Paul on my arrival.

I related our experience to Woolf the next day.

"You cannot imagine the treatment we got at the border yesterday." Woolf laughed,

"Tell me about it. When Olive and I came here six weeks ago we had to spend hours waiting around as these surly customs men went through all our possessions."

"Exactly, we had the same thing and they charged me one hundred pounds in duty! They refused to let us pass until the duty was paid in full. Luckily, I was carrying enough money with me. You know how I am I sometimes, I carry no money at all."

"The Boer Government raised taxes for the *uitlanders*, the foreigners, on everything in Johannesburg. We were being squeezed by the burghers in Pretoria and paying up to ten times more taxes than the rest of the Republic."

"This is a bad business, and I intend to speak to Kruger about it. I was going to write, but I think it best to go and see him," I told Woolf.

"Do you think it will make a difference? He hates foreigners, particularly us British."

"I've heard that said about him, but we seem to have gotten on well together. If this continues, he will stifle the growth of Johannesburg, and we cannot let that happen under any circumstances."

"When will you go?"

"I'd like to go now, I'm so aggravated by this, but I think that is not practical. We've only just arrived. I'll go before the end of the week. Tell me everything that has been going on here in my absence."

"While you were away, President Kruger visited Johannesburg and it was a disaster. More than 10,000 people turned up to hear him speak at the Wanderers Cricket ground. Members of the Town Council were there and wanted to get answers to some of the grievances that we all have; a railway link to the Cape, lack of proper sanitation, the Boer monopolies on food, dynamite and other essentials to life here, and his refusal to give whites not born in the Transvaal, the right to vote."

"Did Kruger address the issues?"

"He opened his speech by calling us *uitlanders*, foreigners and that's when the booing started. He tried to shout down the hecklers, but it was impossible."

"Did he respond to any of the grievances?"

"Not a single one. After about fifteen minutes on the podium, he stormed out of there. According the local newspaper, he vowed never to return to what he called the devil's town."

Woolf's report sickened me,

"That's not good news, I will visit Kruger at my first opportunity and see if I can placate him. We need his support."

"That would be a good idea."

"And now most important, how are we doing with our cyanide plant?"

"It's very exciting, we have it set up and the cyanide easily separates the gold from the pyrite. You know what this means don't you?"

"Yes, we have to go through thousands of tons of tailings and extract the gold. What's our yield?"

"Easily ninety per cent," Woolf said, grinning.

"We have to keep this a secret. I don't want anyone to know about it until we have the chance to buy up more mines. How many men know about it?"

"Probably twenty or so, but I took the precaution of telling them all we will pay a bonus of one hundred pounds to each of them until the newspapers get a hold of it, which eventually they will."

"Good thinking. By then we will have picked up the best mines. I promised Harry that I would not invest any more of our funds into gold mining until we start to show dividends, but I think this is a dividend, don't you?"

"Absolutely."

"We'll keep it to ourselves for now. What else has been going on?"

We spent the next few hours going over the accounts, looking at acquisitions, reports from our geologists, managers and foremen. A staggering amount of transactions had taken place; I calculated we had invested more than one million pounds in a variety of ventures over the past six months. All in all, I was pleased with our progress, but there was the possibility of the slump in the market getting much worse due to the Boer's heavy taxation, particularly on the mining industry.

Woolf told me that my old partner, Louis Cohen, was bad-mouthing me around town. It appeared that he felt that I had cheated him and other shareholders in one of the gold mining companies that I had floated on the market. Considering the number of companies that I have been responsible in forming, I had an excellent record of profits and dividends. However, there was one that was a dud; the Eagle Gold Mining Company. I didn't like it that Louis was telling anyone and everyone he met, that I cheated him. It hurt me. So I went to sort him out.

Louis wasn't too hard to find, as he is a man of habit and liked to drink in the same saloon every day after his evening meal. He didn't look happy to see me. We moved to a corner table, ordered a round of brandies and I offered him a cigar, which he refused.

"I hear you're bad-mouthing me all over town, Louis."

"You hear correctly."

"What's your problem? I have always treated you fairly."

"My problem is that I have been cheated by you.

"How so?"

"I paid six thousand pounds for two hundred Eagle shares. Today, they are worth less than one hundred pounds. Your damned Eagle Mining Company was a sham, there was nothing there."

"Steady on, let's not get nasty about this."

"Easy for you to say, but that was a loss I could not afford to take."

"There is no guarantee of a return when you invest in any kind of shares." Louis flared up.

"At least there is an expectation that a mine will produce something, other than its prospectus."

"The geologist reports were not at all misleading; the reality was that the cost of extraction was too high considering the low yield once we started mining. I'll admit it was a disappointment."

"Huh, that is a huge understatement to say the least. I'm broke."

"I'm sorry to hear that. You're my friend, we're almost like brothers. I'll tell you what I'm going to do to make things right between us. I will exchange your two hundred Eagle shares, for the same number of shares in the New Primrose Mine. I calculate that it not only restores your six thousand, but on today's price that will give you a small profit if you were to sell them straight away. My suggestion to you is that you hold onto them, as they will surely double or even triple in price over the next year. You come to my office in the morning and I will take care of it. "

"That's most generous of you, Barney."

"Considering what you have been saying about me, you don't deserve this," I fired back.

"One more suggestion. Don't invest in any more mining companies. Better still, don't invest in any shares. I can't stand a sore loser."

I stood up, shook his hand and left.

Chapter 42

The Volksraad in Pretoria is the Boer Parliament where the President and the upper and lower houses sit in session. Only the burghers, the original Dutch settlers and their heirs, can become members of the Raad and only burghers can vote. That means that we, the foreigners, were at a distinct disadvantage when it came to making any changes in the law. President Kruger ran the Volksraad with an iron hand. There were rarely any dissenters when it came to what he wanted. I met with him in his spacious and well appointed office. It was just the two of us and his ever present interpreter.

Kruger was not at all receptive to my complaints and responded quite angrily.

"You *uitlanders* came to the Transvaal of your own free will and you chose to settle in our country. It is our mineral wealth that you are extracting, and the profits that you make are leaving the country to foreign shores!"

"Sir, your countrymen also benefit from our enterprises. We employ thousands of men and many of them are Boers."

"Most of the men you employ are *uitlanders*. Boers are farmers, not mine workers. You have to pay your dues for what you are taking away from us. That is the way of the world. The profits you make from your holdings in the *Zuid-Afriakaansche Republiek*, (ZAR) are substantial. You complain to me that you are being taxed unfairly. What do you earn each year, Mr. Barnato?"

"I'm afraid I have no idea, sir. I have accountants to handle my money. I can tell you that in the last six months alone I have personally invested more than one million pounds in mines, property and construction since coming to the Transvaal."

I knew how much I earned to the penny, but I sure as hell was not going to disclose that to him or anyone. I realized that on my visit to meet with Kruger some months ago, I had given him too much information. Now I pressed on.

"There is a danger that taxes will stifle growth in the country. Investors will be reluctant to put their money into ZAR companies. If that happens many people will lose everything and Johannesburg will become a ghost town."

"If it happens it will not affect the Boers one bit, they will continue to farm their land and enjoy a country that we fought hard to settle," he retorted.

"Surely, you don't mean that! Why would you want to turn back the clock when the wealth that this will bring to the Transvaal will be tremendous?"

"I think our conversation has gone far enough. I have much to do today, and I granted you the courtesy of an audience."

"What about our railway connection between the Cape and Johannesburg?"

"As I have said, this audience is over."

With that he turned and walked out of the room. I was stunned by his arrogance and his shortsightedness. I decided to talk to Rhodes about this and see if we could have the British Government put some pressure on Kruger.

Back in Johannesburg, I returned to making money. If these Boer bastards were going to tax me to the hilt, then I was going to make as much as possible and get out as soon as I possibly could.

I went to the cyanide plant over at the New Primrose Mine to see it for myself. It was impressive even if one didn't understand what was involved. The building was about one hundred feet long by sixty feet wide. A rail line ran down the center and there were two intersecting lines. Five huge round tanks about fifteen feet in diameter were sunk into the ground, allowing the rail containers room to tip the pyritic-gold conglomerate into the tanks. Water and potassium cyanide were added, creating a complex chemical process, that released the gold from the rest of the minerals. I'm no chemist, so I had really no idea what actually happened, but I could see the results. Ore that we considered worthless was now productive.

Two and half months went by without anything about the cyanide plant getting out. Secrets only last for a short time before someone lets the cat out the bag. When that happened it made headlines everywhere. In that time we had purchased a number of mines at extremely favorable prices. I cabled Harry to tell him the good news. I knew he would be angry that I broke my promise to him, but this was an opportunity not to be missed. In time, he would see the benefit of my actions.

Every mine in Johannesburg was given a new lease of life. Within a couple of months almost every one was back in production and men were being hired. Wagons full of men were arriving every hour and Johannesburg went from a town that was on the brink of disaster to a boomtown again. In fact, skilled men were in such demand, that for the first time they could negotiate their salaries. The amazing thing to me was that the cyanide extraction process had been around for more than two years before we set it up. I just couldn't understand why other mine owners had not had the good sense to invest in it.

A new boom had started. As the largest holder of real estate in the town, we were in the best position to benefit from it. Our properties in Berea, Doornfontein, Houghton and Yeoville increased tenfold in value. Our construction company could not keep up with the demand for new housing for the skilled workers who could now afford to buy their own homes. To my great delight and that of Harry, Barnato Buildings was full, as were our Market Hall stands. Actually, we could have built twice as many and leased every one.

Our geologists estimated that each one of our deep level gold mines would yield a profit of eight million pounds a year by the end of 1890. So the cost of acquisition and sinking shafts as deep as two or three thousand feet was justified. They further advised me that because the deposits of gold bearing conglomerates spread out, the farther we went underground, we should purchase several farms on the outer edge of the known gold area. It was described to me as an inverted wedge shape. I only had to be told once and immediately got to work with Woolf purchasing the farms that we had identified as suitable prospects.

Once again, Harry cabled that he was not happy with this. It was decided between us that we would float a public company for each new mine. That way the investors would pay the large scale outlay involved to bring each one of these mines into production. It wasn't hard to sell shares in these startup companies. There was a new wave of buying, not just in South Africa but in London as well.

I had not been back in Johannesburg for more than three weeks when I received a cable from David Harris in Kimberley. Apparently, the Standard Bank threatened to dishonor a Rhodes Chartered Company's cheque for more than two hundred and twenty thousand pounds. David who acts on my behalf when I am away, wanted to get my approval to have De Beers Consolidated, guarantee the Chartered Company to stop the bank from bouncing this one and possibly others we did not know about. Harry

Currey, Rhodes private secretary, told David, that any delay would create a devastating blow to Rhodes company, sending it into bankruptcy. The good name of the Prime Minister was at stake, as was the possible collapse of the company and the future of adding new territories to the British Empire. If that wasn't enough, he added that neither Rhodes nor his partner Beit were able to continue to finance their endeavors from their own funds. Mr. Curry had tried unsuccessfully to contact Rhodes who was somewhere in Mashonaland on another of his empire building expeditions.

The three Life Governors in Kimberley approved the De Beers guarantee. David reluctantly agreed and signed a guarantee on my behalf. David was extremely concerned about Rhodes writing cheques for huge amounts of money with absolutely no paperwork to show what it is for, and why they were necessary. It appeared that my partner in De Beers regarded our diamond mining company account as his personal bank account.

It was my intention to find out what this business with the bank was all about. I cabled David that I would arrive in a few days. Anyway, I had to be in Kimberley to chair the annual shareholders meeting. As usual, Rhodes would not be there.

Chapter 43

Our chief accountant Bill Jones was a very mild-mannered and able man. But entered my office at De Beers, visibly upset. David was with him, looking somewhat sheepish. They were both worried how I would react.

"Good morning, David, Mr. Jones." I greeted them.

"Good morning Barney. I'm pleased you are here. Jones and I have gone through the accounts for the shareholders meeting. I have a copy of the signed guarantee for Rhodes Chartered Company. We had to give the bank a seventy thousand pound cheque, and agreed to pay the remaining sum in monthly installments over the next three years. The loan bears interest at five per cent. I think you will find everything is in order."

"Wait a moment. First let's talk about this fiasco with the Standard Bank. Jones why don't you start and tell me how much we are on the hook for."

"Thank God you are here, Mr. Barnato. I really have to say that I was extremely uncomfortable being forced into this situation, Sir. I did everything in my limited power to discourage having to put up this guarantee."

"It's all right, Jones, I am not holding you or Mr. Harris responsible for this."

"Thank you for that. As you know Mr. Rhodes is a bit forgetful at times. He is so involved with so many things, that he often thinks he has given instructions when in fact he has not. I work closely with his private secretary, but Mr. Currey is unable to get Mr. Rhodes to be more organized."

"Jones, I know what he's like. Don't worry. I will make him pay every penny of it back. The real question is how we stop this sort of thing happening again?"

"I'm sure I don't know, sir."

"Okay, you go back to work and I will discuss this with Mr. Harris and see what we can work out." Jones looked relieved.

"Very good, sir. Good morning to you."

Jones shuffled out of the office, probably grateful that I had not shouted at him. I'd get infuriated about things like this. If I had been in Kimberley at the time, I would have done exactly the same as David, gone ahead and signed the guarantee.

"Barney, I agreed to be your stand in, but never envisioned having to make decisions like this. My business is trading in diamonds, not making financial decisions that have long term effects."

"David, I don't blame you for your actions. What we have to do is control Rhodes spending. If I have to, I will break up the De Beers Consolidated partnership. He cannot continue to use it for his own ends."

"That's pretty drastic."

"It may be, but we cannot afford to allow him to drag down our company. He may want to build an empire, but it will not be at the expense of my years of hard work. He has his Chartered Company, and if that is not enough he will have to look elsewhere for funding. I will make sure this is the last time he pulls a stunt like this. No more guarantees from De Beers. And if he fails to pay back the money, I will bankrupt him."

I chaired the annual general meeting of De Beers Consolidated Mines, at our head office on Stockdale Street. There was a good turnout and every seat was taken. Due to the higher cost of sinking deeper shafts, our dividend had dropped slightly from the previous year. However, expectations for the future were high. De Beers' overall control of 95% of world diamond production was finally paying off with higher prices. Supply and demand influence the price that dealers will pay. During the crazy years, when there was absolutely no control, prices kept falling as more and more rough stones were dumped on the market. Now we are able to balance the quantities sold, resulting in a steady increase, by as much as twenty per cent in one year. Our financials were well received. The next day, the price of our shares jumped once again.

I had a couple of weeks in Kimberley before taking my seat again in the Cape Parliament. This is something that I look forward to, although I find it increasingly difficult to sit for long periods of time, during some of the discussions. I decided that I will only attend when there are things of importance to the mining or railway industries.

I realized that more visits to Pretoria to see Paul Kruger were necessary. At least once a month, I made the journey and visited Oom Paul, sometimes at his residence and occasionally at the Volksraad. He and I were not exactly friends, but he liked to get the information about what was going on in Johannesburg and the Cape Parliament first hand. At least that way he was told without any embellishment, or at least none that he knew of. Rhodes and I had strategized on what to present to Kruger so that he would think he was getting a few state secrets.

Throughout 1891, with the help of Sir James Siveright, we were in secret negotiations with President Kruger to extend the Port Elizabeth Railway line to Pretoria with the condition that we have a spur to Johannesburg.

Finally, toward the end of the year, we received good news about our railway connection. The Cape Governor came to an agreement with the Orange Free State to continue the railway to Port Elizabeth by connecting through Bloomfontein. Work had already commenced. Within a few months the railway was right up to the border with the Transvaal. Kruger was as desperate to get a rail link to the coast as we were to get a link to the Cape. He agreed to our plan in principle, subject to the approval of the Volksraad. We knew that was only a formality. It looked like we would get our railway long before he got his Delagoa Bay connection to the sea.

Chapter 44

Rhodes continued to spend money on financing his expansion of the native regions to the northeast from De Beers Consolidated accounts. He had no regard for the rules that we had set out in our charter. I admonished him time and again and finally we met in his office in the Cape Parliament building for a private talk, just the two of us.

"Cecil, I know you are a busy man with many new responsibilities, but I must implore you to consider your responsibility to our company." He grimaced.

"You have no idea how busy I am. As prime minister, I have to work eighteen or twenty hours a day, seven days a week sometimes. Quite honestly, your constant nagging about expenditure is really annoying to say the least."

"Yes, I am sure you feel that way. The problem is that you have a responsibility to our shareholders as well as to me and the other life governors. Either you stop spending company funds on your myriad projects, or you will give us no choice but to cut off those funds."

"You can't do that."

"I'm afraid we can and will."

"My work is for the good of the British Empire and cannot be curbed by a bunch of financiers. I have the backing of the British Parliament."

"That's as maybe, but we have taken advice of a prominent barrister in the High Court and we are confident that in the event of you not conforming to the laws pertaining to public companies, we have no choice. It may well be that you have already broken the law and may face, not only civil penalties, but a criminal prosecution."

Rhodes sat staring at me for a few seconds as he digested this information. He frowned, he glared, he pulled out a pipe and tobacco pouch, stuffed tobacco into the bowl and lit up with clouds of smoke filling the room.

"That would not be good for the prime minister of the Cape to be tried for malfeasance," he sighed.

"It certainly would not."

"Alright, Barney, I will promise to be more accountable in the future."

"Cecil, I'm afraid that is not enough. I have a document here that we request you to sign. In a nutshell, you will no longer be a signatory on any of the corporation's accounts. The banks have been informed. All it needs is your signature and a witness to it."

Again he puffed furiously at his pipe and drummed with his fingers on his heavy mahogany desk.

"I never thought that you, Barney, would try and take my company away from me."

"I am not taking your company away from you, Cecil. Sign the document and you will continue to receive your income and dividends from De Beers."

"And if I don't?"

"Then you know the consequence. It's up to you."

"Give me the damn document," he demanded, his face reddening.

He picked up a pen, signed the paper, blotted it and handed me the pen to add my signature as witness. I blotted the document again, folded it and put it back in my pocket.

"Now get out. I have affairs of state to take care of."

It was not a pleasant exchange but had to be done. I don't think he even gave it another thought. Rhodes could switch off the things he did not like.

I had promised Fanny we would return to England before the end of 1891. So in December, Fanny and I sailed for England on a brand new ship, the R.M.S. Scot. The Scot was the fastest ship on the line between the Cape and England, saving a full week of the voyage. The first class cabins and appointments were far more luxurious than any previous ship that sailed the route.

One of the pleasures of a voyage, or lack of, was the other passengers. Sometimes, they were an incredible bore and had to be avoided at all costs. I like people, but my fame as an investor and financier tempted brief acquaintances, to seek advice. Fortunately, I had the great pleasure to meet Lord Randolph Churchill on this voyage, a man of wealth and education, an interesting orator and statesman. We spent many hours together discussing gold and diamond mining, investing and acquisitions, of which he seemed to know very little. So we talked about horseracing, hunting and government, which he knew everything.

"I think you would make a good politician, Barney."

"I am one, Randolph, in the Cape Parliament."

"Well, I wasn't wrong then."

When the voyage was over, we parted our ways, never to be so familiar again.

Fanny and I received a warm welcome from all the family. Harry had put on some weight and my niece Leah had grown into a fine young woman. She had polish and poise that made her seem older than her fourteen years.

My father looked well, but thin. He still had a full head of hair, which was more than could be said for Harry. Father cornered me in the library of the house we were renting in Mayfair, a stone"s throw from the house we were building.

"Barney, I want you to know that I am incredibly proud of you. Fanny is a delight and I can easily understand how you fell in love with her."

"Thank you, father, I have been very lucky."

"It's not just luck, my boy, it is your personality and passion for life that makes you a success. You and Harry achieved things beyond the wildest dreams of any man, certainly beyond anything that I could have imagined for you. I only wish your mother was here to see it."

We sat in silence for a few seconds thinking about her. There were tears in his eyes that brought a lump in my throat. She had been dead nearly forty years and my recollection of her was somewhat cloudy. Seeing Leah, had set me off when I realized how much she looked like my mother.

It's a strange thing when you see a family likeness in the younger generation. It made me wish that Fanny and I had children. As if my father could read my thoughts, he spoke out.

"I am looking forward to when you and Fanny have children too. Kate and Harry's children are all growing up fast. When are you going to give me more grandchildren?"

"We will, all in good time, dad."

"I certainly hope so. You know, your wealth is in your children." I had to cut him off.

"Let's not discuss this any further, it makes me uncomfortable."

"As you wish. I will not discuss it again, but you know it would make me very happy."

A typical parent. It is never over till they decide. I'm sure if my mother had been alive, I would not have heard the end of it.

The weeks passed quickly with business affairs taking up much of my time. Fanny and I met weekly with the architects designing our house. Weekend parties and family gatherings filled all the remaining time. We managed to attend a number of theatre performances and charity fundraisers. Harry and I went to see a fantastic boxing match. Jack Joel, Fanny and I attended a number of race meetings to watch our own horses place, but not win.

By the end of May, 1892, it was time to travel back to the Cape. I wanted to sail on the Scot again, as we had on our outward voyage but to my surprise it was fully booked, so we took the R.M.S. Moor, an older but comfortable ship. I always think back to my first voyage to the Cape and the rough accomodations and poor food that I was quite comfortable with, how fortune had smiled upon me and time had changed me. I could put up with any condition, I really didn't care, but I loved to spoil my wife who enjoyed every minute of it. Sailing was good for me. It put me in a contemplative frame of mind.

Aboard, my thoughts went back to my father and his desire for grandchildren. Having my own kids had never seemed important before. But now something had changed in my mind. I think it had to do with Leah and how much she reminded me of my mother. I wanted to have a daughter who would look like Fanny. More importantly, I wanted a son who was just like me. Of course, he would have a better life and certainly a better education. After building an empire, a man has to have heirs to hand it on.

July 1892, Fanny broke the good news to me. She was pregnant. I was thrilled. So was she. I couldn't wait to tell the family. I sent cables to them all. Fanny wanted to have the child at home, which I was unhappy about. My feeling was, that in case of any complications, our local doctor just did not have the skill that may be necessary. He was a competent doctor, with many years experience, but I was taking no chances. I told Fanny that it was my intention to take her to England and stay there until after the birth. She put up an argument that women had been giving birth to children in Africa forever. She was healthy and could not see the point in going to so much trouble. As far as I was concerned, there was not going to be any further discussion I immediately booked passage for England.

I had another concern, which I did not share with Fanny at that time. Our marriage in Johannesburg had been a Jewish one. Other than our *Katubah*, there was no official record of it with the Transvaal government. This was not unusual, as many children did not survive, and the Volksraad did not require registrations of births or marriages at that time. Now that we were going to have children, I felt that it was important to have another marriage in London, where I knew that births, marriages and deaths were officially recorded.

I cabled Harry to make arrangements for our second wedding reception at the Savoy Hotel in London, asking him to figure out the guest list: family, friends and business acquaintances.

We sailed in early October 1892 on the R.M.S. Mexican. I still could not get a suite on the R.M.S. Scot, much to my annoyance. Word had got out that it was the best ship on the Cape to London route.

Fanny had to know about our second wedding. She was not thrilled when I told her. She would be five months pregnant by the November 19th date Harry had booked. When I explained why it was necessary she relented, as she understood how important this was for us all. As soon as we arrived, she couldn't wait to go shopping for a suitable wedding dress, accompanied by my sisters, Harry's wife and Leah. She was in good hands. I had no doubt that Fanny would have a great time, as long as they didn't tire her too much.

The wedding took place at the Chelsea Registry office on a beautiful sunny but cold day. A reception and dinner that followed was attended by more than a hundred people, most of them family. Harry had done a fine job, and I thanked him for helping make our second wedding such a successful event.

Chapter 45

A week later I was interviewed by the prestigious Financial News. The paper wanted to know the prospects for the mining industry in South Africa. This gave me a great opportunity to update the financial community in England. As the reporter opened his note book, I said,

"Everything in the position and outlook in the Transvaal was very bright when I left there a month ago and I attribute this, to some extent, to the arrangement between the Transvaal Government and Sir James Sivewright, the present Commissioner of Crown Lands, whereby direct railway communication between the Cape Colony and Johannesburg has been established. By this union of interests, the friction which hitherto existed is wiped out. The loan brought out by Messrs. Rothschild has also improved the financial condition of the Transvaal, and given the general public more confidence."

"How do you see the future of the gold mining industry? He asked.

"As far as the permanence of the gold-mining industry is concerned, that is guaranteed. It has taken time to put down stamps and machinery and secure good management. The companies are now getting the benefit of the preliminary work." As he wrote I went on.

"The Rand is one of the greatest goldfields ever seen, and its position is unequalled. There is plenty of coal and water on the spot, the climate is healthy, and they have a direct railway communication to the coast. As to economical mining, it has been proved that in some cases a profit can be made out of a yield of only 5 dwts. (a quarter of an ounce) of gold per ton."

"Reports show that the September output of gold in excess of 100, 000 oz., is a specially engineered flash in the pan. What do you have to say about that?"

"The September output of gold was 107,850 oz., and was definitely not a flash in the pan, as you seem to suggest. Two years ago, when the monthly output was a little over 40,000 ounces, I predicted to shareholders that it would reach 100,000 ounces in another two years. I am glad to see that my prophecy has come true. Today, considering that in some cases the deeper mines go the richer the ore and with the extra yield from the cyanide process of treating tailings, I have no hesitation in expressing my opinion that in another two years the monthly output will be nearer 200,000 ounces, or close upon eight million pounds a year."

Financial newspapers tend to look for the negative aspect of a situation, and the interviewer pushed hard to find the weak spots that could cause a downward trend in the price of shares. They are definitely the half glass empty people of the world. Johannesburg was thousands of miles away and there were many negative reports about the town, just as there had been in the early days of Kimberley. I knew the question about Johannesburg was coming.

"A lot of mining towns spawn tent cities. How permanent is the town of Johannesburg?"

"The best proof of the permanence of Johannesburg is its suburbs, which might be compared to Sydenham (a London suburb). The houses that are being built are very different to what were put up in the early days. The private houses now being erected, for which there is a demand, cost from £1000 to £4000 each (comparable to Sydenham)."

"Tell me about the diamond industry. How is the demand for diamonds today?" No surprise that this would be the last question.

"I am equally confident about the diamond industry. The position of De Beers Company was never stronger than it is today. The demand for diamonds is greater than the production, and the prices are as high as ever they were. The resources of the company are being strengthened by increasing its holding of Consols and other Government securities, while its debentures are being redeemed and the Wesselton Mine has been paid for out of profits."

At that point I terminated the interview, feigning other commitments. I did not want to have to answer questions about our Johannesburg Waterworks Company for which we had come under intense criticism last year by the shareholders.

A special meeting had been called for the following week at which Sir James Sivewright, the chairman and I, planned to speak. The meeting duly took place before a large number of shareholders at Winchester House in London.

The Waterworks Company was started by Sivewright and I bought into it rather late. It was obvious to me that water was as important to the local economy and well being of the population of Johannesburg. People need water to live. Whoever controls the local water, controls the growth or lack of, as a result of it. Over the past year, the owner of the farm on which our reservoir stood had threatened a lawsuit. The company was already in poor financial position and was on the verge of bankruptcy. The lawsuit would have been the final blow. I couldn't let that happen.

Prior to sailing for England, I went to visit Mr. Bezuidenhout, the owner of the farm of Doornfontein, and put it to him that his lawsuit would create massive unemployment. Furthermore, the whole future of Johannesburg was at stake. Everyone has their price, Mr. Bezuidenhout was no different. I asked him what it would take to drop his lawsuit and how much he would take for the freehold of his property. After all is said and done, everything is negotiable. Doornfontein was mine for the sum of £12,500 and I purchased this for the Waterworks Company. I would have paid double that amount had it been asked.

Doornfontein is only three quarters of a mile from the center of Johannesburg and was without doubt, the most desirable suburb of the new town. I went into great detail about it and the potential value to the Waterworks Company. We owned the most important water rights in the area, an area that was potentially the finest township development. I called it the Belgravia of Johannesburg.

At the end of the shareholders meeting, I received huge applause. They had accepted my report and all previous hostility had disappeared. The Waterworks Company would never be highly profitable, but it was one of my key projects. As Johannesburg grows, so would it. The Financial News the next day gave me a positive write up. Our dividend for the company amounted to six per cent for the year, a far cry from the twenty-five per cent dividend that we were paying at De Beers Consolidated Mines.

On January 1893, the Tati Concessions Land, formerly part of Matabeleland to the north-east of our holdings, was formally annexed by our government into the Bechuanaland Protectorate. I could see Rhodes at work here, but there was no mention of his involvement in any of the newspapers. Anything that happened in South Africa ultimately affected the mining industry. My concern was that it would impact our native labor force. However, I should not have been concerned as there was no shortage of labor at this time.

Chapter 46

Fanny's pregnancy went well. Our daughter Lily was born on March 16th, 1893. She was beautiful. Everyone in the family was happy for us. We celebrated with Champagne, although many of my family would have preferred something stronger. My father was so excited that he had another grandchild. Congratulations poured in from all over the world from people I didn't even know. We put an announcement in the Times daily newspaper and the Jewish Chronicle, a newspaper read by almost every Jew in England.

I felt that Fanny needed time to get her strength back after the birth, so I planned to spend a few more months in England before sailing back to the Cape.

It was hard for me to decide where I considered home, England or South Africa. My affinity was for England, but I had made a name in Kimberley and Johannesburg and felt that both places were also home. Each time we went on a voyage, I knew it was only a matter of time before we would be back once again.

In April, the newspapers announced that Paul Kruger had been elected president of Transvaal for the third time, an excellent result as far as I was concerned. I had built up a good relationship with him and didn't want to have to start with a different head of state. Not that that was going to happen as long as Oom Paul was around.

Then came the bad news. There was panic on the New York Stock Market due to excessive speculation. This could not be laid at our door, but it certainly had some influence. The repercussions were felt around the world. Our shares took a hit. It was time for me to go back to South Africa to manage the fallout. Fortunately, we were able to book passage on the new R.M.S. Dunottar Castle, which made the voyage in sixteen days. Not a day too soon. The New York Stock Exchange crashed the day we arrived back in Johannesburg.

The crash meant there were opportunities for our companies to pick up shares in depressed companies that fit into our holdings. I intended to make the most of it. Our Johannesburg Holdings Company was sitting on a lot of cash, just waiting for the right opportunities. Call it speculation, or good business, our company had the resources to absorb many other entities that complimented us and gave us a wider base of operations.

Fanny, Lily and I returned without delay to our Johannesburg home. Most of my correspondence was taken care of while I was away and only an odd letter was held for my personal attention. One from the United States piqued my curiosity. It was from a John Hays Hammond, a name I had heard of before. Hammond was an engineer and a mining expert. Certainly there was no shortage of mining experts already in Johannesburg, Hammond had some of the best contacts in America and he was looking for a job at an extremely high salary. He had selected my company, as he was convinced he could improve our gold production yields, and he assumed that I would pay the £10,000 pounds annual salary he was asking.

I sent a cable and told him to pack his bags and come to South Africa by the fastest route. I like a man that has confidence in his abilities and is not afraid to seek the best situation. His response by return cable, was in the affirmative and he would book passage immediately.

Meanwhile, we had little bonus in late June. A blue-white diamond weighing 995 carats was found in one of our mines, the Excelsior.

Hammond arrived in mid-August. Our first meeting was cordial and I found I liked the tall American who towered over me. I arranged a contract for him to sign, and allocated one of our new houses in the Doornfontein for his personal use.

He insisted on taking a tour of the mines before signing the contract, which was prudent of him to do. I didn't see him for more than two weeks and I thought that he had got lost. But the man was more than thorough. When he finally returned to my office he presented me with copious notes of his observations and recommended course of action.

"Mr. Barnato, I have had the opportunity to examine all the mines in your current holdings on the Rand. You have competent people working here, but I will want to make changes. There are a number of recommendations that are imperative to improve production."

"I will need a bit of time to go through this voluminous report," I told him.

"Do you want to sign your contract now?"

"Not until I have your full agreement on my recommendations."

"I can assure you I will accept them without doubt. After all, you are the expert."

"If that is the way you feel, I will sign with one addition."

"And that is?"

"My recommendations will be put into practice and carried out within six months. In the event that they are not, the contract will become null and void. I will resign and you will pay me my entire year's salary."

"That does not sound unreasonable. I will have to digest your report before I add that to the contract."

Hammond's notes and recommendations were more than I had bargained for. He certainly knew his stuff. There was a huge cost involved and unfortunately I dragged my feet on this. At the end of six months, less than half of his recommendations had been put into practice. Hammond resigned as he said he would. He did not want to continue working for me. I tried to get him to change his mind, but he was adamant that we stick to the contract.

To my regret, Hammond and I parted ways. I was curious where he was going to next. I was not surprised to find that he went to work for Rhodes as his chief mining engineer, probably at a higher salary than I paid him. Rhodes was spending much of his time on empire building; he was only too pleased to have someone, with such experience in charge.

Matabeleland made the news in late October 1893. The natives were in rebellion against the British who had annexed their land. The chiefs had given concessions to Rhodes' British South Africa Company without realizing that, in effect, they were giving up control of their lands. Lobengula the King of the Ndebele knew his Zulu warriors were no match for the modern weaponry that the B.S.A.C. had in their arsenal. Dr. Jameson fought the local native Ndebeles and massacred many of them. Spears and arrows are no match for modern guns.

Some days later, a mounted column of British soldiers crossed the Umniati River into Matabeleland where they set up camp. Six thousand Ndebele warriors attacked the camp, only to be mown down by the British Maxim machine guns and two seven pounder cannons. Thousands of the Ndebele warriors were killed in the skirmish with only ten British killed or wounded.

This kind of military action had huge repercussions for the mining industry. We were reliant on our native workers and many deserted their jobs to return to their tribes in expectation of a more extensive war. The natives may not have been able to read what is going on in the newspapers, but the bush telegraph was rapid and word got around fast. If anything, the natives knew about the skirmish before we read about it in the newspapers.

Chapter 47

The year 1893 started out as one of the busiest and happiest in my life. My beautiful little daughter and my darling wife, Fanny were my greatest joy. Toward the end of November, Fanny announced to me that she was expecting again. She wanted to have the baby at home in Kimberley, but I refused to allow it.

"We will go to England and you shall have the Queen's doctor to attend to you."

"Really, Barney, it is not necessary to travel all that way."

"I'll not hear any more about it, I will see to it today."

I was not taking any risk when it came to my family. Anyway, I enjoyed the voyage and I was anxious to see my father again. Kate had sent me a letter a few days earlier. She didn't want to worry me, but told me that father's health was failing. He had been sick with a bad bout of influenza, which had left him weak and listless. She felt that if we were to visit it would raise his spirits. I decided to take the next ship to England.

De Beers Consolidated Mines had a very good year and we paid a dividend of 25% for the year. This was an outstanding improvement considering the crash of the American stock market in May. I realized that when the stock market takes a beating, investors flee into gold and diamonds. So we were in a great position with our interests in these areas. Gold was found this year in Kalgoorlie, Australia. Some of the miners left the country on the next ship for Australia. Every man hopes to strike it rich and I didn't blame them for trying. I was the best example of what a lot of hard work and some degree of luck can do. For every man we lost, there were at least two men waiting to take their place.

More trouble broke out with the Ndebeles natives in early December. The thirty-four man Shangani Patrol of Rhodes British Africa Company, was ambushed and almost completely annihilated by an estimated three thousand warriors. Only three men managed to escape. This meant an all out war with King Lobengula. The British Government would not tolerate the massacre of Englishmen and there is no doubt that this rebellion would be put down quickly. The thing that none of us could understand, was how these spear throwing natives could overpower the well armed and trained men of the Shangani Patrol. Admittedly, the Ndebeles had a few rifles, but they should have been no match for the new Maxim machine guns that the Patrol was equipped with.

There also was an interesting report in the newspapers that told of King Lobengula sending two of his warriors to intercept an advancing column of British South Africa Company's Police, the BSAP. These warriors were carrying a box of gold sovereigns that they were instructed to offer to the BSAP in return for them not to attack the king's kraal. Apparently, two officer's batmen accepted the coins and kept them for themselves, not informing their officers of the offer and message.

The two batmen were charged in court and found guilty, even though the evidence against them was inconclusive. They received a sentence of fourteen years hard labor. The money was not recovered and no doubt, if true, these men would be quite wealthy by the time they got out. For most, this would not be worth the agony of hard labor for an extended period of time, but the temptation must have been great. Was the story true? Hard to say, but it was unlikely that the Ndebeles would invent such a story.

The New Year brought an ironical end to the Ndebeles War. King Lobengula died of smallpox in January. Smallpox was brought to Africa by the Europeans. Following his death and the heavy assault by the BSAP, like most native wars in South Africa, the conflict quickly came to an end.

Accompanied by Woolf Joel, we sailed for England on March 3rd. Fanny was six months pregnant and the sea voyage was not too much to her liking, as she was sick almost everyday.

Woolf and I played a lot of poker on this voyage. It passed the time away in the pleasant company of other passengers, who like us, had made this voyage on numerous occasions.

Arriving in England on a cold but dry day, we were all pleased to be on dry land again. Our London house was still nowhere near completion. So we leased a spacious townhouse at 38 Curzon Street in Mayfair on the corner of Hertford Street. Only a few minutes walk to Hyde Park. The house was comfortable and beautifully furnished. We had an excellent housekeeper and highly competent staff. I think both Fanny and I were surprised at the opulence of this house. Once again, my family would be appalled at our extravagant lifestyle, even though they were not only getting used to it, but were benefitting from it.

As soon as we had settled in and Fanny was feeling stronger, we had a party for all the family. It was a very grand affair. My father was happy and pleased to see us, but he looked thin and rather frail. We made a big fuss of him. He held my beautiful little daughter, bouncing her on his lap, much to her delight. Her nanny was appalled at this, standing by, just in case my father dropped her on the floor. I wasn't worried. My father loved to roughhouse with all us kids when we were small. Harry looked really good. The English weather was much more to his liking and he had settled into a comfortable routine that he enjoyed.

My sisters, their husbands and kids roamed around Spencer house, admiring the paintings, furniture and ornaments. It was like living in a museum, not that I have been in many museums in my life, something I regret. It was a wonderful party and when it was time to leave, Fanny was exhausted.

"I think we will postpone any more parties till after the birth of the baby, Barney, she said."

"As you wish my love. It was just too tempting not to have a celebration for all the family and especially for my father. Sadly, he is looking very old and he may have little time left on this earth."

"None of us know how much of our lives we have left. He could surprise us all," she responded.

"I hope so.

The City of London is home to the London Stock Exchange. My presence here caused much speculation about the reason for being in London and not in South Africa. I have gotten used to it, but on this occasion I didn't have any real agenda.

I went to our offices in Draper's Gardens and met with Mr. Benham. A fresh idea had come upon me. Well maybe not fresh, but one that had been percolating in the back of my mind for some time. It was a cordial meeting.

"Mr. Benham, good to see you again."

"Good morning, Mr. Barnato, it is indeed certainly good to see you too. I hope all is well with you and your family?"

"Yes, everything is fine. My wife is expecting our second child and will deliver in three months or so. Thank you for asking."

"Our financial position is excellent and our share prices continue to improve almost daily," he noted.

"Do you have something that the City can get their proverbial teeth into, sir?"

"Yes, I believe so. You know I have always wanted to start my own bank. The Rothschilds have made fortunes with theirs, and I think we can too. You're experienced in banking. Do you think we can successfully float our own bank?"

Benham sat thinking for a minute or two. His expression gave nothing away, but I could sense that this was something he had already considered.

"Yes, I do believe that we can. The most difficult thing will be to get new depositors, but with your reputation I think that it will work. Do you have a name in mind?

"Let's call it The Barnato Bank, Mining and Estates Company."

"Admirable. I will get to work on the paperwork for the formation. Once that is complete may I
suggest an interview with the Financial Times to announce your new venture. That will help to get
things moving forward."

"Thank you, Mr. Benham, I know that I can always rely on you. You are a good man."

My dream of the Barnato Bank became fact, although I was unsure what I was going to do with it or how I would make money from it. All I knew was that it was another string to my bow.

My father passed peacefully away in his sleep a few weeks later. I felt fortunate that I was able to spend time with him during his final days. He had lived to a ripe-old age of eighty-four.

We sat *shiva* at Harry's house. *Shiva* is a traditional mourning that lasts for a week. Hebrew prayers are said several times a day and friends and relatives come and visit. People bring food so that the mourners don't have to be concerned about cooking. It is like a wake, only much longer. I couldn't wait for it to finish.

Fanny was due to deliver anytime, and I was worried about her, even though she kept on reassuring me that everything was fine. Three days after we finished sitting *shiva*, Fanny gave birth to a baby boy. We named him Isaac Henry after my father. It was a very emotional time for me, I couldn't have been happier that I had a son, but my father had died before knowing that he had another grandson.

London is a wonderful city to live in when you are rich. The theatres, restaurants, shops, parks, great homes and estates make it what it is. There are easy railway connections to all parts of England, as well as cross channel steamers to the Continent. So the subject of where we should live came up in conversation now. In the past, neither Fanny nor I had considered anywhere other than South Africa. But now we had two tiny children. We were both concerned about the unhealthy atmosphere of Johannesburg.

The railway connection from Delagoa Bay and Pretoria had brought with it a huge influx of people, many undesirable. It was noted in the newspapers that Johannesburg had more than ninety brothels now. I certainly didn't doubt it, with the ratio of men to women. The prostitutes were doing a roaring business. The center of our town proliferated with gin palaces, where the brawls and noise at night made it impossible to walk there with one's family. Even more disturbing was the choking air filled with dust from the mining operations.

We had experienced all of this in Kimberley, but not to such an extent. Kimberley was now quite genteel by comparison.

One night Fanny asked me directly.

"When we return to the South Africa, are we going to live in Johannesburg or Kimberley?"

"I'm not sure, my love."

"Barney, you are always sure; you're just avoiding telling me."

"Our real expansion is in Jo'burg and I find the excitement there much more to my liking. But I am concerned, as you are, about bringing up the children there. While they are small it might be better to spend most of our time in Kimberley."

"Good, that's what I want. We cannot let our babies grow up in the choking air of Jo'burg.

"Of course, I will be spending a lot of time away from home in Johannesburg and in Cape Town. I still have to go to the Cape Parliament when it is in session."

"I understand that. We've talked about living here in London. Do you think that we might do so in the near future?" I paused.

"You know I love visiting London, but I do get bored after a while and yearn to return to South Africa. That's where I can be me, where I don't have to put on airs and graces that are expected of me here."

"What about the new house we are building in Park Lane?"

"That's for when we stay here, four of five months of the year," I said.

"As much as I miss my family back home, I want you to know I love being here."

Fanny was telling me she wanted to live in London and for the first time in my life, I seemed unable to make up my mind. She continued.

"What's not to love? We're living in the finest house in London, second only to Buckingham Palace. We have more servants than we know what to do with and we are feted by the most important people in England."

"At some point, when the children are older and ready for fine schools, I will consider moving to London permanently. In the meantime, we will go home to Kimberley," I said. The decision was made.

Chapter 48

After our London sojourn, Kimberley looked positively provincial. Fanny and I had gone on a spending spree before leaving England, but it would be a few more weeks before everything would arrive.

The nursery had been completely redecorated for Isaac, who for some inexplicable reason, we were calling Jack. I'm not sure how that happened; something to do with a nursery rhyme that Lily liked me to read to her and she started calling her baby brother Jack.

I spent two weeks in Kimberley, taking care of business, checking on our De Beers Consolidated, which was being run efficiently by dependable staff, leaving little for me to do. I said my goodbyes to Fanny and the children and travelled by railway to Johannesburg.

You leave a town like Johannesburg for a few months and when you return, the town has grown so much, it is hard to recognize some of it. I spent no time settling in, I had to get to the office and see what had been going on in my absence.

Solly greeted me as soon as I arrived. He couldn't wait to bring me up to date on all the new acquisitions, our production figures and some of the new ideas he had for more expansion of our company. He got right to it.

"While you were away, Rhodes passed an Act of Parliament called the Glen Gray Act. It was instigated to establish an individual land tenure for the natives. It creates a labour tax to force the natives, mainly the Xhosa, into employment on farms and mines."

"Will it work?"

"Who knows? It has only just been passed this week. To some extent, this Act was forced on Rhodes by the farm communities in the Cape. But you and I know that Rhodes' ambition is to colonize the entire African continent, including getting the natives under British jurisdiction."

"How is that affecting the laborers in our mines?"

"Well, it's too early to say. My guess is that it will help the mining industry in the long run. Otherwise, Rhodes would have changed the wording of the Act to benefit us all. He knows where his bread is buttered."

"Good. Let's take a tour of the mines and holdings. Now that I'm back, I want to see everything."

Solly and I spent the next few days riding around and looking at our ever growing holdings. One thing I knew: I could rely on him when I went away. He and Woolf were my right hand men, as was their brother Jack working with Harry in London. What would I do without them?

Johannesburg was growing rapidly. In the few months I was away in England, many new buildings had been constructed or were in the process. Our housing developments in Berea and Dorrnfontein, were providing homes for our upper management and executive employee's families. Additionally, we were building schools for the children, a hospital, and places of worship. Most of the early temporary wood and tin shops had been pulled down, replaced by substantial brick buildings. Who says you can't make a silk purse out of a sow's ear?

The Barnato Bank shares were trading twenty per cent higher than the issue price. There was another boom in South African mining stocks, resulting in our net worth increasing daily. It appeared that we could do no wrong. Financial newspapers were estimating my net worth at a staggering one hundred and fifty million pounds. I'm not sure how they arrived at this figure, but I was quite happy to be worth a fraction of this highly exaggerated amount. When we started the Barnato Bank, I put a considerable amount of my assets into the bank, shares of other companies, but not De Beers Consolidated or Johannesburg Investments. The valuation of those stocks amounted to twelve million pounds. Some critics, there were always critics, said I put all my bad holdings into the bank. I refuted this completely.

The quartz bearing veins in all our gold mines were deeper and in many cases, almost vertical. It was necessary to sink ever deeper shafts to extract the gold. As a result, our costs were now considerably higher. Fortunately, the new and renewed interest in our mining stocks allowed us to add more shafts to these lower levels.

We had to maintain a twenty-four hour schedule to make the mines profitable. We used huge amounts of coal to run our pumps, to haul the ore to the surface, pump out water from the bottom of the mines and to move men to and from the surface to the deep levels. Unfortunately, the Transvaal government-appointed railway concessionaire was charging extortionate rates for our coal.

I complained to President Kruger about this problem each time I met with him, but it fell on deaf ears.

Floating new companies specializing in deep-level mining was being done by all of the main players in Johannesburg. I will admit that some of the properties we floated were completely unproven, but we understood the business and investors showed their confidence in our ability to turn these into profits. That was my reputation, making profits where others had previously failed.

I was splitting my time between Johannesburg and Kimberley, with most weekends with Fanny and our two children. She was still of the opinion that Kimberley was healthier and I would not argue with her on that point. Each week I seemed to spend more time there, resulting in my days in Johannesburg down to two or three each week. This suited me fine.

I was re-elected to the Cape Parliament again and when it was in session, I had to attend. I curbed this to the absolute minimum. Making money had pre-occupied my life for years, but now, my time spent with my family became more important to me.

Early in the New Year of 1895, Fanny decided to come with me to Johannesburg, as it had been a while since she had visited. She wanted to take a look at the house and see what was needed to make my life there more comfortable. It really wasn't necessary. I had everything I needed or even wanted. Nevertheless, she insisted and when she insisted, she got her way.

The Transvaal government was becoming extremely protective of its borders, especially with the British Cape Colony. The long border delays we had experienced in the past got even longer. They were on the look out for contraband, diamonds and jewelry in particular, as well as liquor and firearms. These all had huge import tariffs. On one occasion, a Transvaal customs officer had found a revolver in the baggage of one of the passengers on a coach arriving from Cape Town. Shouting at the man and not realizing that the gun was loaded, the officer slammed it down on a counter top. There was a thunderous report as the gun went off. The children screamed and I saw Fanny flinch. Her eyes rolled and she collapsed into a heap. There was blood, a lot of blood and I was unsure from where she was bleeding.

"Quick, get a doctor. My wife has been shot by that idiot."

One of my servants rushed to help Fanny. Easing her down to the floor, I could see that the bullet had hit her in the arm. I was terrified she might die! My very able servant held a compress to Fanny's arm to stop the worst of the bleeding, while we waited for a doctor, who arrived ten minutes later.

Fortunately, it looked much worse than it was and we were both shaken by the event. I'm pleased to say Fanny made a quick recovery. However, the press made a lot of the incident. It was reported that this was a deliberate attack on uitlanders. I received a formal apology from Kruger's office in Pretoria.

I'm not sure that Fanny was ever comfortable in our new house in the Berea district of Johannessburg. We had spent a small fortune on it, more than £500,000.

I had two surprises in February. Vanity Fair published a caricature image of me in its magazine that I quite liked. Most importantly though, Fanny told me she was expecting again. At this rate we were going to have a large family, we already had two children under two years old.

"I guess it is time to go back to England again."

She laughed, I knew that she wanted to get away from Johannesburg.

"I will book our passage straight away."

"Thank you, Barney. I think just us and the children this time, if you don't mind."

"Not at all."

On May 11th, 1895 we sailed to England again.

As on my previous visits to England, I often visit the East End of London, where I was born and raised. It never seems to change very much no matter how much I donate to the charities in the area. The poor are everywhere and there are always children in ragged clothes on the streets. Most don't know how poor they are; I know we didn't when we were growing up. Fortunately for us, there was always love in our home. My sister Kate always made sure of that after the death of our mother. Sadly, for many of the poor and destitute that I see, there is no love. Often they find themselves in abusive situations and drunkenness is a common root cause. I like a drink and my father did too, but never to excess. There are few times in my life when I was really drunk.

The Music Halls of the East End are a big attraction for me. In high society it was considered acceptable for gentlemen to frequent these establishments. The trouble for me these days, is that I wasrecognized everywhere I went. People were always touching me for money. I gave away huge amounts every year and I easily fell for a hard luck story. However, it got to the point where I could not enjoy my evenings in the old quarter anymore.

I decided to make a contribution of £75,000 to the poor, through the auspices of the new Lord Mayor of London, Colonel Sir Walter Henry, whom I had met at some gala ball. Needless to say he was thrilled at the gesture. He wanted to name it the Barnato Fund, or some such nonsense, which I refused to accept. I told him to distribute it how he saw fit and call it whatever he liked, as long as my name was not attached to it.

Our London house was still not finished. I'm sure had I pushed the builder a bit harder, it could have been finished long before this visit. My London solicitor had somehow persuaded the Earl of Spencer to lease Spencer House in St. James's, London for a period of six months. The Palladian style house had spectacular gardens and views of Green Park. This grand house in the neoclassical style and was built for the Earl of Spencer in the mid eighteenth century. It had passed on to successive earls. The current earl preferred his country mansion and estates at Althorp.

I really loved the expansive house and gardens; the close proximity to Green Park and the shops of Piccadilly and Regent Street. The staff were unobtrusive, but always attentive to our needs. Fanny and the children loved the nursery and we all enjoyed taking rides in an open landau around the park when the weather was good.

My family, now more accustomed to the luxuries of life, came to stay at least one weekend each month. Fanny and I were invited to a number of weekend parties at country homes. There were in fact too many invitations and Fanny declined them all, as she grew larger in her pregnancy.

For my personal entertainment there were the gambling clubs in Pall Mall, where I could play poker at night, often till dawn. And there were my horses, ten of them now being trained by Charles Archer, a man with a great reputation for winners. Unfortunately, none of them were mine. I decided that I would buy a winner at my first possible opportunity. To this end, I had my eye on Worcester, a five year old chestnut that had a string of wins behind him. This beautiful horse was great over seven furlongs, slightly less than a mile. Archer agreed that it would be a good addition to our stud. So I bought it.

Twice a week I would go to our office and have meetings with Harry and Jack. The first order of the day was our current share prices. For months they had been climbing during the bull market of 1894 and 1895, but I was worried that their valuation was far too high. Harry didn't agree as usual.

"What are you worried about, Barney? Things couldn't look better."

"That's what worries me. My gut tells me there is going to be a hell of a crash when investors realize that many of the South African mining stocks they have invested in are practically worthless. This crazy speculation in the stocks is going to come crashing down around our ears."

Jack tried to stay out of the discussion, knowing that we brothers rarely agreed about anything these days.

"I don't want to take sides here, Harry, but I think that Barney might be right. Instead of arguing about it, why don't we strategize what we want to do about it?"

"The lad's right, Harry, markets go up and markets go down. What is important is our exposure in the market, not which way it's going."

"Okay, I can agree with that. What do you suggest we do?"

"First, we should not float any new companies for the time being. Secondly, we should concentrate on our winners: Barnato Consolidated, New Primrose, Johannesburg Investments and possibly Kimberley Roodepoort. As for the companies we have floated for newer mines, we should hold off investing in plant, machinery and sinking shafts."

Harry pondered the suggestions. I know that when he does this he generally agrees with me, but at a slow pace.

"I see the merit in this. We have no need to put ourselves in a position where we will be the biggest losers."

"Exactly. We are extremely wealthy on paper and speculation as to our net worth is ridiculously high. But I don't want to be the one who everybody points the finger at. Because when the bubble bursts, there will be a lot of finger pointing."

Cables were sent to our managers, instructing them how we wanted to proceed. We literally shuttered three or four companies, which we knew were hugely risky. Not that the public wouldn't buy the shares, but I didn't want to fuel the already excessive speculation. Let the others do it. We were not going to be the ones.

Unexpectedly, three weeks later Solly arrived in England, having decided that he was not happy with our directions given from the London office. He came to the office in a fighting mood and demanded a meeting. I had no problem with this. If he had something to say, then he was entitled to say it. Harry, Jack and I sat opposite him in our boardroom. He wasted no time getting straight to the point.

"I am disgusted that you three have made a decision to curtail some of our expansion programs without consulting me for my opinion."

"Have you seen the financial newspapers here in London?" I asked.

"Some, yes. But newspapers will always write negative reports when things are going well. That's what sells newspapers."

"You may not be aware of this but there was a scathing report in the Engineering and Mining Journal only last week. It showed South African mining stocks are selling at 408% of their par value. Even at last year's levels, production of gold will barely cover dividends for ten per cent of the one hundred and fifty or so of the mining shares on the London Stock Market."

"Barney, most of our companies are producing dividends."

"Not all. Some are producing dividends because we have sold off property that we don't need, giving us one time profits. Those are not dividends from production."

"That is not the point. You are curbing our ability to make money," Solly charged.

That was too much for me. I blew up.

"You're an arrogant little shit. I make the decisions around here and this was not just my decision, all three of us agreed. How dare you come here and challenge our authority."

"It's obvious to me that you don't have the balls anymore," he chided.

With that he stormed out of the office, slamming the door on the way out. I was so enraged I wanted to run after him and flatten him. But cooler heads prevailed.

Fanny gave birth to Woolf on September 27th at Spencer House. She had the Queen's doctor in attendance and the birth went well. She and the baby were thoroughly pampered by the staff, and we had an excellent nanny to take care of the infant. I was delighted to have another son. Lily was thrilled to have another baby brother and kept calling him Babe until we were all calling him Babe.

As I had predicted, within a couple of weeks, the financial newspapers were full of concern over the excessive speculation in South African mining stocks. Even the daily and evening papers were writing about it. Of course, this negative publicity helped create the slump that followed rapidly. In October, the stock market went into a deep slump. I tried to support our share prices by purchasing as many as I could. After losing more than three million pounds of my own funds in a short period of time, I knew it was impossible to shore up a collapsing market and I had to let things take their natural course. As I had anticipated, there were a lot of recriminations in the press.

Solly stayed away from family gatherings and this upset me a lot. We were very close and I had given him the opportunity of a lifetime. He had worked hard and reaped the benefit just like the rest of us. I knew I was wrong. I should have consulted with him and Woolf in South Africa by cable, before making our decision final. I wanted to make peace with him and knew he was leaving for Cape Town in early November.

I told Fanny what I wanted to do. I would sail with him as far as Madeira. Then catch the next ship back to England. She agreed that it was a good idea.

I met with Solly at the port in Southampton. I had arranged with my valet to pack my things and get them onboard the ship. The look on Solly's face said a lot. He wasn't too pleased to see me.

"What are you doing here?"

"I've come to apologize to you. Solly, I'm really sorry that I didn't consult with you and Woolf. I was wrong. I don't want there to be bad feelings between us."

"I'll accept your apology."

"Thank you."

"I have to go now. My ship is sailing in less than an hour."

"You know, I need a rest, so I'm going to take the ship as far as Madeira, spend a couple of weeks there and then come back to England. Do you mind if I join you?"

"No, not at all."

I knew it was going to take more than a simple apology to straighten things out with him. I was determined to put all this behind us. So I decided, if need be, I would go all the way back to Cape Town. I ended up doing just that, managing to smooth Solly's ruffled feathers.

Chapter 49

I have always tried to steer clear of political conflict. Over the period of a few short years, I have been able to build a friendship with Paul Kruger. He respected my opinion on matters that relate to the mining industry and to problems that we, the *uitlanders*, feel impacted our lives.

The Boer Government have made sure that the laws they passed, excluded the *uitlanders* from voting rights, therefore guaranteeing a dominance of the minority of the population. *Uitlanders* outnumber the Boers by a ratio of six to one. I have expressed my opinion to Oom Paul, that this was causing increasing unrest. In addition, heavy taxation on the gold mining industry added to the problem. He didn't want to keep hearing this from me and often angrily terminated our meetings.

Recently though, the level of unrest amongst some of the more prominent members of the Johannesburg community made me uncomfortable, and as I saw it was leading to insurrection. I expressed this to him in no uncertain terms. He was outraged, but I prevailed upon him to give some concessions or face dire consequences.

On my return from Pretoria, I had a visitor one evening at my home. It was John Hays Hammond.

"Good evening, John, what do I owe the pleasure of this visit?"

"Good evening, Barney. I wonder if I may have a word with you."

"Of course you can. Don't tell me you want your old job back!"

"No, that is not why I am here. You have the ear of President Kruger. The Reform Committee, which I am part of, would like to see if you can talk some sense into him regarding the taxation and representation problems that continue to plague us here in the Transvaal."

"John, I have spoken at length to Kruger on both subjects. He is a stubborn old ox. He will do nothing to improve the position of people he feels are taking his country's natural resources and wealth to Europe. Those are his words."

"The Reform Committee fears that if he does nothing, there will be a war. You and I both know that a war is the last thing our industry needs," John said, his voice rising.

"On my recent visit to Kruger, I told him exactly this."

"How did he react?"

"He gets a bit manic when the subject comes up. His worry, and that of the burghers, is that England will get involved and try to annex the Transvaal."

"Do you think The British Government would get involved?"

"I'm not the person to ask. Perhaps you should ask Rhodes. He would know better than I."

"What's you personal opinion then?"

"Yes. I think they might in the right circumstances. But you are on very dangerous ground here, John."

"There is a plan," he replied with a knowing look.

"Stop right there. I don't want to know about any plan. I am not going to be embroiled in action against the Boer government under any circumstances. Do I make myself perfectly clear?"

"Yes, Barney, quite clear."

"Good. Now let's have a glass of Cognac, cigars and some pleasant conversation."

It was only a matter of time before things would blow up. I had no doubt that Rhodes was mixed up in this somewhere, pulling the strings of his puppets from his office in Cape Town. Of course we did not know the details until after the insurrection.

The Reform Committee had about six hundred men; four hundred were part of the Matabele Mounted Police under Dr. Leander Starr Jameson, who we had read about in the newspapers in 1893. The other two hundred men were volunteers, mostly from Johannesburg. All were equipped with rifles and there were eight Maxim machine guns, the latest in easily portable military weapons. The Mounted Police also had a few light artillery pieces, a seven-pounder and a twelve-pounder.

Dr. Jameson held the position of Administrator General of Rhodes British South Africa Company (BSAC). Rhodes was chairman and was in an expansive mood, having been given control by the British Government earlier in the year of a large area of more than three-quarters of a million square miles of Africa renamed Rhodesia.

At the end of 1895, in preparation for the uprising, Jameson moved his men to Pisani, on the border of the Transvaal. The plan was for the men of Johannesburg to revolt and seize the Boer government armory in Pretoria. I'm not sure exactly how that was meant to proceed, but that was the first part of the plan. The second part was for Jameson to immediately cross the border to restore law and order in Johannesburg, secure the goldfields, then on to Pretoria to take control of the government of the country. A plucky move. They were betting on the apathetic Boer farmers not getting involved.

One of the problems of any insurrection, and this one was no different, is the failure to have agreement of all parties about the aftermath, and the governance of the territory taken. There was disagreement between the Reform Committee and the Johannesburg Uitlander reformers.

Jameson was ready, his men were ready, but the Reform Committee was not. Christmas had come and gone, the New Year was a few days away and Jameson was anxious for the coup d'etat to begin before the start of 1896. A cable to Jameson from the Reform Committee told him to stand down and wait while the differences with the Uitlanders were sorted out. This was not what he wanted to hear, as he was having his own difficulties keeping his men waiting. They were ready to go.

Believing that he could influence the situation and force the hand of the committee, on December 29th, he cabled Rhodes: "Unless I hear definitely to the contrary. I shall leave to-morrow evening." Jameson received no reply and the next day sent a second cable: "Shall leave tonight for the Transvaal."

Unfortunately, the first cable was delayed and both arrived at the same time, creating a lot of confusion. In the meantime, Jameson's men had cut the telegraph wires so that the Pretoria garrison could not cable for reinforcements. When Rhodes tried to send a reply there was no possible way to hold the coup back.

On December 29th, 1895, Jameson and his armed men invaded the Transvaal and headed for Johannesburg. Unfortunately for the raiders, they had cut the telegraph wires to Cape Town, but had failed to cut the wires to Pretoria. From the time they crossed into the Transvaal, the Boer forces were tracking them. The raiders encountered a small Boer outpost on

January 1st, 1896. The bastion was no match for the superior fire power of the raiders. Some forty miles farther at Krugersdorp, a force of Boer soldiers had dug in, waiting for the raiders to come their way. A battle ensued and a number of men were killed in the skirmish.

Towards nightfall, Jameson successfully pulled back in an effort to outflank the Boer force. But the early morning light the next day, the Boer forces spotted them again at Doornkop and blocked the road to Johannesburg. This was the decisive battle in this abortive raid, which went on for several hours before Jameson, realizing that to continue was futile, and in an effort to stem the loss of life, surrendered to the Boer commander. The remaining Jameson force was taken to Pretoria and jailed.

Kruger protested to the British Colonial Secretary, Joseph Chamberlain, in no uncertain terms. He warned them that any foreign force crossing his border again, would result in all out war. Chamberlain's response was to condemn the raid, even though it has been rumored that Rhodes had informed him in advance. Furthermore, Chamberlain had agreed to send armed assistance to Johannesburg in the event of an uprising. Politicians are what they are, and they don't like failure.

Under pressure from the British Colonial Secretary, Rhodes was forced to resign as Prime Minister of the Cape for his role in the affair. Dr. Jameson, his officers and all of the raiders in Boer custody were handed over to the British Government to be returned to England for trial, an excellent move on the part of the Boer Government.

However, on January 8th and 9th all sixty-four members of the Reform Committee were arrested on charges of high treason, and thrown into jail in Pretoria. The men, many of whom were some of the wealthiest in Johannesburg, were allowed privileges far beyond those afforded to the ordinary prisoners. They were allowed to have food brought in and even their own bedding. This was a prison for natives and it was certainly a rude awakening for the members of the Reform Committee. With the heat of the summer, overcrowding and unsanitary conditions, many succumbed to severe cases of dysentery.

As I read through the list of names in my morning newspaper, I found to my horror, my nephew Solly, was among those charged. I had warned him to stay out of this dangerous plot when he had brought up the subject one evening at our house. Now he was facing many years of hard labor and deprivation, or possibly, death by hanging. What was I going to tell my sister?

Many of the most prominent members of the mining community were on the list. There was no doubt that if they all ended up in jail, or worse it would devastate the production of gold mining. Even Rhodes brother was on this list.

The trial of the Reform Committee started on April 27th. Considering the number of men on trial and severity of the crime, it was short, only a few hours. In a bargain agreement with the Boer court, John Hays Hammond, Lionel Phillips, Percy Ferrar and Col. Frank Rhodes, Cecil's brother, pleaded guilty to the charge of High Treason. The other members pleaded guilty to lesser charges. There was little doubt that these men had plotted to overthrow the Boer Government.

At the end of the trial by judge and jury, the four men were all found guilty and given the harshest punishments for the crime. They were sentenced to death. The other prisoners got to two years imprisonment and fines of ten thousand pounds each, or in default, an extra year in jail. They were also banished from the Transvaal for three years after their release.

The trial of Dr. Jameson and his officers was taking place at the same time in London, and the effect of this news must have been devastating for them.

I knew what I had to do. I travelled immediately to Pretoria to visit Oom Paul. He wasn't going to like what I had to say, but there was no choice as far as I was concerned. When I arrived in Pretoria, he refused to see me, but I was not going to let this demagogue have his way. I pushed past his staff, prepared to flatten any one of them that got in my way. He was angry, but not as angry as me.

"What do you mean by barging into my office?"

"That's funny.

I thought you didn't speak English."

"What do you want?

"I want the release of the four men you have just had sentenced to death and the release of the other sixty men, who have been imprisoned unjustly."

"I think you don't know who you talk to."

"President Kruger, I know who I'm talking to. Release these men and

I give you my word that there will be no further action from any of them."

"The ringleaders have been found guilty of High Treason, there is only one penalty for that in the Transvaal. They will die as prescribed by the court."

"What can I say to you that will change your mind, sir?"

"Absolutely nothing."

"Is that so?"

"You have asked, I have responded. You petition is denied."

"Then you leave me no choice. I will shut down my entire mining business in the Transvaal from tomorrow. I have twenty thousand whites on my payroll and one hundred thousand blacks. I will put them all out of work and let them roam the streets. If I close down, I will put more white men out of work than you have burghers in your entire state. We'll see how you handle the revolt that will follow. My concerns also pay out £50 000 every week in fees and taxes, which will be lost to you. Thanks to this political crisis my mines have already lost twenty million pounds in production. Do you want to ruin your country for good and all? You will lose all your revenues from gold mining, I will make sure that all the other mines are closed, even if it is only temporary, but I will not reopen my mines until your government falls."

The look on Kruger's face was one of extreme fear. I had touched a nerve and it was my only chance to convince him. I turned my back on him and walked out of the door. He shouted something in Dutch, but it obviously was not to me. A few seconds later his interpreter tapped me on my shoulder.

"Mr. Barnato, President Kruger believes that there has been a misunderstanding in his translation of your conversation with him. I was unavailable and he made an effort to speak English, but it he is not fluent enough. Please could you return to his office with me?"

"Of course I can."

Kruger rattled off a long diatribe to the interpreter, presumably telling him what I had said to him. The interpreter asked me to repeat what I had told the president, which I did, emphatically. I did not want any doubt as to how serious I was about closing the mines.

"The president says there has to be compensation for the wrong done to the State."

"I will pay ten thousand pounds for each man."

The interpreter gave Kruger this information. Once again there was a long ranting diatribe.

"He says that it is insufficient and wants twenty thousand per man and one million for the ringleaders."

"This is what I'm going to offer. If it is not enough, then I walk out of here and this entire country will go to hell. I will pay compensation of ten thousand per man, plus half of a million pounds for the four condemned men, who are to be released immediately."

Kruger looked like he was going to blow up, his face was red and he was puffing as if out of breath. He looked at me as if trying to make up his mind if he could get more out of this. He spoke quietly to the interpreter, who nodded and translated what he had said to me.

"The president insists that in addition he wants a written apology from each of the men."

"Tell the president I have made my final offer."

Once again the interpreter went through the translation and once again Kruger sat there watching me. He nodded and I knew I had managed to pull it off. We shook hands and that was it. The sentences were commuted. Two days later all the men were released. Of course, it was after I presented Kruger's finance minister with a bank draft for one million, one hundred thousand pounds.

South African mining stocks plummeted as a result of the abortive Jameson Raid. The newspapers were full of recriminations. Interestingly, I was not one of those whose name appeared and my popularity with investors increased. There was no doubt that our stock prices had dropped with all the others. My efforts to shore up our share prices, brought praise from the financial press.

Chapter 50

In the midst of all this, I received some good news from England. My horse Worcester, won the City and Suburban Handicap at Epsom on April 22nd. Finally, I had a winner in my stud. The prize money wasn't bad either, two thousand gold sovereigns. Shame I missed the event.

In the wake of the Jameson affair, I decided to make myself scarce in the Transvaal and go back to England on the next available ship. Fanny and the family were pleased to see me, as I was to see them.

My appearance in London helped stop the run on our shares after I talked with various members of the London Stock Exchange. I reassured them that things would get back to normal quickly, as the leading heads of the mining companies were back at work. News of the threat I had made to Kruger was being talked about. There were questions asked about how serious I was when I gave my ultimatum. All I did was smile and say that I'm a good poker player.

For my reward in this, I was given an honorary membership in the Carlton Club, a highly prestigious Gentleman's Club for Tory members of parliament, peers and gentlemen. A club, that under normal circumstances, would never had given me a membership. I was probably the second Jew to have membership, the first being Prime Minister Benjamin Disraeli, who renounced his faith to attain that high office. Who would have believed that I, Barney Barnato, was rubbing shoulders with the elite of England.

The whole family celebrated Jack's second birthday in great style at Spencer House. We invited many of our newly found acquaintances and sat down eighty guests to a dinner. The weather was beautiful and we had a marquee erected on the lawns. The children ran around, closely watched by their nannies. We even organized a cricket match. Not my favorite sport, but it was summer and that is what the British do in summer.

Our new house was nearing completion. Fanny and my sisters were out shopping almost every day for furnishings. We attended a number of auctions and purchased antique furniture, paintings and sculpture. Fanny and I were looking forward to moving into the house next year on our return to England.

At the age of forty-five, for the first time in my adult life I was seriously considering living in London permanently. The Jameson affair, and the aftermath, had definitely had an effect on me. As much as the excitement of South Africa had driven me for a quarter of a century, I now craved the lifestyle that London had to offer me and the family. Fanny and I talked about this for many hours on our voyage back to South Africa. The stumbling block was missing her family. But that was gradually changing. She also enjoyed London and couldn't wait to move into the new house there.

I returned in time to chair the annual board meeting of De Beers Consolidated Mines, an event I always enjoy. Unlike the gold mines, our diamond mines were producing well. Our dividends for 1896 amounted to forty per cent, a new record.

The meeting was very upbeat and, as usual, Rhodes was not in attendance.

It was rumored that a number of the British irregular forces had disbanded and left to join the new gold rush in the Klondike.

I sent a pair of stone lions to Kruger for his birthday in October as a goodwill gesture. He acknowledged the gift in a short note. Later, I found out that he had them installed on the front porch of his house in Pretoria and pointed them out to visitors that they were a present from me. Who knows, one day I might be able to visit him in a social capacity.

Harry sent me a copy of the Financial News from London that detailed the loss in value of Barnato company shares. I was aware of their extent, but this informed the general public and investors. The picture was not pretty.

The article was sharply critical of the speculation in Mining Stocks. Comparing the value of fifteen of our mining stocks from October 1895 to November 1896, the stocks had lost more than twenty million pounds. A short note from Harry commented that it was a good job we had taken the action we did, but it was too little too late. Well, at least he understood my motives for cutting back. I showed the article to Solly who read it, shrugged his shoulders and threw it on my desk. He was still angry with me for cutting back on our expansion without consulting him, although I thought we had put that all behind us.

Chapter 51

The strain of the last year sapped my strength. I am not the sort of person that worries about his health and wellbeing. I was as fit as any man who has exercised his mind and body for a lifetime. My real fear was that something dreadful would befall my wife and children.

The failure of Jameson and his attempted coup brought down a lot of grief on me. I had butted heads with the most powerful and influential men in South Africa, particularly Kruger and his burghers. Several anonymous threats had been made on my life in the last few weeks. Men were lurking in the shadows somewhere, too cowardly to meet me face to face, where at least, I had a chance to tackle them in my own way. They didn't scare me, but a man can be vulnerable if his family is attacked.

Fanny knew about the threats and was concerned, but fatalistic. She believed that everyone would forget about my confrontation with Kruger. Even though our friendship with him had soured, Kruger would not allow anyone to harm us. After all, my companies were the power house of the Transvaal economy.

I was inclined to believe that was true, but the vitriolic nature of the written threats still worried me, as they were directed not just at me but at my family as well.

We received an official invitation to attend the Diamond Jubilee of Queen Victoria. I considered this to be a great honor and so the decision was made that we should go back to England. We still had to add the finishing touches to our new London house at Stanhope Gate. Maybe this time we could spend an entire year in England to allow the whole mess to blow over. I liked the idea and it settled my mind.

Early in the New Year of 1897, my top financial expert at Johannesburg Consolidated asked if he could see me urgently. This was highly unusual, so I went to see him in his office immediately.

"Mr. Barnato, I am sorry to call you away from your daily business affairs, but I am deeply concerned over something I have found."

"That sounds very ominous, Mr. Brown. Please explain yourself."

"I have found a shortage in the accounts of more than one million pounds." I gasped.

"How is that possible? There are only a handful of people that even have access to any major funds. Other than yourself, my brother, Solly Joel, Woolf Joel and me."

"That is correct, sir. I'm afraid to tell you that I believe, no, I know that it is Mr. Solly that is responsible." I felt blood rushing to my face.

"I can't believe that."

"If you wish to have an independent audit carried out, I am sure you will be told the same thing."

"Absolutely, I am shocked that Solly would do such a thing and that this is even possible."

"I will organize an audit immediately and have the auditor bring you a report within the week."

It was impossible for me to believe that my nephew would cheat me, and if he did, that he would think he could get away with it. But sadly, the report from the auditors showed a pattern of embezzlement over a long period. I was devastated. I had to decide how I wanted to proceed. There was no way I could put my nephew in jail, but he could not get away with it. I called Solly to my office.

"Do you think I am an idiot or something?"

"No, why should I?"

"Have I not been generous to you, made you a wealthy man, given you every opportunity in life?"

"Yes, of course, but what is this all about?"

It was amazing, he was as cool as a cucumber. He faced off with me as if he thought there was no way I had discovered his crime.

"I had a meeting last week with our chief financial officer, which resulted in a complete audit of the J.C.T. books by our auditors. Is there anything you want to tell me, Solly?"

He went pale. I could see the perspiration on his forehead. His bravado disappeared.

"Why should there be?"

"Because your scheme to embezzle in excess of one million pounds has been discovered!"

"How could that be?"

"Because you are not as clever as you thought you were." He hesitated.

"What do you intend to do?"

"I should fire you immediately, or worse, have you thrown in jail. But you're family, and my sister would never forgive me. The first thing you will do is pay all of it back with interest."

"I can't do that I have spent a lot of it."

"How could you have spent a lot of it? We're talking about a huge amount of money."

"Different things I don't wish to enumerate," he said with a slight smirk.

"Whatever you have left, you will transfer to the company accountant immediately. You still have shares in De Beers Consolidated, don't you, or have you gone through those too?"

"I still have shares, of course."

"You will put them on the open market first thing tomorrow and sell enough to cover the balance. I expect you to work out the details with Mr. Brown after this meeting. If you fail to do this, I will have you arrested for embezzlement by the end of the week."

"You said you wouldn't do that." His face reddened.

"I've changed my mind. Do as I say or face the consequences. Now get out of my office."

Solly did exactly as he had been told. Mr. Brown took over his bank account and arranged the sale of the shares. I contacted Woolf, Harry and Jack to let them know what happened and to make sure that none of my family purchased the shares privately or on the open market.

The next day I called Solly back to my office. He was very offhand as he glared at me.

"I have decided to send you back to England, Solly."

"What if I don't want to go?"

"Don't force me into that position you won't win, I can assure you."

"Are you firing me?"

"Not at this point, but I am going bring the matter of your embezzlement before Harry and Jack. Between us we will make the decision."

"Why don't you go and cable me when you have made up your mind?"

"Do you think I'm that stupid to let you have the run of things here while I am away for several weeks? It's bad enough that you have already stolen a small fortune. I don't intend to give you another opportunity to do it again.

"I don't think you are stupid, Barney, just spineless."

He was looking for a fight and if need be I would give it to him.

"I can still have you arrested and thrown in jail. Is that what you want?"

He shrugged, looked angry, but lowered his belligerence.

"I may not be able to get a booking."

"Don't worry. I've already done it. Now clear out of here. I don't want to see you till you are on the ship." Solly stormed out.

The next day I met with Woolf to explain to him what had transpired with his brother.

"I'm taking my family to England next week. Solly will be on the same ship as I want to let Harry and Jack help me decide if Solly is to continue to be part of the Barnato companies.

"Barney, I am so sorry for my brother's action. I voiced my opinion to you when you told me about the matter. Personally, I am shocked as you are. You have my vote to kick him out."

"Thank you. Believe me I'm sorry that he has resorted to this."

"Are you going back to England because you are worried about the threats against you?"

"Yes and no. Of course, I'm concerned that the lives of my family have been threatened. I would like to finish building my new London house and spend some time with the rest of the family."

"I can't believe that you of all people are going to let these bastards run you out of South Africa."

"I'm not running out I will be back when cooler heads prevail."

Woolf sighed, "Sadly, things will never be the same again for you or them. I do think it is crucial that we continue to exert our influence on the affairs both here in the Transvaal and in Kimberley."

"I'm perfectly capable of running our business affairs from the London office. There's nothing wrong with that, is there?"

"No, but keep in mind that we are at a critical stage. Kruger has been weakened by our action and the British government may well push to take over the Dutch Republic. It is a great opportunity to finally establish a Union of South Africa."

"You sound more like Rhodes than my nephew. We are not to get involved with politics. Ever!"

"I hate to disagree with you, but you're wrong. We can influence the outcome of the politics of South Africa by the sheer weight of our business interests. Barney, we've got them by the balls."

"Those ideas are dangerous and put our financial interests at risk."

"We will have to wait and see.."

"With Solly and me out of the country you are in charge now. Look after things."

"Don't worry, Barney. You can rely on me. Bon voyage."

Chapter 52

The weather was mild and the seas were reasonable. There was a six or eight foot swell, but nothing that we had not experienced in the many voyages we had taken now. We had our usual suite on the R.M.S. Scot in addition to extra cabins for the children, nanny and staff that now traveled regularly with us.

I had decided that I was going to find a bodyguard for Fanny and I. Someone who could handle himself in the event of an attack on us. There were plenty of honorably discharged soldiers in England that would be pleased to get the job.

Solly was in a foul mood, I had never seen him in such an unfriendly state. For the most part he stayed well out of my way. I was beginning to regret ordering him along. He was making sure that I would suffer his temper.

I couldn't help watching the other passengers on the ship. What was I watching for? Did I really think that my life was in danger still? The answer was yes, I have my enemies and they could be anywhere, including on this voyage. The real problem is identifying the threat.

We were almost half way back to England and I was starting to relax. Solly had kept out of my way for a week, which helped improve my state of mind. One day, around two o'clock in the afternoon, we sat in the dining room for lunch. Solly decided to join us, and immediately found fault with the food and admonished a steward for no reason at all.

"What right do you have to tear a strip off that poor fellow? He is doing the best he can and you have been extremely rude."

"He's incompetent and does not know his place."

"It seems to me that you do not know your place. I take your attitude as an affront to Fanny, my children and me. It is time that you and I had a little talk."

"If that's what you want. You always get your own way."

"Let's do this now, I am not prepared to let this attitude go on any longer."

We excused ourselves from Fanny and walked out onto the deck, moving far down toward the bow of the ship. There was nobody within earshot as all the other passengers were still at lunch. I'd absolutely had enough of Solly, after all I had done for him.

"You've become a real piece of work."

"I'm fed up with being under your thumb. You want to control everyone and everything. You're a maniac."

"I'm a maniac? You're an ungrateful little prick!"

His eyes glared at me. I'd seen that look before in other men's eyes, he wanted my blood. If he thought he could take me, I had no doubt that he would try. Instead he turned on his heel and appeared to back down. I relaxed and turned to look over the rail of the ship.

"Murder!"

EPILOGUE

Barney Barnato drowned off the coast of Madeira on 14th June 1897. His body was retrieved from the sea by William Tarrant Clifford, the fourth officer of the Scot.

As soon as Barney's body was brought ashore, an inquest was held by a coroner and jury at the South-Western Hotel in Southampton. The date was Friday June 18th, 1897. There were only two witnesses deposed; W. T. Clifford and Solly Joel.

Solly Joel was the first to testify. He stated the following:

"I was a passenger on board the Scot, and the deceased Mr. Isaac Barnett Barnato was a fellow passenger. I was walking on deck with him on Monday last at nine minutes past three in the afternoon. I was getting tired, so I asked him to sit down. He said, "Oh, no, let us walk." We, however, sat down, and he asked me – "What is the time?" I looked at my watch, told him, and then I saw him dash by. I had not time, in fact, to close my watch, or even to lift my eyes when he gave a spring. I threw out my hands to catch him, but only caught the back of his trousers, and he jumped over the side into the sea. I screamed "murder," and saw the fourth officer, who was sitting dozing, and said "For God's sake save him." He said, "I will try." He took his hat and coat off, and dived into the sea, while I stood pointing out where he was. They stopped the vessel, and life-buoys were thrown over. The ship then turned round, and a boat was lowered. The fourth officer was first picked up and then the body. Every effort was made by artificial respiration and other means, but without success."

In answer to further questions, Mr. Joel said: "Deceased at times was not in his right mind. One hour he appeared to be quite well, and the next his mind would wander. On the fatal day I noticed his behaviour, and made up my mind not to leave him, and I did not. I think he had never shown signs of suicidal mania before."

William Tarrant Clifford, the fourth officer of the Scot, was the next witness. He stated: "I had seen and spoken to Mr. Barnato once or twice on the journey, and noticed nothing peculiar either in his appearance or actions. On the 14th, when in latitude 31.8N and 17.13 W., I saw him leap overboard. Mr. Joel said something I don't remember, and I think I said "I'll go," and with that I pulled off my coat and jumped in after him. I did not reach the body, though I saw it some way off. I was subsequently picked up by the ship's boat."

Clifford produced the ship's log, which showed that lifebelts were thrown overboard and that the ship rapidly turned and steamed in the direction of the body.

Answering a question from a member of the jury, Mr. Joel said there was no one beside himself with the deceased when he jumped overboard, and he did not know if others saw him. Mrt. Clifford subsequently explained that the ship's rail was only about three feet high, where the deceased jumped off. When the body was found the face was downwards.

Mr. Solly Joel, before the jury gave it's verdict, intervened and said that the Monday before sailing he received a telegram from Mrs. Barnato asking him to come to Cape Town because of Mr Barnato's mental condition. He left Johannesburg by the next train, and found Mr. Barnato in very bad health. He had eaten nothing nor slept for three or four days, and at times wandered considerably. Subsequently, however, he improved, and was much better when the ship sailed.

The jury, after a short retirement, returned a verdict that the deceased jumped overboard, and met his death by drowning while temporarily insane.

There are a number of troubling things about the testimony at the inquest into Barney Barnato's death.

Who screamed murder? Solly says he did, but it could just as easily been Barney. Solly shouting murder seems to be a strange thing to shout. Why not shout for help?

Solly says that "I saw him dash by. I had not time, in fact, to close my watch, or even to lift my eyes, when he gave a spring, I threw out my hands to catch him, but only caught the back of his trousers." How could he have caught the back of Barney's trousers if he dashed by so fast that he did not lift his eyes?

The only person that could influence the jury as to the state of mind of Barney was Solly, who made the statement that Barney was in bad health and suffering from mental problems. He did this before the jury retired. Had he not done so, they may have come to a different verdict.

In Mr. Clifford's testimony, he states that he saw Barney leap overboard. Yet Solly Joel says he saw Mr. Clifford sitting dozing. How could he have seen Barney jump if he was dozing?

The Barnato family vehemently deny that Barney was suffering from bad health. They had been at sea for ten days and Barney was in good spirits. Fanny Barnato did not attend the inquest and it is likely that she had no idea what had been said in Solly Joel's testimony or for that matter from Mr. Clifford.

Barney Barnato was buried in Willesden Jewish Cemetery on Sunday June 20th, 1897. The funeral was attended hundreds of people; family, friends and business colleagues. The funeral cortege was more than seventy carriages long when it started outside sister Kate Joel's home at Marble Arch. By the time it had reached Willesden, dozens more carriages had joined the procession.

The following week, South African Mining Stocks dropped in value as investors were unsure of the repercussions, but quickly regained their prices.

Barney Barnato left a legacy. Some of his companies are still in existence today and still produce dividends for shareholders.

Woolf Joel, Solly's brother, was murdered by a con-man Karl Frederic Moritz Kurtze on March 14th, 1898.

Solly Joel, became the chairman of Barnato Brothers after the death of Barney Barnato and Woolf Joel in 1898.

THE END

ABOUT THE AUTHOR

Anthony Davis spent 27 years in the gemstone business, purchasing rough gemstones and arranging for their cutting. Involved in a family business which included manufacturing and retailing jewelry, as well as selling gems at a wholesale level. After moving to the U.S.A. he has for the past 25+ years turned his hobby of collecting 19th century photographs into a business and continues to sell on his website www.19cphoto.com . Among the many thousands of original photographs, Anthony has an extensive collection of South African mining photographs from the period of this story.

Distantly related to Barney Barnato through his mother's side of the family and connected to the diamond business on his father's side of the family, he has for many years been fascinated with the life of Barney Barnato, a man who was larger than life.

Currently living in Southern California, Anthony was born in London and knows the city well.

BIBLIOGRAPHY:

B. I. Barnato – A Memoir by Harry Raymond. Published by Ibister and Company, 15 & 16 Tavistock Street, Covent Garden, London 1897.

Rhodes & Barnato – The Premier and the Prancer by James Leasor. Published by Leo Cooper an imprint of Pen & Sword Books Ltd. 47 Church Street, Barnsley, South Yorkshire, United Kingdom. 1997.

Made in the USA
Middletown, DE
20 December 2014